Yeah, maybe

By Joey Hodges

Cover design by Jennifer Wright.

Table of Contents

For Zoe,
Who believed from the very start

PROLOGUE

July 2009

Oh. This was supposed to be exciting. This was supposed to be The Best News Ever. So why did she feel ... disappointed? No, that wasn't the right word. Scared? Nervous? This was what she wanted, wasn't it?

"Uh, hello?" Laurie snapped her fingers in Annie's face. "Didn't you hear me?" It was 10 p.m. on Saturday night, and Laurie had just burst through Annie's bedroom door with the news.

Crap. React. React! she told herself. She squashed the twinge of…whatever that was she was feeling and launched herself off her bed, grabbing Laurie into an excited hug.

"This isn't one of your pranks, is it?" Annie asked as she loosened her grip on Laurie so she could face her friend. "Because I swear, L, my heart can't take it."

Laurie released her, traced an X over her heart then held up three fingers. "Scout's honor."

"But you're not a Scout," Annie teased.

"So what?" Laurie flipped her straight blonde hair over her shoulder. "Their word is still good, right?" Laurie playfully nudged Annie then slung her oversized purse off her shoulder to retrieve a compact from the front pocket and started checking her makeup. Annie was practically falling asleep, and Laurie was *checking her makeup.*

"FYI, I'm crashing here tonight," Laurie continued. "The parentals are having another one of their charity benefit hooplah whatevers, and I swear to God if one more stale-smelling geezer tells me how beautiful I am, I'll barf all over their Valentino shoes."

"But you love being told you're beautiful," Annie said as she collapsed back onto her bed. She looked down at her yoga pants and mismatched socks and ran a hand over her disheveled low pony.

"This is true," Laurie said with a coy smile as she replaced the compact into her bag. Annie had no idea what she was actually checking in that tiny mirror. She'd never seen Laurie look less than perfect. "But it just means so much more when it isn't coming from someone who's knocking on death's door."

Annie let out a half-chuckle. "Forty-five is hardly knocking on death's door."

Laurie looked over at Annie. "Well, it might as well be," she said flippantly. She ran her finger over Annie's DVD collection and slid out the fourth season of *Gilmore Girls*. Binge-watching TV shows was one of the few things they actually had in common. They'd been best friends since they were two – hell, they'd practically been raised as sisters since their parents were always together.

Well, that *had* been true until last summer when their parents had that falling out over the beach timeshare. At least that was what they *claimed*. Annie had to pretend like she didn't know the *real* reason their parents didn't speak anymore.

Laurie opened Annie's dresser drawer and pulled out a pair of pajama pants and a T-shirt, slipping them on. Annie couldn't remember the last time either of them had packed a bag for a sleepover. They basically lived together. Annie pulled her hair from her low pony and retied it.

"Aren't you so excited?" Laurie asked as she grabbed the remote and joined Annie on her bed. The theme music from the

Gilmore Girls intro taunted Annie's mood. It was such a happy tune, and yet internally, Annie was in turmoil. "This is exactly what we've always wanted. What we've always talked about! I can't believe it's actually happening. They *caved* Annie! We did it!"

Laurie had gone to the private school 30 minutes outside of town since kindergarten, and she'd hated every second of it. She said she wanted to have a life *inside* Willow Point, where she lived, even if it *was* like the smallest town ever.

Annie didn't see the appeal in that, having gone to the public school in town all her life, but she was pretty sure half the reason Laurie even cared so much was because she wanted to wear street clothes instead of the hideous (Laurie's words, not Annie's—Annie couldn't have cared less about clothes) uniform she'd worn for the past nine years.

So Laurie had come up with the plan to persuade her parents to allow her to join Annie at Willow Point High for freshmen year, and somehow…*it had worked.* In years past, her parents always shot down her pleas. They had been so insistent on having *the very best and nothing less* for Laurie her entire life. Either they had changed their minds or they had just gotten fed up with Laurie's constant whining.

So why did Annie feel so uncomfortable? Why had she let herself believe that Laurie's parents wouldn't ever go for it, that all of this was just something Laurie talked about but that would never actually happen? Laurie was her *best friend*. She should *want* her to go to school with her, right? She *should* have been excited.

Instead, there was a sick feeling in the pit of her stomach and her nerves felt electric. It didn't feel right. She couldn't pinpoint *what* didn't feel right, but it scared her. Her best friend going to school with her *scared* her.

As that thought passed through her mind, she realized how stupid it sounded. She was being ridiculous. She gazed over at Laurie who was watching the episode intently and twisting her shoulder-length locks into a mock pony with her fingers. Laurie must have felt her eyes on her.

"What?" Laurie asked, releasing her hair, which swung back over her shoulders. "Do I have something on my face?" She brought her hands up to her flawless skin.

"No," Annie said. She grabbed Laurie's hand and squeezed it. "This really is the best news ever. I'm so freaking excited!"

She ignored the panic that continued to surge through her veins.

"I know," Laurie said smiling her genuine smile that crinkled her nose and made her eyes go squinty. "It's going to be the best, Annie. I seriously can't wait."

BREATHE, WOMAN

Annie was pulling her towel off the back of her bedroom door when it swung open nearly smacking her in the face.

"Oh God," Laurie was panicking as she barged into the room. Her face was already made up, but her hair was up in hot rollers and she was wearing a robe. "You seriously haven't even showered yet?" she asked, glancing Annie up and down with clear distaste.

"Did you seriously just run across the street like that?" Annie asked mockingly, rolling her eyes. "And relax. Unlike *some* people I know, it doesn't take me a century to get ready."

"Well," Laurie huffed as she swung Annie's closet door open. "It should. By the way," she continued as she pulled a bright orange tank top from the side of Annie's closet full of unworn clothes. "I'm wearing this." Laurie yanked the tags off the tank and flung off her robe revealing a lacy pink bra and an adorable pair of white shorts. "It's not like you're ever going to wear it anyway."

Well, that was true. Annie's mom, Lisa, was constantly buying trendy clothes for her that always went unworn. Annie couldn't help it, she just preferred the comfort of her worn-in Rainbow flip flops and a good old-fashioned T-shirt. She would have sworn her mom wished she were more like Laurie. Like *that* would ever happen.

"I'm hopping in the shower," Annie said. "And L?"

"What?"

"Breathe, woman!"

"Whatever," Laurie fidgeted with her top and looked in the floor-length mirror she had insisted Annie hang on her wall two summers ago. Laurie had a tendency to get panicked and jittery when she was excited, and that happened pretty damn often.

Annie walked back into her room wrapped in a towel after her shower to find Laurie riffling through her CDs.

"Uh," Annie spit, startling Laurie who jumped. "Could you not?"

Laurie glared at Annie. "What good is all this crap anyway if your best friend can't even borrow them every once in a while."

"Look, you know the rules. If you want to listen to something, which let's be honest we both know you don't, I'll burn you a copy. But don't touch my CDs."

Laurie threw her hands in the air. "It was just a couple scratches! Sheesh, let it go already!"

"A couple scratches? L, it sounded like The Avett Brothers had the freaking hiccups! When are you going to replace that album anyway?"

Laurie put her hands up and backed away from the CDs. "Whatever," she said as she collapsed onto Annie's bed. "Are you going to let me do your hair?"

Annie squeezed excess water from her hair with a second towel. "Nope."

"Aw, c'mon! Please?" Laurie folded her hands.

"Not a chance. It's a thousand degrees out there anyway. What's the point?"

"Well, then at least let me put some makeup on you."

Annie glared at Laurie, then swung her closet door back open. She grabbed a pair of khaki shorts from the shelf and a fitted (for her) plain white tank.

She slid on a pair of underwear and her shorts without dropping her towel, then turned around and snapped on her bra. The bra was useless since her boobs were practically non-existent, but it was the one thing her mom left on her bed a few weeks ago that she'd actually taken the tags off of. "You're not touching my face." Annie spun around and pulled her top on.

Laurie fished her makeup bag out of her giant purse and unzipped it.

"L, I told you," said Annie. "You're not putting any of that stuff on my face."

"Listen, okay?" Laurie retrieved a mascara tube from the bag and twisted the cap off. She approached Annie and handed her the wand. "I know you don't like makeup. And the lucky thing is, you don't really need it."

"You don't exactly need it either," Annie defended, inspecting the wand. "And you wear *so much.*"

"Yeah," Laurie said, "because I like it! There's nothing wrong with that, is there?"

"Well, no." Annie said, meaning it. "But I don't like it. I wouldn't know what to do with all that stuff anyway."

"Okay, here." Laurie pulled Annie over to the bed and set her on the edge of it. She took the wand from Annie and held it up to her eye. "Blink."

"What?" Annie questioned, jerking her head back and away from the wand.

"Hold still," Laurie said lining the wand back up over Annie's eye. "And blink."

Annie blinked.

"Blink again."

She blinked again.

"And now the other eye, okay?" She realigned the wand and commanded Annie to blink. She did. Twice. "Alright, do you trust me?"

Annie sighed. "Yeah, I guess. Just don't go hog wild, okay?"

Laurie dropped the mascara tube back into the bag, rocked back onto her heels, and clapped her hands. "Yay! Okay!" She riffled through her bag and selected a few products. Annie sat mannequin-still while Laurie did her thing.

"Okay, ready?" Laurie asked encouraging Annie to open her eyes. Laurie pulled Annie off the bed by her wrist and nudged her towards the mirror. "Take a look. If you don't like it, we can take it off."

Annie stumbled toward the mirror. She inched forward until she was as close as she could get, inspecting herself.

"L —" she said in disbelief. "How did yo—"

She cut herself off and touched her face. She looked like herself. The makeup wasn't caked on, and she looked…what? *Pretty.*

"You definitely don't need makeup," Laurie said quietly. "But you sure are a knockout with it on, huh?" She stood just behind Annie with her hands folded together and tucked under her chin.

Annie turned around to face a beaming Laurie. "You do good work," she said, and before she could stop her, Laurie was squeezing her into a tight hug.

"Ooookay," Annie said, patting Laurie's back.

"Okay!" Annie demanded, pushing away and releasing herself from Laurie's grip. She pulled herself back, putting space between them. "Gushy moment is over."

Laurie just laughed. Annie glanced at the clock then back to Laurie who still had her hair up in rollers. "When were you planning to leave?"

Laurie touched a roller on her head. "We'll leave soon. The Bonfire technically starts at 8, but we're going a little late." She

---

started unrolling her hair. The strands fell into perfect loose curls.

"We are?" Annie asked.

"Uh, yeah," Laurie said making the one syllable *yeah* into two. "You never show up on time to a high school party, Annie."

"Oh, well that's news to me." Annie sat in her computer chair, swiveling from side to side.

"Plus, no offense, I love you and all—but I'm not going anywhere with you until your hair dries." Laurie approached the mirror and started fluffing her hair. She dumped the curlers into her bag. Annie sighed audibly.

The Bonfire was at Misty Lake Park, next to the middle school. Which was next to the high school. Which was within walking distance from Annie's house. Willow Point was a small town—a *really* small town.

The Bonfire was a kind of final send-off for the graduated seniors on the Friday before the high school started back. And it was kind of a big deal.

It was also the first time the rising freshmen got to experience *high school.* It wasn't exactly Annie's nature to go to this type of thing, but she would have been lying if she'd said she wasn't at least a *little* excited to see what it was all about.

Her brother, Drew, was now a rising senior at NC State University, and she was just a kid when he was in high school. He always made the Bonfire seem like The Greatest Thing Ever, though. So somewhere, deep down, she'd been anticipating this night for years.

"Earth to Annie," Laurie snapped. "Can I please take a blow dryer to your hair? I swear I won't do anything fancy—I'll just get that mess dry."

Annie sighed, rolled her eyes, and handed her brush to Laurie. Whatever. Laurie usually got her way anyway; why even bother trying to fight it?

"Have at it."

As the girls approached the park, Laurie turned to Annie and sashayed along excitedly. "Oh, gosh! Okay," she said. "When we get there, you have to tell me about everyone, deal?"

The familiar panicky feeling lodged itself in Annie's throat. She swallowed it. What *was* that?

"There isn't much to tell," she said as the park came into view. It was beautifully lit, the trees were draped with white Christmas lights, and colored lanterns were hanging from tree branches. It was gorgeous.

"Of course there is!" Laurie insisted. "You *know* these people. And I don't want to feel like some outcast. Tell me everything!"

Laurie had never seemed like an outcast, Annie thought. Nonetheless, she agreed. They stepped under the canopy of trees into the twinkling forest.

There were picnic tables scattered across the field, kids sitting at most of them, sitting on top of them, and standing near them. There were people everywhere, and most were holding a red Solo cup as an accessory. A few girls were gathered around the bed of a guy's truck.

Annie noticed that he had sharp features and hypnotizing eyes — obviously the reason for his fan club. One girl stumbled into him, chanting, "I'm so drunk. I'm *so* drunk!"

Annie's brother once told her that was the standard mating call of the sorority girls at his college. Seemed legit.

"Okay," Annie said reluctantly. She linked her arm into Laurie's and began the breakdown. She pointed out the seniors. She pointed out the guy she thought would be Senior Class President, Dave Watson.

She explained who the AV (audio/visual tech) kids were. She was surprised to even see them there — but then again, she was there. She supposed that everyone participated when there was booze involved.

And then she spotted them.

A girl was gesturing wildly with her free hand, the other clasping a Solo cup. Maddie Burns. Annie could hear her talking about her summer vacation with her rich aunt in the Hampton's.

Figured.

"Now them," Annie gestured towards the girls. "Those are the ones I've told you about." Annie couldn't stand them. The girls had been a problem for as long as she could remember.

"Wait," Laurie said excitedly. "*They're* the ones who call themselves The Elite?" Laurie's eyes were wide, as if she were getting to see fictional characters from her favorite book before her very eyes.

Annie told her countless stories about *The Elite* over the years. They were ridiculous, really. They were mean. And they were stupid. And, well, they were just *horrible*.

"So wait," Laurie was saying giddily. "Which one is Olivia?"

Annie pointed out the petite, blondish brunette with fierce brown eyes. Her eyes were so dark they almost looked black. *Fitting*, Annie thought, *considering she probably has no soul.* Olivia was the Queen Bee. The head bitch. The meanest of the bunch.

"Uh," Laurie interrupted, "who is *that?*" She indicated a guy who had just walked up to the group of girls with a cup in one hand, the other in the pocket of his khaki shorts. His shaggy brown hair had a slight curl to it, making it seem more messy than curly. His eyes were piercing, even from across the park. Ice blue.

"Josh. Watson? His brother is that soon-to-be-class president guy. You know, the one I told you about earlier? Dave?" Annie faced Laurie who had stars in her eyes.

"Well isn't he just a tall glass of mother-may-I?" Laurie gushed as she fanned herself with her hand, flushing.

Annie let out a laugh.

"I guess," she said. She honestly never noticed him that way before.

"Oh, c'mon. I know you're not into the whole social scene thing," Laurie put air quotes around *social scene*, "but even you can't deny that guy is H-O-DOUBLE-T hott."

"Okay," Annie admitted. "Fine, yes. He's good looking.

Good for him."

Before Annie could continue filling Laurie in, Sally Harnett approached them. She was Annie's one school friend, if she could really even call her that. Annie pretty much kept to herself, but Sally was friendly with everyone.

"Annie!" Sally squealed as she approached. She gave Annie a quick hug as she looked around. "Can you believe all of this?"

"I really can't," Annie answered, meaning it. The park was completely transformed. The rising seniors must have worked all day — or for *days*, really — decorating.

The girls stood quietly for a moment, and suddenly Annie felt the awkwardness. "Oh, sorry!" Annie said, flustered, turning to Laurie. "Sally, this is Laurie Wentworth. She'll be at Willow Point with us this year."

Sally greeted Laurie and complimented her outfit, and just like that, the girls clicked. They gushed excitedly about school and their back-to-school shopping and who they had for which classes.

"Have you guys made it to the keg yet?" Sally eyed their hands, answering her own question. "No? Okay, me neither," she said way too excitedly for Annie's taste.

"It's over this way," she nodded in the direction of the keg and led the way. The girls got in the keg line as Sally and Laurie continued their excited conversation.

Annie stood there watching them, and she just felt…out of place. Nerves surged Annie's system, and then it hit her. School was her sanctuary. She'd gone to school with these people her whole life, and she'd gone mostly unnoticed, which was exactly how she liked it.

Laurie, on the other hand, was not the type to go unnoticed, *ever*. She lived and breathed for attention. That dynamic of their friendship worked at home. They'd been friends for so long that it didn't really matter that they had very little in common; they appreciated each other for exactly who they were.

Going to school together would change things. Annie couldn't deny that deep down she was afraid that going to school together would change *everything.*

She pushed the thoughts from her mind and told herself to stop being so dramatic. Everything would be fine.

The line inched forward, and then it was Sally's turn to fill her cup, but she was deep in conversation with Laurie about how it seemed almost pointless to style their hair in this humidity. So Annie skipped ahead and started filling her cup.

She stood to the side of the keg and waited for Laurie and Sally. A loud cracking noise startled her, and she turned abruptly to investigate. Annie's heart slowed when she realized it was just a car backfiring.

"Oh, jeez," she exhaled, rattled, turning to face the girls. "That scared the crap out of me!"

But they were gone.

Annie scanned the crowd but couldn't find them anywhere. *What the hell*, she muttered to herself. *It's already starting.*

She tried to force the thought from her mind and continued to search the crowd as she made her way to the fence lining the perimeter of the park. There was still no sight of the girls. She tried her best not to feel annoyed — they probably just wandered off. They'd find her, she was sure.

She leaned against the fence and watched the party. It seemed like everyone already had a place. They somehow just knew where they belonged, and to *whom* they belonged.

Annie held her cup close to her chest and scanned the crowd hoping to spot Laurie. No luck. She always knew her place at home; she knew she and Laurie belonged to each other at home. But would that translate at school? She didn't see how that would be possible.

She struggled to pull herself up onto the fence to sit on the top rung. Being short did have its perks, but her climbing ability was definitely not one of them. There were so many people she could hardly see through the crowd.

There were cars and trucks parked along the opening of the park all in the grass, and she couldn't see the truck where she witnessed the *sorority girl mating call* earlier, but she could hear it. It was the main source of music with bass so intense she could see the truck vibrating when they entered the party.

The music was awful. One minute it was some God-awful rap song followed by Dierks Bently's *Sideways*. This town was so confused when it came to music. It seemed there wasn't a girl in attendance that was immune to the music—they were all moving, some full on dancing while others swayed as they flirted and flipped their hair over their shoulders.

Several minutes and songs passed before she finally took a sip of her beer. She immediately spit it out.

"Yeah, it takes some getting used to," a voice said over the music with a half chuckle. She looked up, surprised, to see Josh approaching her. Dang, he was way taller up-close than she'd figured. He had to be 6'1, 6'2?

"I'm Josh," he said casually as he flicked his hair out of his eyes with a smooth shake of his head.

"I know," Annie said dropping her eyes to the ground. She silently cursed Laurie for pointing out how attractive he was— because she probably wouldn't have ever noticed otherwise, and now that she did, there was a lump in her throat.

"Annie, right?" He sat on the top rung of the fence and she laughed to herself. He didn't even have to pull himself up. He was tall enough to just *sit* on it.

"Oh, yeah — sorry," she said indicating her lack of introduction. "It's Annette, but Annie."

"Well hi, Annette but Annie," Josh said smoothly with a smile. He took a sip from his cup and gazed out over the crowd.

"Hi," she said bashfully into her cup, taking another sip. She spit it back out. "I'm sorry," she said, wiping her mouth. "It's just so bad."

"Yeah." He tilted his cup towards her. "Water. No one ever asks, so promise not to tell, K?" He smiled again, and this time his eyes crinkled. It did something to the pit of her belly. Oh God, Laurie was right. He *was* hot.

"So is that a new girl you were with?" He asked.

Oh. *Of course*. He'd noticed Laurie. Everyone always noticed Laurie.

"Sort of. She's new to the school, but she's lived in town forever."

"Gotcha," he said, taking another sip of his water.

She was uncomfortable, and she felt kind of stupid. Of course he didn't approach her for *her*.

"Listen," she said, springing off the fence. "If you want her number or something, I could introduce you. You know, when I find her."

Josh looked at her, puzzled. "Wait, what?"

"Laurie. She's around here somewhere. Actually, I don't really know *where* she is because she kind of just ditched me, but I'm sure she'll come around at some point. I mean she can't be *totally* missing…" Crap. She was rambling.

Josh held up his hands. "Whoa, whoa, whoa!" he laughed. "Slow your roll. I was just making conversation." He leaned forward and grabbed her wrist, gently pulling her back towards the fence. "Have a seat. Stay a while." *There was that smile*.

"Sorry," she said sheepishly as she attempted to pull herself back up onto the fence. It was an embarrassing struggle.

Josh took her cup, allowing her to use both hands. He dumped out her beer then poured half of his water into her cup. When she got herself situated, he handed it back to her.

"I just thought —" she waved her free hand generally, "you know," she said with a sigh.

Josh nodded knowingly. They were quiet for a moment, watching the chaos of the party. "So you got ditched, huh?" He took another sip of his water.

"Sort of, I guess. I don't think she meant to."

"Well, if it makes you feel any better…I sort of got ditched too."

She looked at him, surprised. "*You* got ditched?" She had a hard time believing that.

"Well, sort of," he replied. "They're all doing shots with my brother and his friends. I opted out."

"Hate to break it to ya," Annie said, "but that hardly counts as getting ditched."

"Sure it does." He nudged her with his shoulder playfully. "So do you —"

A commotion of laughter interrupted Josh as a group of guys approached. Annie recognized them as graduated seniors. With them was Dave, Josh's brother, and Brandon, who Annie recognized as Josh's best friend. And behind Brandon was—

"Laurie?" Annie exhaled. Laurie was gazing up at one of the graduates and teetering on her feet. She was giggling uncontrollably and sloshing the contents of her cup as she swayed. The graduate, who Annie heard one of his buddies call Doug, had an arm wrapped around Laurie's waist—he was practically holding her up. Sally was nowhere to be seen. *Awesome.*

"You know, boys," Laurie shouted, addressing the crowd of guys. "I'm wearing the cutest little thong you'll ever see!" Josh spit out a mouth full of water.

"Laurie!" Annie shouted, hopping down from the fence. "Good lord, how much have you had?" She unwrapped Laurie from Doug and stood with her hands resting on Laurie's shoulders, trying to get her to look her in the eye.

"Great," Annie exhaled. "You're trashed. Come on." She draped one of Laurie's arms around her neck and tried to support her weight. "We're going." Annie took Laurie's cup, and it spilled in the process.

"Oh no! My happy juice" Laurie cried.

Annie sighed, making eye contact with Josh who looked

apologetic. He hopped off the fence and went to the other side of Laurie. Laurie wrapped her other arm around his waist excitedly.

"Oh, hi! You're cute! I'm Laurie!" She leaned into his chest and walked off center.

Annie peered around Laurie. "Look, I've got her. Thanks, though."

"Let me walk y'all home. Please. It's my buddies who got her drunk—it's the least I can do."

"No, really. We're good. Thanks though." Josh gave her a look to clarify if she was sure.

"Really. I've got this. Stay. Enjoy the party." Josh untangled himself from Laurie and hung back. Laurie draped all her weight onto Annie and coughed.

"Where are we going," Laurie asked with her eyelids drooping.

"Home, L. We're going home."

"Aw, c'mon Ans. Don't be such a party pooper."

Before Annie could respond, Josh called after her. "Hey Annie!" She paused and turned around, still supporting Laurie's weight.

"See you Monday." He flashed her a smile and her insides

twisted.

"Yeah, sure," she said. "See you Monday."

I GET THE PITY INVITE

"Annette," Annie's mother hissed as she walked into the kitchen. Annie jumped, startled. She'd put her head down on the kitchen table for just a moment, and she must have dozed off. It was entirely too early.

Annie's mom, Lisa Mackey, was a tall woman with platinum blonde hair who was currently hovering over the coffee pot as if willing it to drip faster.

"Oh," Lisa said with obvious disappointment, turning around and scanning Annie's outfit. "Didn't you see what I bought you last week? I thought maybe you'd like to wear one of those tops today."

"I'm fine in what I'm in," Annie said through a yawn. She was wearing denim shorts with a plain yellow T-shirt and her Rainbows. Her chocolate-colored hair was tied back in a low ponytail that she could already feel frizzing in the NC humidity.

Lisa gave Annie a pointed look.

"Really, Mom. I'm good," Annie said.

"I don't know, Annie," her mother said. "I just thought maybe now that Laurie's joining you at school you'd..."

"What? Change completely?" Annie interrupted. "Give me a break. What I'm wearing is fine."

Lisa huffed as she drew the coffee pot from the machine and poured the entire contents into a large thermos. "Fine," she rolled her eyes in resignation. "Listen. I'll be..." she hesitated, "working late again tonight. But your dad should be back soon after you get home."

Lisa was a lawyer, and she was practically never home. Annie was certain her mom cared way more about her job than she did about anything else, her family included.

Annie's dad, Jason, was gone a lot, too. But he traveled for work. He was a photographer who did a lot of branding work with big companies. On the side, he photographed weddings.

Annie always teased him because he was an absolute hopeless romantic and had somehow managed to find a way to make money off the trait. It was actually kind of ironic, his hopeless romantic tendencies, now that she thought about it in regard to what she wasn't supposed to know. But either way, Annie spent a lot of time in the house alone.

"Kay," Annie answered flatly as she got up from the table to peruse the pantry. She held on to the pantry door and rested her foot on the calf of her other leg, or as Laurie liked to say, she stood like a flamingo.

Lisa hustled out of the kitchen and was halfway out the door before she even remembered to call out for her daughter to have a nice day.

"Yeah, you too," Annie muttered to herself as she reached for the box of Pop-Tarts.

Laurie swung open the door that Lisa had just exited shouting, "Thanks, Mrs. Mackey!" Her light pink summer dress was flowing behind her and her sling-back gold flats clacked against the tile floor. Her blonde hair was carefully straightened.

She turned her attention to Annie. "Girl – your mom looks *fierce.*"

"Of course she does," Annie spit out, rolling her eyes as she placed the box of Pop-Tarts on the counter.

"What's wrong?" Laurie asked, approaching her.

"Oh, you know. Just the same old same old with Lisa." Annie could hardly stand to call that woman "Mom." It wasn't exactly like she'd *earned* the title.

Laurie waved her hand flippantly through the air. "Oh, don't let her mess with today. Seriously," Laurie flashed her megawatt smile. "You know how she is. And today's a big day for us!"

Annie wouldn't have exactly classified the day as A Big Day, but maybe Laurie was right. The start of high school was kind of a big deal. Part of her really wanted to be excited. Having Laurie at the same school should be like a dream come true, right?

But she was still feeling panicked about the idea. And if Friday night was any indication of how this year might go, she wasn't sure she was up for the challenge.

As the girls walked to school, Annie had to remind Laurie twice that she herself hadn't actually *attended* the school before. She knew the people, sure, but this was her first day at this particular school also.

"Oh, yeah!" Laurie giggled. "I keep forgetting!"

"I think we'll be fine," Annie was kind of tired of discussing it all and she wished it were just any other day. The *first* of anything always came with a bit of anxiety for her. And this day, in particular, wasn't any better, especially with the added worry of how things would work out with Laurie.

"Of *course* we'll be fine," Laurie ensured her friend. "In fact, we'll be *better* than fine!" Laurie adjusted her large Vera Bradley tote on her shoulder and slid a stray hair behind her ear.

As the girls approached the school, Sally spotted them and waved frantically. She was standing with her twin brother, Evan, and a few other freshmen. The girls walked over to the group, and Sally grabbed Laurie into a quick hug.

"Oh, em gee!" She said. "I was so worried about you when I couldn't find you on Friday night!"

Laurie looked a little embarrassed. "Oh," she said with a wave, "it was nothing. I guess those shots just went right to my head. Annie says I was trashed, so we just went home." Sally directed her attention to Annie, who now felt ultra-uncomfortable. Why did she have to come across like the strict parent ruining Laurie's fun?

"Well, you *were* kind of throwing yourself at a bunch of older guys and embarrassing yourself," Annie said. "Not to mention *describing* your underwear. I'd say it was time to go."

Laurie flushed beet red. When she'd sobered up that night, Annie asked her what the heck happened and why they'd ditched her. Laurie explained that Evan showed up and dragged Sally off to where the guys were doing shots. Laurie followed them, assuming Annie had as well. By the time she'd realized Annie wasn't with them, she couldn't spot her. Harmless enough, Annie told herself.

"Oh," Laurie said excitedly, "I forgot to tell you, Annie! Sally and I have first period together!"

Annie's heart dropped into her stomach. *No.* But that should have been a good thing! What should she care if Laurie and Sally had a class together? Sally chimed in, "Yeah! ELP with Mr. Jenkins."

"Whatever that means." Laurie swatted the air as if she didn't even *care* what ELP meant.

"*Economics, Law* and *Politics*," Annie explained to Laurie giving her an exasperated look. "We've been over this," she huffed then laughed nervously. She fidgeted for a moment then shifted her weight from one foot to the other. "Well, that's cool," Annie said. Frankly, she didn't know what else to say. She didn't typically care what anyone else's schedule was. In fact, she didn't normally have anyone's schedule *to* care about. This was already feeling weird. *Shake it off*, she told herself.

The first bell rang, and the sea of students started

migrating off the front lawn toward the front doors.

"See ya! Good luck!" Laurie called out to Annie with a wave as she walked off with Sally to the History wing of the school.

"Yeah, you too," Annie said flatly as she broke off toward her own class down the hallway.

"Wait!" Laurie shouted, and Annie turned around. "I'll meet you at the picnic tables for lunch?" Annie's chest tightened, and she felt a little better.

"Kay," she said, trying not to sound too desperate.

The girls didn't have any classes together during the first half of the day, but they *did* get the same lunch period. Laurie actually ran in on Annie in the shower when she'd gotten her schedule in the mail.

***

"We have the same lunch!" Laurie squealed. "And Science! We have Science together, third period!"

"Uh, hello—" Annie said, sticking her head out from behind the shower curtain. "Trying to shower here. Wait —" Annie's brow furrowed. "How do you know?"

"Oh, I stalked the mailman," Laurie said, "and I grabbed your letter on my way in. Duh."

"You opened my mail?" Annie would have felt violated but she wasn't even surprised.

***

Annie's first two classes, Algebra I and English, went by quickly. When she'd finally snatched her schedule from Laurie's hands that day, she'd winced when she saw she had Algebra first thing. She wasn't a math person at all, but she'd convinced herself that maybe it was a good thing — that way, it would be out of the way first thing and she would be rewarded with her favorite class just after.

She had Mr. Beal for English. She'd taken a Creative Writing seminar with him one summer, and he was…well, he was good-looking, to say the least. That made learning just a *little* more fun. She was used to his teaching style, which was one little comfort in the midst of a whole new experience.

When the lunch bell rang, her stomach was growling so hard it practically hurt. Annie had abandoned the Pop-Tarts on the counter that morning in Laurie's haste to get to campus early. She made a mental note never to skip breakfast again.

Annie was the first to arrive at the picnic tables. She put her backpack on the table and pulled out her agenda. She was glancing over the pages when she heard Laurie's voice. It was high-pitched, and she was talking quickly like she always did when she got excited or nervous. Or both. Annie turned around and couldn't believe what she saw.

Laurie was walking with Olivia. *Seriously*? All those years, all those stories, and Laurie was *giggling with her.* Annie instantly felt betrayed.

She knew Laurie didn't know about *the incident,* she had done her best to bury it deep inside hoping the humiliation would die, but Laurie *did* know that Olivia was an awful person. The way she treated people was disgusting.

Once, Olivia locked a girl in a janitor's closet for carrying the same Coach bag as her. Half the school day went by before the assistant principal heard the crying from inside the closet and let her out. The girl *and* her reputation were ruined by the time she was released.

Olivia had a weird power, and Annie couldn't stand her or the idea of her. And she *really* couldn't stand the idea of Laurie becoming buddy-buddy with her!

Laurie laughed loudly and then skipped over to the picnic table where Annie was sitting as Olivia sauntered over to her entourage. Laurie had an eager look in her eyes as she slid onto the bench next to Annie.

"You'll never believe this," Laurie said excitedly.

Annie rolled her eyes, "You actually remembered what ELP stands for?" Annie was annoyed. No. She was *pissed*!

Laurie giggled and waved her hand dismissively. "Oh, shut up. No! Olivia and I hit it off in first period! And better yet, we have all of our morning classes together! She's actually a very sweet girl. I can't even believe all those stories you told me! There's no way that's the same girl."

Annie stood from the table and grabbed two dollars from her backpack.

"Well, it is. And listen, I know you like to be the girl who is friends with everyone, but you have to trust me when I tell you she's not someone you want to be hanging out with."

"Oh, Annie." Laurie playfully hit her on the shoulder. "Don't you think you're being just a *little* dramatic? Maybe things can be different for you now that I'm here, 'kay?"

"I don't need for things to be different," Annie said. "I'm going to grab some pizza. You comin'?" Laurie shifted her gaze to the ground.

"What?" Annie huffed.

"Well, it's just that — Olivia said I could eat with her and her friends today if I wanted." Laurie looked up at Annie with hopeful eyes, like a child asking for a sleepover.

"...And?" Annie couldn't even believe this. The first day wasn't even over yet, and already things were going exactly as she'd feared they might.

"Well, uh," Laurie fidgeted. "I told her I wouldn't if you didn't come with me."

"Oh, gee, that's great, L. I get a pity invite."

"It's not a pity invite if I'm inviting you!" Laurie insisted. "Come sit with us!"

"Us? So what, you're like one of them now?"

"That's not what I mea–" Laurie was starting to get defensive.

Annie turned and stormed off toward the pizza line. Her heart was tightening, and she was willing herself to take deep breaths. It wasn't like her to let people bother her so much, but this was different. School was *her* world. She knew exactly who she was and where she did and didn't fit.

She'd never been the kind of girl to fall into a certain

group—but that didn't make her a loser. It just made her, well, *her*. She'd made it through the last several years in school by just being friendly with everyone but *friends* with no one.

She didn't *need* anyone, not really. She liked school. She liked learning. And she liked that she could go home at the end of the day to a different world that belonged to just her and Laurie. This messed everything up.

When Annie returned to the picnic table with her pizza, Laurie was gone. Annie's throat tightened and suddenly she was completely self-aware. She thought about her feelings of paranoia and how it had made her feel stupid, but now she felt totally justified in feeling like this was going to be one big mistake.

She'd known from the moment Laurie had told her they'd be going to the same school that it would mean trouble. Fine. *Whatever.* She'd sit and eat her pizza in peace. She pulled a Sarah Dessen book from her backpack and settled in.

Annie wasn't three sentences into her book when she felt someone sit next to her. She looked up.

"Oh, Josh." She cleared her throat. "Hi?"

Annie closed her book and flipped it over. He didn't need to know that she wanted to know *The Truth About Forever.*

"You're sitting alone," Josh said. "That's lame." He flashed a smile. Well, gee. Wasn't he a peach?

"Yeah, well," Annie said, "Laurie ditched me. Again." Annie waved toward the table of girls, who had been joined by Brandon.

"Yeah, saw that," Josh said. "Seems to be a trend, huh? You okay?"

Annie's heart clenched like it did the night of the Bonfire. His eyes were just so intoxicating.

"I'm fine." Josh held Annie's gaze a little too long. She looked away. "I'll be fine," she corrected.

"Why don't you come sit over there with us?" he asked.

"Oh, I don't know." Annie looked over at the table. Brandon had just zipped a "that's what she said" line, and the girls had their perfectly coiffed heads tossed back in laughter. "I'm pretty sure I don't fit there."

"Sure you do! You're a tiny girl and there's plenty of room at the table. You'll fit just fine!" Josh smiled. "But really," he said joking aside, "what if I asked you to?"

"Why?"

"Because it's the first day of school, he said, "and you're sitting all by yourself. That's why." Josh was already picking up

Annie's backpack. "C'mon."

Josh's smile melted the ice around Annie's heart. Laurie smiled at Annie and gave her a quick wave as Annie sat at the other end of the table with Josh. Laurie was too caught up in her conversation with Olivia and Maddie about the importance of changing nail polish colors every three days to say anything, though.

Olivia glanced at Annie from across the table and trapped her in her stare. In that one look, Annie knew everything she needed to know. She was not welcome there.

"Brandon," Josh said, tilting his head toward the guy sitting next to her, distracting Annie from Olivia. "Annie," he tilted his head back toward Annie, as a way of introduction, for Brandon's sake.

"Sup," Brandon said with a mouthful of pizza. *Classy.* Annie flashed him a weak smile. She was panicked for what to say, but Josh swooped in.

"I take it Laurie made it home from the Bonfire okay?" Josh asked, pulling a brown paper bag from his backpack. He dumped the contents onto the picnic table. A sandwich, a Ziploc bag of pretzels, and a can of Cheerwine. She found it absolutely adorable that he had a sack lunch.

"Oh, yeah," she said then took a small bite of her pizza. She covered her mouth partially with her hand. "I made her crash at my house. She was fine. A little hungover the next day. Nothing major."

"Well, that's good. I was a little worried that you guys would get in trouble. Hard to hide a drunk girl."

Annie's eyes narrowed.

"Not that I would know anything about that." Josh flashed a smile then took a swig of his soda.

He had worried about them? He had thought about them after they left? Annie willed herself not to blush.

"Nah," Annie replied. "My parents are pretty MIA."

"Gotcha. I know how that goes." Josh wiped his mouth with the back of his hand. Annie watched him, and something deep in her stomach fluttered. He had this air of confidence about him, but he was also just so…normal. Down to earth. Himself. Or something like that.

"Your parents gone a lot, too?" Annie handed him one of her napkins. He took it without really even paying attention and wiped his mouth. She immediately felt comfortable with him. She looked over at Brandon who was trying his best to interject into the girls' conversation at the other end of the table.

"Dad works from home when he can, but he's on the road more than he'd like, I think. It's usually just Dave and me." He popped the last of his sandwich into his mouth and chewed quickly. "Mom's been gone almost five years now," he added through a mouthful of food.

Gone. Annie wondered what he meant by that. Wondered if his mom had quit his family like hers seemed to be doing. Either way, she instantly felt like maybe he could get it. Get *her*. He didn't offer any more than that, and she didn't ask.

Before she could say anything else, Brandon slammed his hand down on the table in a fit of laughter, startling her.

"A little jumpy, are we?" Josh chuckled.

"You could say that," Annie said with a shy smile. Josh held her gaze for what felt like a second too long. His eyes crinkled at the edges, making her stomach tighten. What *was* that? Was he flirting with her? No, definitely not. Although, she wouldn't have had a clue even if he were – that wasn't exactly an area she had any experience in.

Joey Hodges

"So tell me about Annie," Josh said, unzipping his backpack that rested on the bench next to him. He pulled out two fun-sized Snickers. He extended one toward her, and she smiled.

"Thanks," she said. Okay, she didn't want to admit it, but he'd gone full-on adorable on her now. A sack lunch *and* dessert? She unzipped the front pocket of her brand new backpack and pulled out a Ziploc of M&Ms. She opened the bag and placed it on the table between them.

"Well, okay. I guess for starters – any time I eat something salty, I almost always have to have something sweet." She giggled and flushed.

"Ditto." Josh crumpled the Snickers wrapper and tossed it into his brown paper bag.

Annie surged with excitement. It had been a long time since she'd met someone she had anything in common with.

"I'll admit this," she said, getting excited. "There are times I practically have to force myself to eat real food just so I can get to dessert."

Josh laughed. "Yup," he agreed. "I'd totally survive on cakes and candy if I could." Josh dipped his hand into the bag of M&Ms

and took a small handful. "So you like dessert. What else?"

Nerves flooded her system. Why did he even care? Was there anything harder than having to sum yourself up into just a few bullet points? Who was Annie? How the heck should she know?

"Music," she muttered as if she were ashamed of her answer. Josh looked up at her.

"What was that?" Josh asked.

"Music," she said a little louder.

"Oh, cool," Josh said matter-of-factly. "So you kissed a girl and you liked it?" He asked, teasing.

Annie almost choked on an M&M. "I'm sorry, what?"

Josh cracked a smile. "Katy Perry? That sort of thing?"

"Oh, gosh, no!" Annie regained her composure and took a sip of her water. "I wouldn't exactly call *that* music."

Josh looked at her inquisitively. "What exactly *would* you call music?"

Immediately, she regretted even bringing it up. Music was such an intense subject for her, and it was something that had pretty much always been hers, and hers alone.

"I dunno," she said quietly, hoping he'd drop the subject. "You know, just less commercial stuff. Real music." She waved her hand generally. "Probably stuff you've never heard of."

"Try me," Josh said folding his hands and resting them on the table. He raised his eyebrows and cocked his head.

Annie's heart was racing. She shouldn't have said anything. She should have been sitting by herself at a picnic table. These worlds weren't supposed to collide. She wasn't some cookie cutter girl, and Josh would see that in 3…2…1…

"Okay," Annie said, taking a deep breath. "For instance, Bon Iver. He's a brilliant musician. Or Ben Howard." Annie looked over at Josh, certain she'd lost him, but he actually looked interested.

"Nice," Josh said. "I'm impressed."

"You actually know what I'm talking about?" Annie was shocked. In her experience, she'd found if music hadn't been auto-tuned or couldn't blow out speakers, no one she knew had ever heard of it.

"Of course I do. *For Emma, Forever Ago*? Classic album." He leaned back, stretched his arms up over his head then leaned back in, resting his elbows on the table.

"Okay, here's one," he said, inching closer. "Have you heard of The Avett Brothers? They're from North Carolina originally."

Annie could hardly believe her ears. "Of course I have!" Annie pulled her iPod out from her backpack and slid it across the table. "*Paranoia in B Major* has been on repeat pretty much since June."

He *got* it. The part of her world no one else seemed to understand. This brown-haired, blue-eyed doll actually *got* it. Maybe that meant he could get *her*, too.

Annie knew better, though. Things were never as good as they seemed. Josh was handsome, and he was a part of *them.* This was a mistake. Sitting there, talking to him, *bonding* with him. It was all a mistake.

Brandon swiveled around and faced them. "Don't let him bore you with his nerdy taste in music," he said. Josh flashed Annie a knowing smile and handed back her iPod.

"Yeah, you know me," Josh said to Brandon. "Just trying to save the world one song at a time."

"I don't know how many times I've had to tell him," Brandon said confidently. "The ladies aren't going to dig all that whiny emo shit." He shoved his fist into Annie's bag of M&Ms and poured the handful into his mouth. "Dude, Usher. *Love in This Club.* *That's* a hot song," Brandon said through a mouthful of chocolate as the bell rang. Annie looked at Josh who just looked amused. He shrugged his shoulders and smiled at her. She couldn't help but smile back.

Annie threw her stuff into her backpack quickly after she said goodbye to the guys. She could hear Laurie giggling. She looked up to find Laurie *hugging* Olivia. Annie's blood boiled.

Laurie approached Annie excitedly.

"Don't even start –" Annie huffed, taking off for the Science building. Laurie had to hustle to keep up.

"What?" Laurie asked innocently, practically jogging next to Annie who was speed walking.

"You totally ditched me back there!" Annie yelled, her voice echoing through the hallway. "You just left me sitting alone at a picnic table. What the hell?"

"Don't turn this around on me," Laurie said defensively. "I totally invited you—it's not my fault you said no."

"You *ignored* me the entire period! This is crap, Laurie!"

"Oh, please. You looked perfectly content, chatting it up with that Josh guy. Which, *by the way*, has you breaking all kinds of girl code. I totally called dibs on him."

"*What!?*" Annie was completely baffled. How was this even a conversation they were having? "What in the hell are you even talking about? What *dibs?*"

"At the Bonfire, I said he was cute. And then there you go, running off with him."

"Okay, whoa, wait a minute here. First of all, calling someone cute is not the same as calling dibs. Secondly, I'm not *running off* with anyone."

"Could have fooled me."

"Don't try to change the subject, Laurie. Nothing is happening with Josh, but there *is* something happening with you. Those girls? They're awful people, Laurie. They're mean. They're shallow—"

"You're *so* judgmental," spit Laurie.

Annie tossed her head back in frustration and forced herself to take a deep breath. "I'm not being judgmental! I'm just *so* careful about who I let in, Laurie, and we've been just fine on our own, you and me. Why are you so set on *being* somebody*?* Can't you just be you?"

"This *is* me, Annie! I like making friends! I like being social! So sue me!"

"I'm not saying you can't make friends!" Annie was growing painfully annoyed. "I'm just concerned about you making friends with the wrong people! I swear; if you hang out with those girls— and you become one of those little bitches—"

"Whatever, Annie," Laurie said, dismissing the conversation. "You're being ridiculous."

The girls entered the Science room and Laurie stomped over to an empty black top table that seated two. Annie scanned the room and realized the only empty seat in the entire room was the one next to Laurie.

"I'm not sitting here by choice, *I hope you know*." Annie spit out.

"*Whatever,*" Laurie said coolly, rolling her eyes. "You'll get over it. You always do."

Class started and they sat quietly while Mrs. Swanson explained her expectations for the year. Annie couldn't focus on Mrs. Swanson, or anything, really. Her frustration with Laurie was so distracting, and the last thing she wanted was to be sitting *next* to her. Annie could almost *taste* the tension in the room between them. She sat and watched the minute hand of the clock tick by.

Annie jumped when the bell rang, startled. She must have zoned out. By the time she threw her notebook into her backpack, Laurie was nowhere to be seen. Annie didn't expect anything less. Laurie always pulled away and used the silent treatment when they fought.

Annie was one of the first to arrive to Gym, her last class of the day. She sat on the third row of bleachers and put her backpack at her feet. She watched her classmates trickle in, and she was actually happy to see Sally walk through the doors. She waved Sally over.

"Hey," Sally said, taking a seat. "How's your day been?"

"Eh, could have been better, Annie said. "Could have been worse. Yours?"

"Definitely nothing to write home about."

"Yeah, tell me about it." Annie and Sally sat and watched the rest of their class arrive. Once everyone was seated, though the bell hadn't rung, Ms. Connor stood from the bleachers and began calling roll.

As the bell rang, Annie saw Josh and Brandon walk through the doors. They were horsing around, but as they passed her to get to the top bleacher, Josh gave her a nod and smiled softly. Sally nudged Annie and flashed a wide smile. Ms. Collins handed out a syllabus and began talking sports.

When the final bell rang, Annie felt relief wash over her. She said goodbye to Sally and headed for the exit. She had just gotten outside when she felt a tug on her backpack. She turned to find Josh smiling.

"Hey, so what'd you think?" He asked.

"Um, of the gym? Annie looked around hesitantly. "It's okay I guess. Kind of smells like dirty socks."

"Of your first day, you dork!" Annie felt that twist in her stomach again.

"Oh, uh, the jury's still out on that one," Annie answered nervously.

"Ah, well," Josh said. "Maybe you'll have more of an opinion tomorrow."

"Yeah," she said, "maybe."

"See ya," he said, turning to catch up with Brandon.

"See ya," she called out to him.

—

Annie was starting for home when someone called out from behind her. "Annie!"

She turned to find Laurie running up to her, out of breath. Annie stopped and adjusted the straps of her backpack. Laurie caught up, and the two began walking home in silence.

"Listen," Laurie said quietly. "I get it. I know I can be a little…" she hesitated, "overwhelming at times. But I really didn't mean anything by clicking with Olivia."

Annie sighed. "I know."

"She's really not that bad once you get to know her," Laurie began her hard sell.

"And what?" Annie interrupted. "You think you *know* her now?" Annie rolled her eyes.

"You know what I mean," Laurie sighed. "Look, just give her a chance okay?"

"We don't have to do this, you know," Annie said not looking at Laurie, keeping her head forward.

"Do what?"

"The whole school thing," Annie said. "I get it. We're different. We've always been different, but I guess it just didn't really matter until now."

"What are you talking about?"

"The friends at school thing. It's okay. Maybe it just can't work."

"Hey," Laurie reached out and grabbed Annie's arm gently, stopping her. She tilted her head in sincerity. "Don't be ridiculous, Annie. You'll always be my friend. At school. At home. Wherever. It doesn't just turn on and off, you know."

"I know," Annie said, "but I'm never going to fit into that world. And you fit in *everywhere.*"

"Annie. You can fit in where ever the hell you want to. And I want you where I am. Wherever that is, okay?"

Annie hesitated then sighed. As usual, there was really no use arguing with Laurie. "Okay," she said.

"Now, don't be mad…"

Annie rolled her eyes but couldn't help smiling. "What now?"

"Well, there's this party. On Friday?"

Annie sighed in resignation. Laurie skipped ahead, clapping giddily, and turned around to walk backward, facing Annie. "It'll be so much fun, I promise!"

HIGH SCHOOL: FROM THE PERSPECTIVE
OF A TARGET

Annie spent the whole first week battling herself internally. The thing was, she knew better. She knew better than to even *bother* trying. So the fact that she'd spent every lunch period for a week at The Elite table? It was just as mind-blowing to her as it was to anyone else.

She knew Laurie was being sincere when she tried to assure Annie that their differences didn't really matter. But after a week at that table, she was pretty certain they *did* matter. They mattered a lot. And just in case she let herself forget that even for just a second, Olivia was there to remind her.

Like on Tuesday, for example. Annie slid in beside Josh at the table at his coercion, with her pizza on a paper plate and a bottle of water. She was twisting the cap off her water when Olivia suddenly felt the need to question Annie's knowledge on just *how many* calories were in that one greasy slice of pizza.

"It really doesn't matter to me," Annie said casually. "Everything in moderation, right?" She tried to brush it off, to deter Olivia from causing a scene.

"Well," Olivia said, haughtily. "I would think *you* should care." Olivia then made a show of eyeing Annie's body up and down. Annie knew she was a slender girl, but Olivia got inside her head. The next day Annie brought a sack lunch like Josh, with fruit and a plain turkey sandwich. She hated herself just a little bit for it, too.

By Thursday, things weren't much different, except, Annie sat proudly next to Josh with her greasy pizza, and she enjoyed every last bite. Just before the bell rang, Annie allowed herself to think she was home safe, but Olivia cleared her throat, demanding the attention of the table. Josh sighed audibly.

"Hey, Josh?" Olivia nudged Laurie and stage-whispered "Now!" Laurie rubbed the sore spot on her arm and smiled shyly but hesitated.

"What, Olivia?" Josh was irritated and Annie realized she

still couldn't figure out exactly what Josh's place was in that group. He was cute, yes, but he was just…different from all of them, even Brandon, who Annie had come to know a little better during the previous week.

From what Annie could tell, Brandon was three things: 1) a troublemaker 2) obsessed with Olivia, and 3) Josh's lifelong best friend.

"Actually, Laurie has something for you," Olivia said. Annie's throat tightened. *What the hell?*

Laurie glanced at Annie with a flash of panic in her eyes before shifting her gaze to Josh. "Oh, well, it's nothing really," she said, clearly embarrassed. Olivia nudged her again.

"Don't be so shy! Actually, Josh, we baked you cookies last night! You know, we both know how much you just *love* dessert." Olivia slid a paper plate with a dozen or so homemade chocolate chip cookies on it, secured with Saran Wrap across the table.

Annie sat there, unable to speak, as Josh accepted the plate and casually thanked them. Before she could react, the bell rang. She felt territorial. *Betrayed.* She tried to tell herself she didn't have a reason to feel that way as Laurie joined her, and they walked to Science.

"Cookies? Really?" Annie couldn't keep the agitation out of her voice.

Laurie waved her off. "It was nothing. Olivia's idea."

"Oh, I'm sure!" Annie said sarcastically. "So you two hung out last night?" She *hated* that she sounded like a jealous girlfriend.

"Well, yeah!" Laurie said excitedly. "She actually invited me over when she got home from cheer." Annie had been pleased to see Laurie was making the effort to meet her at her locker every afternoon so they could walk home together. Annie told herself it was Laurie being sincere, but she had a nagging feeling things would be different if Olivia and Maddie didn't have JV Cheer after school. She appreciated that Laurie was trying, but it was clear she was struggling to keep balance.

Finally, it was Friday. Annie already struggled through Algebra, and she happily settled into a desk in her English class. It had only been a week, but it was already her favorite class.

Mr. Beal was young, probably in his early thirties. It was nice to feel somewhat comfortable with him and his teaching style thanks to that writing seminar she had taken. Plus, it didn't hurt to have him personally greet her the first day. She could practically feel the jealousy radiating from every girl in the class, because well, he was hot!

Granted, he was hot in a nerdy way, but still, hot was hot. His golden brown hair was short but somehow always a little disheveled. His ocean blue eyes were crystal clear behind his frameless glasses. He wasn't particularly tall, probably 5'9 or 5'10, but his height suited him. He was energetic and passionate, and he did this thing where he tugged at his hair when he was trying to deliver a big point.

The bell rang, but that didn't stop the chatter in the classroom. Mr. Beal didn't seem bothered by it, and he started writing something on the whiteboard. When he was finished, he turned around and cleared his throat. The class quieted down.

Emotional Portfolio

A collection of experiences: A lesson in perspective

"So what exactly does this mean?" Mr. Beal asked gesturing toward the board. "Well," he clasped his hands together and started pacing the room. "You're teenagers. I bet you guys think you have it all figured out right here right now. But you don't. Or maybe you do, I don't know. Either way, whatever you think you do or you don't have figured out will change about a thousand times before you put on that cap and gown in a few short years. So what's an Emotional Portfolio?"

Joey Hodges

Elyse Highsmith raised her hand, but Mr. Beal waved it down. "It was a rhetorical question, Ms. Highsmigth." Elyse tried to hide her embarrassment.

"An Emotional Portfolio is a collection of things you experience this year and your feelings and perspectives on those experiences. The point is to get you to try to see things from outside of yourself, to identify what it actually *feels* like to be a teenager. I've taught this class, and many others, for a couple of years now. And every year I think to myself *damn* – pardon my French," the class giggled.

"Anyway, I think to myself, damn, I've really forgotten what it's like to be a teenager." He paused and looked intently around the room. "And the thing is, these are some pretty important years of your life. They're not the *most* important, but they're years that you'll probably always remember. You do a lot of growing in the four years of high school. You start to find yourself. You explore your interests. Maybe you get boyfriends or girlfriends. Most of you won't be the same person you are today when you graduate. Life happens to you. What goes on in the four walls of this school will change you. It'll change your perspective on things. It might even change your perspective on yourself. And I want you to document that."

Elyse Highsmith raised her hand again, though warily this time "Ms. Highsmith," Mr. Beal called on her.

"So you want us to keep a journal?"

"Well, if you want to look at it that way, sure," said Mr. Beal, "but I want it to be a little more than that. Collect moments, photos, keepsakes, whatever strikes you as important or meaningful. I want you to document your year, and I want you to be as real and as honest as you possibly can be. That's the only way this exercise will really mean anything in the end."

"That's…that's not fair!" Elyse complained. "I don't want you reading my diary. That's *private*."

"Touché," Mr. Beal said. "I understand that completely. That's why you'll pick five entries on which you'll be graded. The exercise is not for me to get a glimpse inside your teenaged brains; it's for *you* to gain a better understanding of the things that happen this year. Those entries can be as personal or as generic as you'd like. I assure you I will only read the entries you designate. I want to encourage you to be as candid with this project as you can be. I also want to encourage you to write as much as you possibly can. You'll never have the same perspective as you do right now."

Annie was thinking about the assignment, which she was eager to start, as she walked to her locker to meet Laurie after Gym. The project was *so* right up her alley. She had always kept a journal full of dreams, thoughts, song lyrics, everything. She had tried to make it a habit to start a new one around the time of every birthday, and even though her last birthday was a few days before the Bonfire, she hadn't had a chance to pick out a new one yet. This was going to be the easiest A she'd ever make in her life.

Annie's smile dissolved as she approached her locker. Panic bubbled up inside and she could hear her blood pumping in her ears. She frantically looked around to see if anyone was watching, then lunged forward and ripped a piece of paper from the front of her locker. She crumpled it up and held the ball with such force that her knuckles turned white. She blinked back the tears that stung her eyes and took a deep breath. *What the hell?*

Annie twisted her combination into the padlock and put her backpack on the ground, shoving the crumpled piece of paper into the bottom of her bag. She put her Science book from her locker on top of it. As she zipped up her bag, Laurie yelled from down the hall,

"We did it! We survived the first week!"

Several students stopped, looked and giggled before continuing on to their weekends.

"Yup," Annie said quietly. "We *sure* did." Her voice dripped with sarcasm. Laurie turned her combination into her own padlock on the locker next to Annie as she spoke.

"Okay, well. I've got to get home and clean my room before my mother has a cow. But I'll text you the second I'm finished, K?"

"Mmmhmm," Annie scanned the students rushing from the building. She was checking to see if anyone's gaze lasted a little too long. She was sure it was a waste. She had a pretty good idea of who was behind it.

Laurie looked at Annie. "Then you'll come over, right? We'll get ready for the party together."

"Sure." Annie was distracted, hardly paying attention.

"And Annie?" Laurie's expression was excited but concerned.

"What now, Laurie?" Annie looked straight at her friend with annoyance filling her eyes.

"Well, I invited the girls." Laurie started emptying her backpack and filling her locker. "Olivia and Maddie?" She posed it almost like a question as if Annie wouldn't know who "the girls" were.

"Of course you did," Annie said, irritation in her voice. She wasn't even a little bit surprised.

Annie was pulling on her jeans when her phone chirped.

Laurie: **All done! Get over here!**

Annie: **Chill, boss lady. Be there in a sec.**

Annie found Laurie panicking around her room when she walked in.

"What are you doing?" Annie asked, sitting on Laurie's bed. She watched Laurie riffle through her closet.

"Looking for something to wear!"

Laurie scooted shirt after shirt over on their hangers. Annie looked at the clock. It was 7:45.

"I thought we were going to the party at 9:30?" Annie reached over and grabbed an issue of *Us Weekly* off Laurie's nightstand.

"We are," Laurie said with a huff, "but Livi and Maddie will be here at 8!" Annie chose to ignore the pang of annoyance she felt at hearing *Livi*. "I can't let them see me like *this*!" Laurie was dressed in sweatpants, the makeup she'd worn to school washed off, and her hair was up in a loose ponytail. Laurie was naturally pretty. Annie thought she looked just fine.

"Aren't they coming over to *get* ready? Doesn't that mean you shouldn't be ready before they get here?" Annie glanced up from the magazine into Laurie's full-length mirror. She saw herself sitting cross-legged on Laurie's bed, wearing no make-up. Her dark jeans were a little tighter than what she normally wore, and she'd actually taken the tags off another shirt from the unworn side of her closet.

Laurie ignored Annie's question and, after three failed attempts, finally settled on an outfit. All that effort just to pick out an outfit to wear *while* picking out an outfit. Annie was exhausted just watching her.

Laurie looked great, even if the outfit would never make it outside. Her hair was still up, but in a tighter ponytail at the crown of her head. She had only a light swipe of brown eyeliner on, which made her green eyes pop slightly without it being obvious that she had any makeup on. She was wearing a light blue racerback tank top over a white fitted tee with dark skinny jeans. Her navy ballet flats had silver sequins dotted around the toes.

The doorbell rang, and Laurie leaped down the stairs. Annie was nervous and annoyed that she even let herself get into this situation.

She didn't have any desire to spend any extra time with those girls, but if she was being honest, she missed her friend. She and Laurie hadn't spent much quality time together since school started, not in the way they used to anyway. So maybe this was the compromise she had to make to keep her friend. What was the alternative, really? Losing Laurie?

She contemplated an escape route through the window, but the girls bounced through the doors too soon.

"Oh, my gosh!" Maddie squealed. "Your room is so freaking adorable," Maddie made a show of looking around.

Laurie's room was painted light pink, and her bed had a pale blue comforter on it. Her curtains were hot pink, and she had a purple lamp on each of her two nightstands. Laurie's room was…colorful, to say the least.

"Do you not have an attached bathroom?" Olivia asked, looking around. "Where are we supposed to get ready?"

"Oh!" Laurie looked panicked. "I thought we could use my vanity mirror on my dresser and my floor-length mirror."

—

"You *do* realize this isn't the best lighting to apply makeup in, don't you?" Olivia tossed her duffle bag onto the bed, almost on top of Annie. "Well," Olivia looked at Laurie's face, "maybe you don't."

Annie glanced up at Laurie and could see she felt attacked, but she recovered quickly.

"We could always use my parent's bathroom," Laurie said. "It's huge with lots of good lighting!" Olivia's face contorted into a half-smile, the daggers in her expression made it clear she was displeased with the suggestion.

God, that girl was so heinous.

"Or..." Laurie was panicking. It was probably awful, but Annie was secretly hoping that Laurie was finally getting a taste of how Olivia could really be.

Before anything could escalate, Maddie jumped in. "That sounds, like, totally awesome!" She was over-eager, and that sort of annoyed Annie, but it was also kind of...endearing?

She'd never spent any time with Maddie at all, but from what she'd observed, Maddie was a little like Laurie – giddy, peppy, just excited about everything. Annie had always wondered how a girl like that ended up under Olivia's thumb, but then again, it was happening with Laurie right under her own nose.

Whether Annie wanted to admit it or not, Olivia had some kind of power, and Annie questioned Olivia's motives for keeping Maddie around. She was clearly annoyed by her.

Maddie was certainly pretty, and she had a cute sense of fashion, Annie supposed. She couldn't tell how much of that was Maddie and how much of it was her copying Olivia, though. She had stick-straight, dirty blonde hair that lay thick against her shoulder blades. Her beautiful, deep blue eyes were huge, almost doe-eyed, and she was tiny, probably the tiniest of them all, both the skinniest and the shortest.

Maddie collected some of Laurie's makeup then turned to Olivia as if to ask for permission. Olivia rolled her eyes and then nodded. Once they were all in the bathroom, Annie humored Laurie by applying some blush and mascara. After some persuading, she sat down on the toilet seat and let Laurie apply eye shadow and lip-gloss. When Laurie was done, Maddie gasped.

"Shut! Up!" Maddie exclaimed. "Annie, I don't think I've ever seen you with, like, makeup on. You look...so totally different. Doesn't she, Livi?" Maddie turned to Olivia, who was leaning into the mirror, applying mascara. Clearly, they had missed her at the

Bonfire, Annie thought. Olivia turned and glared Annie down. It practically sent chills down Annie's spine.

"Well," said Olivia, turning back to the mirror and waving the mascara wand through her lashes again. "It's definitely an improvement."

Annie re-tied her hair into a low pony but Laurie came up behind her and pulled the elastic from her hair. She held up a straightener and Annie sighed. "If you must," she said, resigned.

"So tell me," Olivia said. Annie wondered if the girl had any tones besides *bitchy* and *I'm better than you.* "What exactly is going on with you and Josh?"

At the mention of his name, electricity shot through Annie's veins. She did her best to ignore it.

"Nothing," she said with a wave of her hand. "It's nothing." She could feel herself cringe under the lie—or at least what she *hoped* was a lie. Maybe she actually wanted something to be going on. But either way, at that moment, she was just thankful she had him as a friend.

"Of course it is," Olivia spit. "I just wanted to make sure *you* knew it's nothing. He'd never go," Olivia looked Annie up and down again with distaste, "for a girl like you. Trust me."

Bile rose in Annie's throat, but she swallowed it down. She made eye contact with Olivia in the mirror and squinted her eyes into her own bitchy smile; as if to say *thanks for the info, pal*. Before, she had been pretty sure Olivia taped the note to her locker, but now she was certain. Olivia was the only person Annie knew who could be so vile.

It was Dave's party they were going to, and because he was Josh's brother, Annie figured the party was as much his as Dave's. That thought made her stomach knot up with excitement despite what Olivia had said. He was, after all, half the reason she'd let Laurie wrangle her and paint her face.

The party was already in full swing when the girls arrived. They made a beeline for the keg. Annie followed them and filled her cup when her turn came.

She grabbed Laurie's arm as they made their way into the chaos of the party. She had to shout to be heard over the music. "Hey, I gotta pee. I'll —"

"Okay! I'll go with you!" Laurie lunged forward, but Annie pushed her back.

"No, no! It's okay, really. Go! Mingle! I'll catch up." Laurie gave her a look as if to remind her of the last party they attended together. Annie held up both hands, one clutching a Solo cup full of beer. "I promise. I'll find you."

Reluctantly, Laurie agreed. The house was huge, and there were people everywhere, but Annie found the bathroom after some searching. She dumped her beer into the sink and refilled her cup with water, silently thanking Josh for the tip. Honestly, she probably could have used the buffer of the booze if she was going to have to hang out with Olivia all night, but it tasted so bad.

Annie ventured back into the party and couldn't find the girls, but she did spot Brandon making a fool of himself near the keg line. She wandered around, telling herself she was looking for the girls, but deep down knowing she was looking for Josh. He was probably in his room, avoiding the party completely, or out on the back porch, simply enjoying the night. It wasn't like him to be the center of attention.

There were people everywhere, from every grade. It was loud – too loud. The music pumped through the big screen TV in the living room and surged through the entire three-story house.

People were paired up and grouped off. Everyone seemed to have a place. It didn't matter who it was – geeks, the drama kids, the popular crowd, or the band dorks – these people just seemed to know who they were.

Annie never ever cared about belonging before. She'd never felt like she *didn't* belong before. But now that Laurie came in and mixed things up, she felt more lost than ever.

Annie walked onto the back porch to get some air. She found the potheads out there, but no Josh. The smell of the weed made her light-headed, and the group of stoners never looked up. She remembered that Josh's bedroom was in the basement – he'd mentioned it one afternoon at lunch.

She wandered back through the party and kept an eye out for the girls, not that she'd actually stop even if she did spot them. Maybe it would be best if she tackled this party on her own.

Butterflies filled her stomach as she descended the stairs to the basement. It was comforting that the blaring music grew muffled the further down she climbed. It was relatively quiet, almost peaceful, in the basement.

The main room off the stairs was set up like a mini-living room. It had a decently sized TV, which was muted, a re-run of *The Office* playing in silence. There were a few people sitting on the couch in the middle of the room, in the midst of a heavy conversation about the homecoming float. She spotted a door that had to lead to Josh's room. It was open, but only a crack.

As she approached, she stopped dead in her tracks when she heard *I Would Be Sad* by the Avett Brothers growling from inside. She knew it. She knew he'd be down here, in his own little world. In that moment, she couldn't deny it anymore. She liked him.

She stopped just outside his door to take a breath. Or two. Or possibly three. When she heard a familiar voice, her heart stopped.

"Oh!" the girl exclaimed giddily. "The Avett Brothers! I've always loved them! This is one of my favorite songs ever!"

Laurie.

In Josh's room.

Lying her ass off.

What. The. *Hell*?

Against her better judgment, Annie pushed the door open. Just then, Laurie leaned herself across Josh's body on his bed and...Oh, God! She was kissing him!

A gasp or a moan or something must have escaped from Annie's mouth because suddenly, they were both looking at her. Josh's mouth was moving and Laurie looked panicked. They both stood up, but Annie couldn't process any of it. It sounded like her heart was beating in her ears. Ice was running through her veins. She backed away slowly.

"Annie!" She heard Josh call, but she turned and ran up the stairs. She heard Laurie stop Josh.

"No! I've got this!" Laurie shouted back at Josh.

She must have been chasing Annie, but Annie didn't stop to check. All she could think was that she needed to get the hell out of there. *Now.*

She threw herself through the front door, onto the front porch. She paused for a moment then propelled herself forward, off the porch and onto the driveway.

A massive cramp in her side stopped her. The pain was splitting through her abdomen, and she doubled over to catch her breath. Laurie flung herself through the doorway and joined Annie on the driveway. She opened her mouth, but Annie cut her off.

"What is *wrong* with you?" Annie seethed in between gasps of breath.

Laurie looked shocked. "*Me*? Are you even *kidding* right now? I called dibs and then you had to go off and throw yourself at him! And to think I was actually coming out here to *apologize* to you!"

"Please!" Annie spit, straightening herself and holding her side. "Don't let me interrupt you!" She spun on her heels and walks off.

"Annie, wait!" Laurie huffed. Annie stopped and turned around slowly. She couldn't hide the tears in her eyes.

Laurie stayed put but mouthed *I'm sorry* with her palms out as she backed away toward the house. Then she turned around and walked off.

Annie just stood there and watched Laurie re-enter the party, probably to go find Josh. She felt her heart splitting and she struggled to catch her breath again.

"Oh, no!" Annie heard someone call out from the front porch in a sugary tone. She scanned the crowd and spotted Olivia sitting on the railing. "I'm sorry. Did you *actually* let yourself believe you *belong* here?" The eyes of the entire crowd were on Annie and she was growing light-headed. Her heart was pounding. She turned slowly to head back home.

"Run along home now, heifer," Olivia called out to her.

When Annie got home, she ran straight up to her room. She didn't want her Dad to see her crying. She pulled out an empty binder and placed a giant stack of loose-leaf paper onto the rings and snapped the rings shut.

She pulled the crumpled piece of paper from the bottom of her backpack and flattened it out. A ballooned cartoon girl stared back at her. Written beneath the drawing was:

Annie Mackey: Heifer

She rubbed a glue stick across the crumpled back and smoothed the sign onto the first piece of notebook paper in her binder. She picked up a pen and wrote across the top.

High school: From the Perspective of A Target.

August 28, 2009

On repeat: The Avett Brothers: *Paranoia in B Major*

I knew the second Laurie burst into my room telling me she'd be at Willow Point this year that everything would change. I tried so hard to convince myself otherwise, but in my gut, I knew it was true. We're one week in and already everything is so screwed up. *I'm not even sure I can describe how I'm feeling. Everything feels cold and tight and nothing—and I mean* nothing—*seems fair. I feel out of control. Like I don't have a choice in how all of this goes down. It won't matter what I do—how I dress—who I hang out with—it's as if my fate has already been sealed. And* that's exactly *what makes all of this so much worse. It's not up to me anymore, and I have no idea what I can do to pull myself out of it.*

WHAT EXACTLY ARE PEOPLE SAYING?

After the party, Annie sat up in her bed half expecting Laurie to come barreling through the door armed with apologies. But she didn't.

Annie had to fight the urge to text her. Or call her. Or run across the street and barrel into *her* room. She needed to know what was going on, and she needed to figure out why her heart felt so twisted and mangled. She needed her best friend to help her walk through the sticky situation, but her best friend caused *this* sticky situation. Maybe that was why it hurt so much.

Despite their differences, Laurie was the one Annie would run to under any circumstances. When she heard her mom whispering "I miss you" into the phone when she knew her dad was on the couch watching golf, Annie ran to Laurie in tears. It was Laurie who had told her to suck it up and power through, that the affair was her parents' problem, not hers.

For the first time though, Annie couldn't run to Laurie. And honestly, if anyone should be doing any running, it should be Laurie.

But Laurie never showed up. She didn't call or even text the entire weekend. She might have been a pain in the ass, but that really wasn't like her. She didn't show up Monday morning to walk to school together either.

When the lunch bell rang that Monday, Annie felt nauseated at the thought of sitting at The Elite table, so she went to the library and blocked out the world with the help of her earbuds and Kings Of Leon. Every time her stomach growled she grew angrier with Laurie.

She decided during lunch that she no longer had any desire to sit near Laurie in Science. By not showing up all weekend, Laurie made it pretty clear she didn't have anything to say. So Annie didn't even want to give her the chance to whisper a half-assed apology in the middle of class.

Annie got to Science early and took a seat next to Ron, the kid who always answered Mrs. Swanson's questions correctly, usually without even raising his hand. He might have been annoying, but at least he wasn't Laurie.

When Laurie finally appeared in the doorway, Annie's heart raced and her fingertips felt numb. She averted her eyes as Laurie took a seat at the back of the room.

Josh wasn't in Gym that Monday. As much as she thought she might want to see him, she was relieved that he wasn't there. She wasn't sure what she was supposed to say to him anyway, and she really didn't know if she wanted to hear what *he* had to say. They definitely weren't together, and maybe it had been utterly foolish of her to fall for him, even a little bit.

He was probably just a nice guy. Maybe he didn't treat her any differently than he treated anyone else. Annie was foolish to believe it made her special.

When the final bell rang, Annie couldn't get home fast enough. Nothing had been resolved, but at least she survived the day. Avoiding people was exhausting. It was also pretty clear that Laurie had nothing to say to her, and that made Annie's blood boil. She felt like she didn't even know her best friend anymore. She'd never seen that side of Laurie until now.

Annie set her iPod into the dock. Coldplay's *Death and All His Friends* crooned while she buried her face into her pillows. She couldn't help but feel like the lyrics were speaking to her, telling her to be patient, that someday this might make some sense. That was why she loved music so much. It had a way of saying exactly how her heart felt when her mind couldn't make any sense of it.

She didn't actually hear the door open, but a sad little sniffle caused her to glance up at the doorway, where she saw a tear-stained Laurie. She immediately felt every emotion in the book. She hated seeing Laurie cry. Laurie was always so upbeat and positive, almost to the point of being annoying, that her tears were always a jarring sight.

She instantly felt bad for her friend. But then anger set in. Jealousy. Betrayal. Hurt. She didn't know what to say. She didn't even know if there was anything she *wanted* to say. Laurie walked over to the iPod dock and turned off the music. The silence between them hurt Annie's heart even more. She'd never not known what to say to Laurie. She'd never looked Laurie in the face seen a stranger.

Laurie sat on the edge of Annie's bed but kept her eyes forward. It was like she couldn't even look at Annie. The only sound was the tiny little sniffles Laurie huffed every few seconds.

Finally, Laurie turned to look at Annie, and in that moment, Annie's heart felt wrecked. She wanted to lunge forward and grab

Laurie into the tightest hug, a hug that would stop all of the pain for both of them. But it was more complicated than that.

"I need to explain," Laurie said in the quietest voice Annie had ever heard her use. "I know I hurt you. I *know* what I did hurt you. And I don't really even know what to say except to explain, okay?"

"Okay," Annie said, breathlessly.

"The thing is," Laurie started. She twisted herself all the way around to face Annie, bringing her legs up and folding them. "I know you like Josh. You might not say it out loud, but you do. And I did it anyway, and that makes me the crappiest friend ever." She trailed off, and Annie hoped that wasn't her full explanation, because if so, it was the crappiest explanation on the planet. A non-explanation.

"I could tell you that it wasn't all my idea," Laurie continued, "which it really wasn't. But none of that really matters, I guess because it all just boils down to the fact that you're my friend and I knowingly and willingly did something that would hurt you."

Laurie sat, wringing her hands in her lap, head down. Annie couldn't really tell if Laurie was finished and if it was her turn to talk. But even if it was, she didn't know what she was supposed to

—

say. She couldn't stop the tears that slipped down her cheeks, and she wiped at them quickly, as if to deny they had ever been there.

"And," Laurie continued, "I'm sorry." She threw her hands up in the air in annoyance. "God, those words seem so empty," she said almost to herself. "I feel like I need bigger words. Louder words. I've said I'm sorry to people before, and it always felt like enough. And really, sometimes it felt like *too much.* But in this moment, I feel like there aren't two less meaningful words on the planet. But they're all I have, I guess. And so I'm sorry." She sniffled.

Annie sat and watched Laurie wipe at her tears and she felt empty, just like Laurie's words. She wanted to believe Laurie. She didn't have much of a reason not to believe her, but she'd never had to deal with anything like this with Laurie. That was the benefit of keeping school out of their friendship; it kept the world out.

Annie cleared her throat. "I thought you said you were going to explain."

Laurie looked up at her confused. "I just–"

Annie held up her hands. "No. I don't need to hear you say *I'm sorry.* You're my friend; I can kind of assume that you're sorry. At least I hope I can if you're any kind of a decent person. What I need to hear is *why* you did it."

"It's going to sound like I'm making an excuse." Laurie stopped crying.

"I don't care. You need to tell me why you did it."

Laurie shifted her weight on the bed and leaned back on her hands. "Okay," she said in resignation. "When I was at Olivia's last week, you know, when we made the cookies?" She stopped as if waiting for Annie to validate. When she didn't get anything from Annie, she continued. "Well, Olivia pretty much told me that Josh was just being nice to you because you were by yourself that first day. She said he had some kind of thing for stray dogs."

Annie reacted and Laurie was quick to correct herself.

"No, no. I'm not calling you a dog. That's not what I meant at all. It's just that Olivia said that he's big on making sure everyone feels included, you know?"

Annie still didn't respond.

"Well, she said it was kind of sad how obvious it was that you liked him, and she was worried that you were going to get your feelings really hurt if you kept believing you had a chance with him." Laurie paused again, and Annie felt the words twisting in her stomach. She felt like she might get sick.

—

Laurie leaned forward and gestured, "that's why she said what she did that night at my house, too. Although she could have said it more tactfully, I guess." Laurie leaned back onto her hands.

"So anyway," Laurie sighed heavily. "She told me that I was more of Josh's type, and then I told her that I actually thought he was cute—and that I'd mentioned that to you, too." The expression that flashed Laurie's face was obvious guilt. "She got all up in a tizzy about how there was girl code and all that. And basically told me that it was my *right* to pursue him. None of this fixes anything, I know that. And it doesn't make any of it better, but Olivia just got in my head, and part of me believed her, you know?"

"Oooh," Annie said with an eye roll. "I didn't realize that you were actually doing me a *favor* by kissing Josh! Gosh," she continued sarcastically, "how *foolish* of me to even be upset with you. Thank you, Laurie. You really are just, oh, I don't know, the *best friend ever*." Her voice dripped with feigned sweetness.

"I told you it was going to sound like I was making an excuse."

"Then just be straight with me!" Annie got off of the bed and walked to the door hoping Laurie would take her lead, but she didn't. "Don't give me an excuse! Just tell me why you did it!"

"I told you. Olivia told me it was the right thing."

"Geez, Laurie. Just stop it! You're not the victim here! Olivia didn't *make* you do anything. You *wanted* to kiss Josh!"

"Yes! I did! Of course, I did! What's so wrong with that?" Laurie jumped up from the bed and walked toward Annie. "Is that what you want to hear? That I like him? That I wanted to kiss him? Because of *course* I wanted to. I wouldn't have done it if I didn't want to. I just didn't think you'd get this upset over it! Olivia—"

"Just shut *up* about Olivia! Seriously. I knew this would happen." Annie put her hands up in defeat. "I knew she would change you."

Confusion painted Laurie's face. "She's not changing me! You're so convinced that Olivia is this awful person…she's *not*!"

"Maybe you're right," Annie said quietly, walking back over to her bed and sitting on the edge. "Maybe she isn't changing you. Maybe this is how you've always been and I was just too stupid to see it." Laurie stood by the door, clearly wounded by Annie's words.

"You don't mean that," she said. "Don't be like that."

"Don't be like that? Are you even kidding me right now? I'm the same person I've always been, Laurie. I'm the same person at home as I am at school. I'm not the one *being* like anything. If someone needs to stop *'being like that,'* it's you!"

Laurie opened Annie's door, then turned back. "This is getting us nowhere. Maybe it was a mistake coming over here.'

"Yeah," Annie said defiantly. "Maybe it was."

And that was just Monday. Annie stayed in the background as much as she could the rest of the week. Josh was back in Gym on Tuesday, but aside from a shy smile and a quick wave, they really hadn't talked.

She made a habit of going to the library for her lunch, but she at least got smart enough to start bringing food with her. She may have been trying to avoid Laurie and the rest of The Elite, but she wasn't going to starve doing it.

Days turned into weeks. Two weeks, to be exact. It was the longest she and Laurie had ever gone without talking. They'd had fights before, sure, but nothing like this. Not even close. Usually, neither of them could stand not talking to the other, and the fights were almost always over before they even started. This time was different. Annie wasn't sure how they would come back from this, or if they even could.

Laurie kept her seat in the back of the room in Science while Annie became entirely too friendly with Ron the Know-It-All. As for

Josh, he had practically fallen into radio silence. She couldn't believe he was the same guy who'd been so friendly at the beginning of the year. He didn't ignore her completely, but he definitely wasn't warm.

As a matter of fact, he seemed skittish, jittery, and awkward when she was around. Sure, the kissing situation kind of sucked, but they weren't a couple, and it seemed like his guilt was just a tad overboard. She couldn't make heads or tails of him.

When the house phone rang that Thursday evening, Annie was doing homework and didn't reach for it. Phone calls were always for her parents, anyway, or it was some stupid telemarketer.

So when her mom yelled up the stairs that it was for her, Annie was surprised. She hesitated and stared at the cordless phone resting in its cradle, covered in a slight film of dust, before deciding to pick it up.

"Hello?" Annie put her pencil down on top of her notebook.

"Annie? Uh, hi. It's Maddie."

Annie was silent.

"From school?"

"Yeah, I know who you are. Just a little caught off guard is all. What's up?"

Annie could hear Maddie fidgeting on the other end before she spoke again.

"I got your number from the phone book. I hope that's okay." When Annie didn't say anything, Maddie continued. "Anyway, I uh—well. I, like, don't know if this is really the right thing to do or not, but I mean, if it were me I'd totally want someone to tell me."

"Maddie, what is it? What's going on?" Annie immediately felt guilty for snapping at the girl but she couldn't help it.

"I just thought you should know what's being said about you," Maddie finally blurted out.

Annie's heart stopped. What *now*? She immediately thought of Olivia and rolled her eyes.

"And what exactly are people saying?" Annie managed. Her cold tone surprised even her.

"I don't know how to say it without it sounding like I believe it. But, did you try to kill yourself after the Watson party?"

Annie fell silent on the line. She had known things would be weird with Laurie at her school, but she'd never imagined any of this. She knew it had to be Olivia behind it all, the sign on her locker, this rumor. And Laurie was getting all chummy with her! It made Annie feel sick to her stomach.

"Annie?" Maddie sounded genuinely concerned. "I'm sorry. It's totally rude of me to even ask. But either way, that's what they're saying. And I, like, thought you should know."

"Where would people even get that idea?" Annie's voice was smaller than she would have liked.

"Well, it's just that, like, some people are saying that when you left the party that night, that you went home and tried to slit your wrist. Something about the whole Laurie and Josh situation?" Maddie sounded unsure of herself, and also like she wished she hadn't called.

"That's crap!" Suddenly, Annie thought back to Josh's behavior over the last few weeks. His guilt. Guilt that she thought was a little overboard. *Oh, man.* He'd heard the rumor. He thought she tried to kill herself because he kissed someone else. Panic practically closed her throat.

"I totally thought so, too," Maddie said, "but then, like, the other night, Laurie said she'd confirmed it." Annie could almost *taste* her anger. Her so-called best friend was fueling this rumor? That was *it*. She didn't even know Laurie anymore. How the heck had they gotten to this place so fast?

"Confirmed it? What is that even supposed to mean?"

"She said she saw the scar in Science last week."

Annie pushed back her sleeve and examined the scar running across her wrist. Even if it *had* been a suicide scar, instead of an oven burn, it didn't give much leverage to their story. The "cut" went the wrong way!

"Maddie, I burned my wrist on my oven while pulling bread out one night." Annie pulled her sleeve back down as if to hide the scar from Maddie even though she knew she couldn't see it. "This is so crazy," she huffed out in a whisper.

"It really is. And I totally believe you! But people are taking this pretty seriously. They think you're, like, obsessed with Josh or something. You know, like stalker-level obsessed. And it's pretty much all anyone can talk about."

Annie's stomach felt sour. She hadn't done anything to deserve this. And the fact that Laurie was fueling the rumor made her feel like she could actually throw up. She didn't know what to say, and the silence filling the line must have been all too telling to Maddie.

"Listen," Maddie said quietly. "I'm, like, really sorry, okay? I'm totally not even sure if this was the right thing to d–"

Annie stopped her. "No, it was. Thank you." She almost

couldn't believe Maddie had the decency to tell her, and it made her question even more how these seemingly nice girls got mixed up with Olivia.

Maddie said goodbye, and Annie hung up the phone. She sat staring at it for a second. What the heck was she supposed to do about this? Was there even anything she *could* do?

The next day at lunch, Annie was sitting at her now-usual table in the library with her earbuds in. Chris Martin was singing away her anxiety as she tried to finish the last of her Science homework from the night before. If there was one benefit to skipping lunches at The Elite table, it was the extra time she had to get her homework done.

She was so focused that it took her a minute to realize someone was standing over her. Startled, she glanced up and yanked her earbuds from her ears.

"Shit," she stage-whispered to Maddie. "You scared the crap out of me."

Maddie giggled quietly. "Sorry," she whispered with a bounce. "I just, well, I wanted to check on you."

"I'm fine," Annie lied.

"I figured. I just wanted to make sure. I hate that you don't sit with us anymore."

Annie was surprised. The girls never even talked to Annie when she was squeezed in at the end of the table—it was like she was invisible to everyone there except Josh, and sometimes Brandon. "Do you blame me?"

"No, I totally don't," Maddie said. She gestured to the seat across from Annie. "Do you mind if I sit?" Annie looked dumbfounded. Maddie read the puzzled look on Annie's face. "I just can't stand to listen to their crap today."

"Sure," Annie closed her Science book and slid it into her backpack. A question was burning in the back of her throat, but she almost didn't want to know the answer. "Are they still talking about me?

Maddie dropped her eyes to the table and fidgeted with her hands. "The thing is, you avoiding everyone all this time? They're like, taking it to validate their story."

Frustration gripped Annie. She threw her hands up over her head, forgetting for a moment that she was in a library. "What the hell am I supposed to do? Why would I *want* to sit with those people?!" She was yelling. The librarian glared and shushed her. She could see that her words had stung Maddie. "Sorry, no offense."

Maddie was quiet for a moment. "None taken. You're right," she said. "It seems like a totally impossible situation."

Annie thought it over. "It is. It really is."

Annie took her new normal seat beside Know-It-All Ron. The clock was inching closer and closer to the tardy bell, and Laurie still hadn't shown up. Annie wondered if maybe Laurie was out sick, but then reminded herself that she didn't care.

The classroom filled up, and Annie noticed a girl taking Laurie's new normal seat at the back of the class. Laurie walked in *just* as the tardy bell rang, and Annie watched her scan the room with panic in her eyes.

Laurie was not a fan of not knowing her place, and the only seats left were at the table directly behind Annie and Know-It-All Ron.

"Annie!" Laurie whispered as Mrs. Swanson called the class to. Annie kept her eyes forward.

"*ANNIE!*" Laurie whispered more loudly. Annie felt a few eyes flash in her direction, so she turned around.

"What?" Annie hissed. Laurie hadn't spoken to her in weeks.

She knew, though, there was one thing Laurie couldn't handle.

"Get your stuff. Move back here with me." She hesitated a moment. "Please?" She almost sounded genuine.

"No."

"Annie, c'mon! Don't make me sit alone."

Annie's blood boiled. She'd seen more of Laurie's selfish side in the previous month than she had in the thirteen years they'd been friends, and it made her question their entire friendship.

Had she been fooled all this time into thinking Laurie was a decent person? She couldn't even believe that girl used to be her best friend. She didn't even recognize her anymore.

Annie turned back around and opened her notebook to the page with her completed homework answers.

She heard Laurie gasp, "Eff! Annie! There was homework?" Annie couldn't help but smile to herself. She turned back around.

"I burned my arm on my oven," Annie said then turned back around.

"What?" Laurie spit.

Annie turned around once more. "It's a burn mark, bitch."

Anger boiled in her heart. Anger, with a dash of hurt. A *ton* of hurt. She couldn't take it anymore.

Joey Hodges

"Oh, whatever," Laurie whispered back. "Who cares? It's just a rumor!"

Annie turned to face forward so quickly her chair squawked against the tile floor. She was pumped with adrenaline, searching for a quick response, but when she opened her mouth, she heard Mrs. Swanson's voice.

"Ladies! Outside! *Now!*" The entire class sang out "oooooooh" in unison as Annie pushed her chair back. She could hear Laurie's heels *click-clack* quickly against the tile as she tried to catch up with Annie. When the girls got out to the hallway, Mrs. Swanson's face was red.

"Do you ladies have something you find more important than reviewing last night's homework?"

"No, Ma'am," Annie said quietly.

"Well, actually, yes!" Laurie said indignantly. Mrs. Swanson shot Laurie a surprised look.

"Alright, then. What is it?" Mrs. Swanson crossed her arms and awaited the answer with a curious smirk on her face. Annie could tell she didn't get *that* response to her question often.

"Annie is mad at me because some girl started a rumor, and I just don't think that's fair!"

"You *went along with it*!" Annie yelled. "You're supposedly my *best friend* and instead of *defending* me, you *fueled* it!"

"Oh, whatever, Annie! It's just a rumor!" Laurie shouted again. Mrs. Swanson held up her hands before speaking.

"Ladies, ladies. I have a classroom full of students who are eager to learn. Do you mind keeping your mouths shut during my class and handling this at another time? If not, I'd be happy to assign you both to detention, and you can sort out your problems there."

Mrs. Swanson led Annie and Laurie back inside, where the entire class greeted them with wide-eyed stares. It made Annie long for the days, pre-Laurie when she was invisible at school.

The girls took their seats without another word. Nothing was resolved by their episode. Nothing at all.

Annie couldn't leave the gym fast enough when the final bell rang. She was thankful to have made it through the day alive, and she was even more thankful she had the next two days off.

She'd gotten entirely too good at avoiding people. Josh tried to approach her in Gym, but she'd made sure to dodge him. Same with Sally. Actually, she'd hardly spoken to Sally at all since the beginning of the year.

It was almost funny to her. Now that Laurie was with her at school, she had no one. That wasn't how it was supposed to go at all.

The streets of Willow Point had never looked more inviting. She took a breath of the fresh September air and forced herself to relax.

She was almost home when she heard footsteps running behind her. She tensed a little but didn't turn around. Hope had her thinking it was Laurie, running to catch up so they could finally hash out whatever was going on between them.

But Laurie had been wearing heels that day, so Annie was sure it wasn't her. She wouldn't risk ruining a pair of her expensive shoes to salvage a friendship. At least the *new* Laurie wouldn't.

"Hey!" she heard a voice call out from behind, shaking her from her thoughts. Annie turned around and was floored.

"Josh." Annie could hardly squeak out his name. "What are you doing?" She stopped walking, and he finally reached her.

"Annie! Hey!" Josh wiped the glistening sweat from his brow. Annie couldn't help but notice, *again*, how handsome he was. His yellow polo shirt was un-tucked, and his jeans were a perfect shade of dark blue. His eyes were soft, but with an anxious look in them.

"Do you have a minute? I think we need to talk."

IF YOU'RE ASKING OUT OF PITY

"I'm sorry, what?" Annie stood baffled in front of Josh, who had finally stopped babbling and spit out the question he'd been dancing around.

"Would you like to go to Homecoming with me?" Josh repeated.

"You want me to go to Homecoming with you?" Annie hesitated. "What? Why?" Annie shifted her weight to her right foot, adjusted her backpack straps, and glanced behind her. She hated to sound so shocked, but could anyone blame her? She was sure Josh's posse was hiding, snickering behind the trees. But she saw no one. Either this was real, or Josh's friends were good hiders.

"Well," Josh looked slightly confused, "because we're friends? At least, I think we're friends. We're friends, right?" Josh looked wounded. "If, um, you don't have to if you don't want to. I just wanted to ask." He kicked a pebble.

"You're serious? Like, you actually want to take me to the dance?"

"Well, yeah. Why else would I be asking?"

"Okay, I can't lie. I'm a little confused." She hated that she couldn't just let herself be excited, but she needed some answers. Maybe he'd be a little more upfront than Laurie had been. "You've basically been ignoring me for weeks."

Annie thought back to the comment Olivia made about her being a stray dog. Josh looked embarrassed. He straightened his posture and hiked his backpack up to readjust it on his shoulders.

"Not to mention the whole kissing my best friend thing." Annie was shocked by her own bluntness, but she'd learned that unless you call it like it is, people would run with whatever story best suited them.

"I know," he said shyly. "I'll be honest, the Laurie thing shocked me, too. I was downstairs in my room, minding my own business and she just paraded right in."

"Yeah," Annie said knowingly. "She has a tendency to assume familiarity with basically anyone, anywhere."

"I didn't mind her being down there," he explained. "I knew she was your friend. I just figured maybe you sent her down for recon. You girls do some weird things."

Annie chuckled.

"But then it was pretty obvious that she had other plans. I didn't exactly know what to do. I didn't want to come across as rude, but I also really didn't want to give her the wrong idea. I swear that girl has a one-track mind."

"It's true," Annie agreed. "She does. It's pretty hard to stop Laurie once she has her mind made up about something." That was a quality Annie *used* to admire about Laurie, how she always went for what she wanted and never made any apologies for it. Now it seemed more like a flaw.

"I don't want to be some jackass standing here telling you that your best friend put the moves on me—but—"

"No," Annie stopped him. "I believe you. She did. We talked about it. She wanted to kiss you. And when Laurie wants something, it's rare that it doesn't happen."

"Yeah, well. I didn't really know what to do. I wanted to go after you but she told me not to—that she'd handle it. And then I heard…" he trailed off.

"The rumor," Annie said flatly. "At least I *hope* you know it was a rumor."

"Yeah, okay. Yes." Josh said. "I heard the rumor. And I'll admit it spooked me at first. If we're being honest, I didn't know you all that well, and the idea that I could cause something like that freaked me out." Embarrassment painted his face. "But after a while, longer than I'm proud of I'll admit, I considered the source. I knew from even the first time we talked at the Bonfire that you were..."

He hesitated.

"I don't know, different. *Good* different. You're not like the other girls. And I liked talking to you. I *like* talking to you. You're just, I don't know, who you are and I like it. So when I really thought about it, what I'd heard really didn't seem all that likely.

"And I'm sorry I avoided you. It was really a jerk thing to do. But, geez, I don't know. I didn't know *what* to do, you know? Either way, I'm sorry. But I felt like I needed to give you and Laurie some time to figure out whatever it was that was going on. I know you two are friends. And I really didn't want what happened between her and me to come between *you* and her."

An honest answer. Annie wouldn't have believed it had it come out of anyone else's mouth. But Josh was different. "I screwed up," he said sheepishly. "And maybe I didn't handle everything the right way, but I really thought giving you some time would be best. I understand if you want to say no. But I'd really like it if you said yes."

Annie couldn't help but smile at his honesty and charm. "Well, then I guess I'm saying yes."

Josh made a fist and punched the air.

"Alright!" He exclaimed. Annie giggled at his enthusiasm.

"Great!" He clapped his hands together. "I'll call you with the details once I hammer everything out." He started to walk off, then turned around excitedly. "Thanks, Annie. We'll have fun, I promise."

Annie was left standing just a few feet from her driveway with a dopey smile on her face and nerves in her stomach. She must be crazy. She had trouble avoiding drama and humiliation in the halls on a regular school day. A school dance? That's a breeding ground for drama and humiliation!

But she couldn't deny being a *little* excited that Josh had asked her. She had a week to figure everything out. For the moment, she decided to just let herself be happy.

When Annie got inside, she found her brother playing X-Box

in the living room.

"Drew!" Annie dropped her backpack and ran toward him. "What are you doing home?"

"Eh, you know." Drew paused the game and received his baby sister in a hug.

"After about thirty phone calls a week from Dad, I caved." Drew reached forward and turned off the TV.

"Plus," he said, "Jamie had to go home to Boone to help her parents with their Appalachian Homecoming tailgate booth." Drew met his girlfriend at orientation freshmen year, and they've been dating ever since. Annie loved the two of them together, and she envied their relationship. It was practically the only normal, functioning relationship she knew of.

"Why didn't you go with Jamie?" Annie asked. "I'm sure her parents could've used your help." Jamie's parents were both born in Boone. They had attended Watauga High in Boone, and, when they'd graduated high school, they'd both went to Appalachian State University, also in Boone. They were what people referred to as "Booneites." Now they ran the Alumni Foundation, and Homecoming was their biggest event of the year.

"Well," Drew looked uncomfortable.

"What?" Annie interrogated. "What did you do?"

"She just needs some space. She, uh," Drew half smiled, "needs time to cool off. We're fine. We'll *be* fine."

"Drew!" Annie punched his arm. "What did you do!?" She giggled but also felt her heart ache. She really liked Jamie. She was probably the only female older than herself with whom she had any kind of real relationship.

"Seriously, Annie. It's nothing. I just made a joke that she didn't find all that funny."

"And what joke was that?" Drew was a prankster, but he could definitely take it too far sometimes.

"Well, a lot of our friends have been getting engaged lately. And even though we've had the 'It's coming, bear with me' conversation, she has ring and engagement envy. She's ready now. I get it. But a guy's got to wait for the perfect moment, you know?"

"Well, yeah." Annie furrowed her brow, unsure of where his story was going. "The Perfect Moment. I think that's what every girl wants, right?"

Annie always knew that Jamie and Drew would eventually get married. They've always had that kind of relationship. In fact, her whole family decided when Drew brought her home for the first time, during Fall Break of their freshmen year, that Jamie was *the one*. They just meshed well. "So what happened? What'd you do?"

"Well," Drew said again, looking embarrassed, "a few weeks after we had the discussion, Jamie came over to the apartment. She was telling me about another one of her friends who had gone ring shopping. I could tell, despite her efforts to seem nonchalant about it, she was jealous. So I thought I'd loosen the tension with a joke."

"Oh, Drew. You didn't."

"We went out to dinner that night, and as we were walking into the restaurant I grabbed her hand to stop her, knelt onto one knee and asked her if she'd....wait while I tied my shoe. I saw it on a TV show. I thought it was funny!"

"*Drew!*" Annie hit his arm. "You didn't!"

"Oh, I did. And she was pissed. She grabbed my keys, got in my car and drove off. I had to walk four miles home."

"Wow," Annie sighed. "Are you sure you guys will be okay?"

"Oh, yeah. She's just a little peeved right now. It'll work out. Now it gives me a chance to catch up with my little sis."

He sat back down on the couch, and Annie sat in the La-Z-Boy across from him. "How's it going? You know, with everything?" He asked pointedly. She knew exactly what he was asking.

"It's okay." She hesitated, hoping to change the subject.

"Yeah, that was convincing," he quipped as he leaned back into the couch, waiting for a better answer.

"Okay, honestly? It kind of sucks."

"You expected that, didn't you?"

"The sad thing is, yeah. I did. How awful does that make me? My best friend finally gets to go to school with me, and I assume it means disaster."

"Well," he said, "it's no secret the two of you are...different." He hesitated. "I think it would have been stupid to think there wouldn't be *some*, uh, adjusting."

"Oh, there's been *adjusting*," she said, using air quotes. "Trust me."

"I wouldn't doubt it. Everything okay, though?"

She thought about her brother's question. Was everything okay? She thought over everything that had gone on since the Bonfire, and she wasn't really sure. Nothing was how it used to be. But was she okay?

"Yes and no. I don't even know if Laurie and I are friends

anymore, honestly. School is weird. Different than it ever was before, at least for me. I used to like school, now I just kind of …survive it."

She filled him in on everything that happened. She hadn't realized how much she'd really needed to talk. By the time she was done, she felt lighter.

"I'm going to be frank," Drew said, "and it might hurt your feelings. But as your older brother, I feel like if it's anyone's place, it's mine. I think you're better off without her. She's never been my favorite person, and I've always, *always* thought you were better than her. Don't let her or any of this crap drag you down, do you understand me?" He was using his authoritative, protective big brother voice and it made her smile to herself.

"I'm doing my best," she said, meaning it. "And anyway, Josh actually just asked me to Homecoming."

Drew looked surprised. "You think that's a good idea?"

Annie felt stung as if even her own brother thought there was no way someone like Josh would ever bother asking her to a dance without some kind of ulterior motive.

"Why wouldn't it be? We talked. We worked everything out. I believe him."

"I don't know, Annie. It just doesn't seem to add up, if you ask me."

"What the heck is that supposed to mean?" She wished she hadn't told him. At least that way, she could pretend in her heart that Josh simply asked her because he wanted to go with her. She didn't want to think he'd do anything to hurt her. He was better than that.

"He's friends with those people, right? A person's friends say a lot about who they are. I'm just saying."

"That's crap and you know it! What would it say about me that Laurie is my friend? *Was* my friend," she corrected. "Maybe he asked me just because he wants to go with me. Isn't *that* possible?"

"Sure," Drew said timidly. She couldn't tell if he meant it or not.

"What, you think I should cancel?"

"I'm not saying that," Drew defended. "I would just, I don't know. Just be careful, okay, Annie? You never know with guys like him."

"You don't even know him," Annie snapped, feeling defensive and attacked. Why couldn't her brother just be happy for her? There was a part of her that didn't want to admit that he could be right.

"You're right. I don't." He leaned forward on the couch and rested his elbows on his knees. "It's just, I *was* a guy like him in high school, Annie. And I'm not proud of it, but I wasn't exactly the best person on the planet back then."

Annie was quiet, not sure how to respond.

"I guess all I'm saying is be careful, okay?"

Monday morning came more quickly than Annie would have liked. Having Drew home for the weekend had been awesome, despite the little spat on Friday afternoon. Truthfully, it had just been nice to have someone to hang out with. She'd missed that kind of company since the blow up with Laurie.

When lunchtime rolled around, she felt a little conflicted but made her way to the library. She'd see Josh in Gym, and that was enough, right? She was walking down the hallway when someone came up behind her and grabbed her sides. She squealed and hit the ground.

"Oh crap! I'm sorry!" Josh was laughing.

"Yeah, sorry. I go fetal whenever someone tickles me. Always have." Annie took Josh's hand and pulled herself off the ground. "It's okay," she said as she brushed herself off, "go ahead and laugh." She cracked a smile.

"Listen," he said, draping his arm around her shoulders. Her stomach tensed and she thought maybe he'd changed his mind about the dance. Of course he had. "Would you do me a favor?"

What? "Uh, sure," she agreed hesitantly. "What's up?"

"I was hoping maybe you'd sit with me today. The table's been sort of lonely without you. There's only so much conversation I can make with Brandon, you know?"

Her stomach dropped and she really wanted to say no. "You could always join me in the library."

"Yeah," he said, "I could except I really have to give Brandon his homework."

Annie gave him a puzzled look.

"Trust me, don't ask." He chuckled. "Please? Sit with me?" She could feel the ice around her heart melting. She gave in.

Annie slid into the picnic table beside Josh. Laurie looked up from her conversation with Olivia but didn't say anything. When Brandon arrived, he slid in next to Annie.

"Oh. I can move," Annie said, "you know, if you want to sit next to Josh." Annie started to stand.

"Nah. I'd rather sit next to a pretty girl than a stinky dude." Annie felt the blood rush to her cheeks and she tried to decipher his tone. Was he being serious, or was there a hint of sarcasm in his voice? Annie never knew where she stood with these people.

Josh leaned over her toward Brandon, "Did you ask Olivia yet?" She could feel his breath on her neck, and it sent shivers down her spine. She looked from Olivia to Brandon. She just didn't get it. What did he see in her?

"Not yet," Brandon said. "I was planning on asking her later today. Maybe tonight?" He slid in closer to Annie. "We're all going in together on a limo, right?"

Annie felt panicked. They were all going together? No. No, *no*. She couldn't do that. She leaned into Josh and whispered, "Can I talk to you for a second?"

He looked at her. "Sure," he said in his normal volume. "What's up?"

She looked around. "Not here," she hissed then smiled, trying to disguise her panic. She asked Brandon to excuse them, and he slid out, letting them pass. She led Josh over to a tree near the table but not *too* near. "What's going on?" he asked nervously. "Everything okay?"

"I guess. Sort of. It's just…everyone's going to the dance together?"

"Well, yeah. We thought it would be fun to get a limo. You know, do the group pictures and dinner thing before the dance?"

"Right," she dropped her gaze to the ground. She tried to think of any other way to handle the situation, but she came up dry.

"I'm really sorry, but maybe you should ask someone else." Her throat was closing up, and she could feel the tears prickling. Josh read her expression and was instantly concerned.

"Why? What's going on?"

"I'm really sorry. I just don't think this is a good idea. I'm *so* not comfortable going with everyone. And I don't want to stop you from having fun. Seriously. Ask someone else. It's totally fine. It's not your fault, I promise. I just don't think I can do that."

He held his hands up in self-defense. "Whoa, whoa, okay," he laughed. "Relax. It's alright." He said casually, and her heart dropped. He was agreeing to ask someone else.

"We can always just tag along with my brother," he continued. "He and his girl are going to Storie Thyme beforehand. Have you ever been there?"

She had, for her birthday once. With her family and…well. Never mind. "Are you sure?" she asked as she shifted her weight from one foot to the other and leaned back against the tree, ignoring his question. "Really, I don't want to ruin your night."

He smiled. "The only way my night would be ruined is if you ask me again to take someone else." He squeezed her arm and his eyes crinkled as he grinned. He draped his arm over her shoulders again and led her back to the table.

Olivia looked up from her conversation. "What was all that about?" She nodded her head toward the tree in disgust.

"Nothing," Josh said casually as he and Annie slid back in at the end of the table next to Brandon. "Just making our plans for Friday."

Olivia scrunched up her nose as if she'd smelled something awful. "You're going with *her?* Are you mental?"

Before Josh or Annie could say anything, Brandon piped up, saving them both. "Hey, Olivia!" Brandon got the attention of the entire table and fiddled with a Dorito. "You wanna go with me?" Annie could have hugged him for the distraction.

"With you?" Olivia looked caught off-guard and disgusted.

"Yeah. Why not?" Brandon dropped the Dorito and glanced around the table. Everyone was watching him.

"Um," Olivia grew quiet for a moment, and her face softened. "I'll let you know what color my dress is so you can coordinate your suit and arrange for the proper corsage, okay?"

"So," Brandon asked, "is that a yes?"

"Whatever, Brandon. Just be at my house at 7."

On Thursday afternoon, Annie was messing around with chords on her blue sparkly Daisy Rock guitar her dad had given her for her 13th birthday. When Laurie walked through her bedroom door, Annie looked up, shocked.

"What are you doing here?" Annie asked, removing the guitar strap and laying the guitar next to her on the bed.

"Yeah, I figured you'd be surprised to see me." Laurie had a happy smile across her face and a pep in her step as if nothing had gone awry between them. She plopped herself down in Annie's orange butterfly chair in the corner.

"No, really. What are you doing here?" Annie didn't like or trust the excitement that welled up inside of her. She hated that something that used to be so normal in her life had now become a source of suspicion. She missed Laurie – the *real* Laurie.

"I just thought I'd come by and see what you were up to. Do you have a dress yet for the dance?"

"Oh, what?" Annie spit, "Olivia didn't need you up her butt tonight?"

"Shut up." Laurie gave a stern look but kept her smile. "I'm trying here, okay? This is me trying."

Annie stopped herself. Maybe this was just as hard for Laurie as it was for her. It was all new territory, she guessed.

"Listen," Annie started, but Laurie held up her hands.

"Can we not? You know? Can't we just agree that we're both sorry and move on?" She leaned forward, resting her elbows on her knees. "I really miss you," she said genuinely. "And honestly? Fighting with you is *exhausting.*"

Annie smiled. She knew the feeling.

"Truce?" Laurie held out her hand, pinky extended.

Annie leaned forward and wrapped Laurie's pinky with her own in a pinky promise. "Truce." She noticed there were tears glistening in Laurie's eyes. She stood and yanked Laurie up from the chair. They pulled each other into a tight hug. They were both crying and laughing at the same time.

"This is stupid," Laurie said, pulling herself out of the hug and wiping at her eyes. "God, I really hated not talking to you."

"I know," Annie said happily, sitting back down on her bed

and wiping at her own eyes. "Me, too. You're kind of a bitch when you want to be."

"It's a crown I wear with pride," Laurie said jokingly, and the girls laughed. "So seriously, do you have a dress for Friday?"

Annie stood from her bed, walked over to her closet, and pulled out a plain black knee-length dress with a high neck and sleeves. "I thought I would just wear this."

Laurie looked from Annie to the dress and back to Annie. Annie could see the wheels in Laurie's head turning. "What?"

"I don't want to fight again," Laurie said with a smile.

"You hate it," Annie stated, no question necessary. Annie looked at the dress.

"Well, I mean, you're going with Josh, right? Don't you want to look, I don't know, like a knockout?"

"Are you okay with that, by the way?" Annie asked, ignoring Laurie's question. Laurie waved her arms dismissively.

"Water under the bridge, girl," she said genuinely. "Seriously. I've moved on, *trust* me." There was a sparkle in Laurie's eyes.

"Forget the dress," Annie said, hanging it back up and returning to the edge of her bed. "Spill."

"There's nothing to tell, exactly. I'm just noticing that junior and senior boys are *hot.*"

Annie laughed and rolled her eyes. "Anyway," she sighed, "what did you have in mind for a dress?"

Laurie grinned and stood up. "Grab your purse," she said. "We're going to Magnolia Girls!"

When the girls arrived at the shop, they headed directly to the back to raid the clearance rack.

"I don't know," Laurie sighed as she took another dress out of Annie's hands. "I'm just not seeing anything *wow* enough."

"What about this?" Annie held up a plain champagne-colored cocktail dress.

"That could work," Laurie exhaled, clearly not sold. Annie slipped behind the curtain of the dressing room. She was squirming into the dress when Laurie threw another over the top. "Try that one, too."

Both dresses only received a heavy sigh when Annie modeled them. "You've got such a great body," Laurie said, walking up to Annie and pulling the fabric on the second dress, gathering it at the back to show off Annie's waist. "I'm just not seeing anything here that's going to do it justice, you know?"

The shop attendant walked up, an older lady with a style Annie could only imagine Laurie would describe as *fierce*. She had a feeling that's exactly how Laurie will look when she's in her thirties.

"Can I help you with anything?" The woman grinned, but Annie could tell she was a little annoyed.

"I don't know," Laurie said, both to Annie and the attendant. "I just don't think you're going to find what you need on the clearance rack," she said to Annie directly.

"Yeah, well. I can't exactly drop hundreds on a dress, L." She felt suddenly defensive. She had a little bit in savings, but she didn't want to dip into it too much for a stupid dress, even if it *would* make her look like a knockout. She was saving for college. UNC wasn't cheap, and who knew if she'd get the kind of scholarships she needed to attend.

Laurie's eyes lit up. She jumped up and down, clapping her hands. "I have an idea!"

"Oh, God. What now?" Laurie and her *ideas* usually meant some kind of trouble for Annie.

"Let me buy you a dress. I mean, seriously. It's the least I can do after…" she waved her hands vaguely, "you know. All that stuff we aren't going to talk about."

Annie thought for a second. "I don't know, Laurie. It's really not necessary."

"I *know* it's not necessary. I *want* to do it. Please?" She held her hands together and put the tips of her fingers underneath her chin. She widened her green eyes into a perfectly executed puppy dog expression.

"I really don't want to spend your money, L."

Laurie waved her off. "It's hardly my money, and you know that." She had a point. Her parents were, well…they weren't exactly the parenting kind of parents. They were more of the throw-money-at-your-kid-and-hope-it-works-out-for-the-best kind of parents.

"Alright," Annie resigned and stepped back behind the curtain to change. Laurie squealed and told the attendant to help her pull some dresses.

Annie stood behind the curtain as Laurie brought her dress after dress. She modeled every single one, and each time, Laurie sent her right back into the dressing room.

"We will find the perfect one," Laurie shouted to an exhausted Annie. She thought shopping was supposed to be fun.

She heard the attendant say something to Laurie, but she

couldn't quite make it out. "What?" she shouted.

"Hold on," Laurie said, distracted. "Susan thinks she might have something in the back."

Annie sighed and waited. She was standing in nothing but her underwear when Laurie slid behind the curtain, joining her with a dress draped over her arm.

"This is it!" she said excitedly. "I know it." She helped Annie into the dress, and the girls walked out together to find Susan waiting anxiously. Laurie nudged Annie in front of the three-way mirror. Annie could hardly believe what she saw.

The dress was a deep plum, almost metallic, with a greenish sheen to it. It was strapless and cinched at the waist, letting out into a skater skirt that hit a few inches above her knee. It was nothing like anything she would have ever picked for herself, but Laurie was right – it was perfect. She instantly felt 100% more confident.

She reached under her armpit to pull out the price tag, but Laurie swooped in and ripped it off before she got to it. "My treat, remember?" Laurie turned her attention to Susan. "You mentioned it was on hold?"

Susan looked down at her watch and glanced back up, catching Annie's eyes, which were filled with concern. "Oh, don't worry," she said. "These girls came in over the weekend and put the dress on hold. But that hold expired 30 minutes ago. They're clearly not coming."

"Sweet!" Laurie exclaimed.

"Let me at least give you some money," Annie said to Laurie as she headed back into the dressing room and rummaged around for her bag. Laurie pulled the curtain closed and shouted "Not a chance!"

Before Annie could argue further, Laurie had sauntered off. Just as Annie was zipping up her jeans, her cell phone rang.

"Hello?" Annie balanced the phone between her ear and shoulder as she gathered the dress and her purse and exited the dressing room.

"Hey, it's Josh." Excitement surged through her body. "I've got the details for you."

"Great." Annie tried to play it off as if his call wasn't the highlight of her life. Annie mouthed "Josh!" to Laurie, who smiled and simulated clapping her hands.

"I talked to Dave. He's cool with us tagging along, so don't worry about the rest of the group, okay?"

Annie smiled. "Thanks," she said sheepishly. "I really

appreciate it."

"Not a problem, seriously. Anyway, we'll pick you up around 7 then head to Storie Thyme. We made reservations."

"Sounds great," Annie said, getting excited.

"Perfect!" Josh sounded genuinely pleased. "This'll be fun," he said encouragingly as if he knew Annie might need the extra push.

"It really will be," she agreed. He said goodbye, and Annie could hardly catch her breath when she hung up.

"You are seriously glowing," Laurie said. "You are just so smitten, aren't you?"

"No, no," Annie said. "He's just a nice guy. And we're just friends."

"Yeah, right," Laurie scoffed, making a dramatic show of rolling her eyes.

Susan walked to the opposite side of the counter and took the dress from Annie, hanging it in a protective clear plastic bag. She scanned the price tag she took from Laurie, and the price appeared on the register. Annie gasped.

"Three hundred and fifty dollars?" Annie was horrified. "Laurie, you're crazy. That's way too much."

Laurie casually handed her card to Susan. "Shut up. I owe you." Laurie took Annie's hand and squeezed it.

Susan handed the dress back to Annie and smiled genuinely. "You girls have fun tomorrow!" she called out as the girls walked to the exit. The chime on the door called their attention, and Annie tensed as she saw Olivia and Maddie enter.

"Livi!" Laurie squealed. "Oh Em Gee! You have to see the dress we just got Annie for tomorrow night. You'll die!" Laurie ran up to the girls and hugged them both quickly. Annie stood back, watching the scene unfold before her. Maddie smiled warily at her.

Olivia glanced at the dress that Annie was carrying and then glared at Susan. "You sold my dress?"

Then Olivia looked at Laurie. "And what the hell are you doing with *her*?" The expression on Olivia's face terrified Annie. She stood paralyzed in front of the girls. What the heck was happening? No, no, no. She felt her lungs tighten. She couldn't breathe.

Before Annie could say a word, Olivia turned on her heels, walking out.

"It's on, bitch!" she exclaimed, the door slamming shut behind her.

STUPID GIRL DRAMA

"Annette!" Annie's mother shouted, pounding on her bedroom door. "Get up now! Laurie's already here! You're going to make her late!" Lisa turned to Annie's father, who was climbing the stairs to the second floor. "I don't have time for this crap," she said, sliding her purse onto her shoulder. "You deal with her." Lisa descended the stairs.

Annie could overhear Lisa's sugary sweet tone, one she never, ever used with Annie, telling Laurie to go on ahead.

"Don't let her dramatics make you late, love," Lisa said, and Annie let out a heavy sigh. She heard Lisa and Laurie click-clack their way to the front door. The door slammed shut behind them. Annie buried her face deeper into her pillow to stifle her sobs.

"Annie? Sweet?" Her dad rapped his knuckles lightly against

her door. "Are you okay?"

"Please don't make me go," Annie whimpered. She almost hated herself for how pathetic she sounded. She *did* hate herself for how weak she felt. "I just can't do it today."

The door opened slowly and her dad stood in the doorway. His bushy eyebrows were knitted, and his deep, rich brown eyes were sad. "What's going on, Sweet? I've never seen you like this." He was right. He'd never seen her like this. *She'd* never seen her like this. But the truth was, it was all just too much. The weeks of torment and torture had caught up to her, and she just couldn't do it anymore.

"I think I need a mental health day," she said quietly as she sat up in bed and wiped the tears from her eyes. "I know what you're going to say, that school's so imp—"

Her dad held up his hand and stopped her. "No," he said, "School *is* very important, and I know you know that. But I *also* know how seriously you take it, and if you're asking for a day off, then you need a day off."

He walked slowly into her bedroom, wary of making the wrong move and setting her off into another crying fit. He sat gently on the edge of her bed and reached out to tuck a strand of her wild bedhead hair behind her ear.

She dropped her chin to her chest and sniffled. "Thanks, Dad."

There was not a single person on the planet more important to her than her dad. He just got her. And ever since she heard her mom on the phone that dreadful night, she'd felt particularly connected to her dad, like it was her job to love him enough for herself *and* her mother. She'd heard girls at school talk before about how their dads were just these ghost creatures who were in and out in the dark hours of the night, bringing in big paychecks, but little else. Her dad wasn't like that. Never had been.

Her mom, on the other hand, was the most un-nurturing person ever. Annie hardly ever saw her. She couldn't care less about what was going on in her own daughter's life. She had no interest in their family at all anymore, it seemed.

"I'll tell you what," Jason said, reaching over and patting her knee. "How about I make a call and play hooky and we get out of here?" Annie's heart lifted. He always knew exactly what she needed.

"Yeah?" She leaned her face into his palm as he reached to wipe a tear. "I'd really like that."

She hadn't spent good, quality time with her dad in what felt like forever. She'd been so distracted by everything at school, and he'd been so busy with his work travels. So as Jason started the car and threw the heat on that uncharacteristically cold and dreary North Carolina September morning, Annie felt a twinge of happiness. There was something about spending time with him that always helped her reboot.

They hadn't been on the road long before her dad turned and headed west on I-40. She realized then that he was taking her to Chapel Hill, her favorite place ever. It reaffirmed her faith in her dad and just how well he knew her. She closed her eyes and leaned her head against the seat. Her eyes felt swollen, and her heart felt tired.

She must have dozed, because the next thing she knew, Jason was resting his hand on her shoulder and asking her about breakfast. She opened her eyes cautiously and peered out the window.

They had left the rain behind in Willow County and it was a bright, cool day on the streets of Chapel Hill. The car was parked just outside her favorite breakfast spot: Breadmen's.

"Thank you," Annie said as the waitress placed the coffee pot on the table. "I think we're ready to order. Right, Dad?" Annie looked across the table at Jason, who nodded.

"Okay, um." She scanned the menu for her selection. "I'd like the egg breakfast with … um," Annie paused. "With the home fries and a biscuit." Annie closed her menu and handed it to the waitress. "Oh, and could I get a side of gravy for the biscuit?"

"Sure thing," the waitress said, jotting Annie's order down on a small pad then looked up at Jason with a kind smile. "And for you?"

"Yes." Jason scanned his menu. "May I have the corn beef hash breakfast?" Jason folded his menu and handed it to the waitress with a smile. "Thank you."

Annie tapped her spoon on the rim of her coffee mug. "Should we have called Drew?" she asked. "We're not far. He'd be pissed if he knew we were out this way and didn't call."

"It wasn't exactly planned, Sweet," Jason said, looking at his daughter with a sly smile. "I won't say anything if you don't."

"Deal."

"Besides, doesn't he have lab on Friday mornings?"

"Oh, yeah." Annie had forgotten that it was a school day for a second. Dance day. Her heart ached at the thought. She guessed she wasn't going. Panic clung to her throat when she thought about having to bail on Josh. She shook the thoughts out of her head. She'd deal with all that later.

Jason watched her expression shift. "Annie," he asked, "what's going on?"

"I don't know, Dad." Annie drew another sip from her coffee. "It's nothing more than stupid girl drama. Nothing you'd be interested in."

Her dad smiled faintly. "Try me." Jason leaned across the table and tucked a loose strand of hair behind Annie's ear. "Whatever it is seems awfully important to you," he said, "so it's important to me."

"Alright," she said, unsure as she put down her coffee mug. "I'm almost embarrassed that all of it bothers me as much as it does. You know I've never ever cared about any of that drama crap." Jason nodded.

"I take it the transition of having Laurie in school with you is a little…challenging?" His eyes crinkled in a knowing smile and he took a sip of his coffee.

"Yeah," she chuckled, "you could say that. It's just—I don't care about any of the same things she cares about. And it really never mattered before, you know? But now, all of a sudden it's like all I can see are our differences. It's kind of...heartbreaking."

"What do you mean?"

"It just sort of feels like I'm losing my best friend. I know she's trying—and I'm trying too, but I don't think it's going to work. She's hanging out with the worst people. I really can't even stand them. And there's this one girl, God she's *awful,* Dad. Seriously."

"You think she's getting herself mixed up in some kind of trouble?" It was obvious Jason was concerned. Annie's dad had always liked Laurie, and Laurie's own parents never really cared where she was or what she was doing, as long as she was out of their hair.

She shrugged her shoulders. "I don't think she's going to get herself into any kind of real trouble. It's not like that exactly. It's more like—I don't know, I feel like that girl, Olivia? I feel like she's *changing* her. But maybe she isn't. Maybe Laurie has always been this way and I just didn't know. It's always just been me and her— we've never had any outside forces highlighting our differences, you know?"

"High school can bring out a different side of people too, Annie." They sat quietly for a moment as the waitress delivered their food. Annie hadn't realized just how hungry she was until her dish was in front of her. They both dug in and ate in silence.

"I just feel kind of lost, I guess." Annie put her fork down and wiped her mouth with the napkin from her lap. "I like keeping things compartmentalized, and having Laurie there just … it screws all of that up. And that Olivia girl? She hates me, Dad. Like, 'wants to make my life a living hell' kind of hate. And I just don't get it."

"Why would she hate you?" Concern painted his face as he took another sip of coffee.

"The thing is there's really no reason I don't think. And that almost makes it worse because it's not like I can just fix XYZ and resolve everything. That's the thing about these girls, Dad. They don't *need* a reason to hate someone. They just pick out some random target and enjoy themselves as they torment them. And I'm one of the lucky targets, I guess." She sat back in her chair and watched her dad mill over what she'd just told him. "It's hard to explain."

"No," he said, placing his napkin in his empty dish. "I get it. I was in high school too, once." He winked at her. "The only advice I can really give you is to not lose sight of what you want. Of who you are. Because you're right — there are always just going to be people who are miserable human beings. And Annie? How that girl treats you says a lot more about her than it does about you. Understand? It shows her character. But how you let it affect you shows *yours.*"

"Yeah," she said quietly. Inside, though, she was anything but quiet. She was experiencing a sort of...revelation. "You're exactly right," she said, more confidently this time. Her dad chuckled, clearly pleased with himself.

Annie grinned.

"What is it?" Her dad asked, reading her expression.

"I want to go to the dance."

He looked puzzled. "What? What dance?"

"The homecoming dance. It's tonight. And a guy asked me. I still can't really tell what he has up his sleeve. And I know this isn't anything I'd typically ever want to do—but I actually want to go."

"So go!" he said with a laugh.

"When I woke up this morning, I was sure I'd have to bail on Josh. Something happened last night," At this, her dad's eyebrows knitted with concern, but she waved it off. "It's not important. But anyway, something happened last night with that Olivia girl that made me think I couldn't go. But you're right. Why should she get to decide what I get to do?"

"Bingo!" Jason said with a confident grin. "I think my work here is done." He paid the check then draped his arm over Annie's shoulder as they walked out to the car. She stopped him just before they reached their parking spot.

She squeezed him into the tightest hug. "Thank you," she exhaled into his chest.

"You got here all on your own, Sweet."

Josh: **Everything okay? We still on for tonight?**

Laurie: **Where are you?**

Laurie: **Are you sick?**

Laurie: **Dropped by after school, no one was home. What's going on?**

Laurie: **Answer your phone, hooker.**

Laurie: **Officially worried about you. Wanted to come by and at least do your makeup before tonight.**

Laurie: **You better not bail on Josh. That dress is too fierce on you to sit in a closet. I'm off to get ready at O's. Better see you at the dance! XOXO**

Annie had a little damage control to deal with when she got

home. She quickly replied to Josh's text letting him know that yes, they were still on — she'd just had some bad allergies that morning. A lie, sure, but he didn't seem like the type to be interested in any of the drama.

She also texted Laurie, thanking her again for the dress and telling her that no, she wasn't bailing. She'd just needed a Daddy/Daughter day. Laurie replied that she was jealous and to have a fun night with Josh.

Annie took a record quick shower and actually blew her hair dry in order to be ready in time. Because the dress *was* fierce, she bothered with some of the makeup she rarely used and even ran the flat iron over her hair.

Everything was now under control. As she stood in front of the full-length mirror, she couldn't help but think that Laurie would be proud of her. She looked like herself, but prettier, kind of like how she'd looked the night of the Bonfire and the Party. She just hoped the night would have a better ending than either of those nights had.

"Goodness," Jason said as he poked his head in her door, "You look so grown up." Annie saw the tears form in her dad's eyes, and she tried her best not to mirror them.

"Thanks, Dad." She turned back around toward her mirror and flattened her dress with the palms of her hands. Then she turned back to her dad. "You really think I'm doing the right thing?"

"Absolutely, Sweet. You've got to live your own life. You don't want to look back and have regrets. Trust me." He got quiet and shifted his gaze to the ground, just for a moment, then looked up at Annie and smiled. She couldn't help but wonder if her mom was one of his regrets. "I love the person you are, Annie. Don't let other people change that."

Before Annie could respond, the doorbell rang. Her heart tightened and her nerves surged through her veins. Ready or not.

"Wow," Josh said as he stood in the doorway. He glanced Annie up and down. "You look," he cleared his throat, "just wow," he said bashfully. Annie's dad introduced himself and then proceeded to embarrass her by insisting on taking at least a hundred pictures.

"Dad." Annie sighed, "We should probably get going," she muttered through her smile as he snapped yet another.

"Alright," her dad resigned. He shook Josh's hand and hugged Annie tight. "I'm sorry your mother missed this," he whispered into her ear. She shrugged. She'd expect nothing less.

"Have a wonderful time you two," he yelled out the front door after them.

Josh led Annie to the green Ford Explorer that sat idling in the driveway and opened the door to the back seat for her. She climbed in, and Josh scooted in next to her.

"Dave, this is Annie. Annie, my brother Dave. And this," Josh nodded his head toward the front passenger seat, "is Dave's better half, Amanda." Everyone exchanged hellos and Dave backed out of the driveway.

Dave looked like Josh, just a tad older. Annie was sure they must sometimes get confused for twins. Amanda, Annie could tell despite her being dressed up, is gorgeous in a natural sort of way. Her jet-black hair was thick, pin straight, and glossy. She had milky white skin dotted with light freckles. Her green eyes were lined with black kohl. If she didn't have such a sweet smile, she would have been absolutely intimidating to Annie.

Annie sat back and snapped her seat belt. "Thanks for letting us crash your night," she said to Amanda and Dave.

"Are you kidding?" Dave caught her eye in the rearview mirror as he made his way down the street. She could tell by the way his eyes crinkled that he was smiling. "I'm just glad to see this kid hanging out with a girl who can spell her own name."

"To be fair, it is a pretty simple name," she teased. She rocked her shoulder into Josh's, and he rocked back into her, playfully. She felt happy and included. She was really glad Josh was so cool about the whole "avoiding the group" thing. She was definitely much more comfortable here.

They arrived at Storie Thyme, and it was beautiful. The walls were painted a deep red, almost burgundy. The lights were dim, and the room was glowing, giving the impression you were standing inside a fire. It wasn't a big place, but it was charming. Romantic. The small tables, mostly for two, were covered in elegant white tablecloths with small, flickering, votive candles in the center.

They all stood at the hostess stand while Dave gave the name on the reservation. Now that they were out of the car, Annie could see Amanda's dress, a plain black, floor-length silk gown. While the dress lacked detail, it clung to Amanda's curvy body in all the right places. She was wearing the dress, rather than the dress wearing her, and she looked like royalty. Annie felt a little silly in her "party dress."

"Your dress is amazing!" Amanda said, interrupting Annie's thoughts. "I can't even tell what color it's supposed to be!" She reached out and rubbed her fingers on the hem. "That taffeta material really plays tricks with the color. It's so beautiful. And it fits you really well!" Annie hadn't been showered with compliments like that in ... well, ever. She didn't really know how to respond, so she just thanked Amanda shyly as the MAÎTRE D' led them to their table in the middle of the small dining room.

They were almost finished with their crab cake appetizer, which Josh had absolutely insisted that they order when Annie saw the front door to the restaurant open. Her blood ran cold. The Elite girls, trailed by Brandon, Laurie, and a few guys Annie didn't know, entered the restaurant. Her initial reaction was to drop her eyes to the table and hope to go undetected, but Laurie caught her eye just before she was able to look away and lit up excitedly. The rest of the group stood at the hostess stand as Laurie ran up to Annie's table.

"Oh, my gosh! I didn't know y'all were coming here too!" She collected Annie into a hug then pushed her back to arm's-length and checked her over.

"I'm impressed," Laurie said with a smile. "You look awesome. Hi," she leaned over the table and squeezed Josh's shoulder. He stood up and hugged her casually, and Dave waved and introduced Amanda.

Laurie looked fierce. Her sparkly silver dress was skin-tight, and she'd paired it with black strappy heels that had to be at least four inches high. Her hair was loosely curled and her makeup was on point.

"You're here alone?" Annie asked, scanning the group. "I thought you'd snag one of the hot juniors or seniors?" Annie playfully nudged Laurie's arm.

"Nah, not for a silly dance. This is just for fun." Before Annie could respond, the group walked past Annie's table, and Olivia hissed at Laurie to come on. Laurie turned on her spiked heel with a wide smile and waved to Annie over her shoulder as The Elite gang took their seats at a table just across the restaurant.

During dinner, Annie tried not to be distracted by The Elite table. Dave was telling funny stories about Josh and his dad, and Annie really wanted to pay attention, but The Elite table was loud. And obnoxious. Annie felt a little embarrassed for them. This was a nice restaurant, and they were being *rude.*

She focused on the boys and forced herself to ignore the others. They weren't her problem. Josh reached over and put his hand on her knee under the table. Her stomach clenched. She looked over at him, and he leaned into her.

"You okay?" he whispered. His closeness made her skin tingle.

"Yeah, of course." She put her hand over his and smiled up at him. "This is great, really." She meant it. It wasn't his fault The Elite crashed their party, and it wasn't like she had to sit with them. The waitress approached the table and asked if anyone wanted dessert. Josh squeezed Annie's hand and took the menu from the waitress.

"Of course we do!" he said excitedly. "What are you thinking, Annie?" He held the menu open between them so she could peek over. She spotted the chocolate molten lava cake and was about to mention it when he interrupted her thoughts. He caught her eye and smiled wide. "I'm eyeing that molten lava cake. You want to split it?"

She smiled and closed the menu in his hands and handed it back to the waitress. "Absolutely," she said. Dave and Amanda ordered a slice of key lime pie to split, and Annie excused herself. Her nerves always made her extra thirsty, and now she had to pee like a racehorse.

She was in the one functional stall when she heard the door swing open and Laurie's unmistakable giggle. Someone pushed on the stall door but gave up when they saw it was locked.

"I really have to peeeeee!" Laurie sang out.

"Look what I snagged," the other voice said. *Olivia.*

Laurie gasped. "Oh em gee! Olivia! Where'd you get that?"

"From the bar. The bartender walked away, so I just reached over and snatched it. Here." Annie heard a cap twisting. "Have a swig."

"I don't know," Laurie hesitated. "What if we get caught?"

"Don't be such a loser," Olivia snapped. "Take it."

It was quiet for a moment then Laurie coughed. "Oh geez," she said, "that's awful!"

"Awful? Are you kidding? It's top shelf tequila!" Olivia was quiet, and Annie assumed she was taking a sip. "You'll get used to it. Here." She must have handed the bottle back to Laurie. "Have some more. You need to loosen up a bit before the dance."

Laurie gagged. "It doesn't make you feel like you're going to throw up? I can hardly handle that stuff."

"You're supposed to take it with lime and salt, but you know—we have to make do with what we've got," Olivia said confidently. "Have another."

"I don't know," Laurie said quietly. "I really don't like it."

"It doesn't matter if you *like* it. You'll like how it makes you *feel.*"

It was quiet a moment. Annie flushed the toilet and walked out of the stall to find Laurie sipping from a handle of Patron.

"Do you really think that's a good idea, Laurie?" Annie ignored Olivia, who was glaring at her. Laurie thrust the bottle back to Olivia.

"Oh, my gosh, Annie! Thank God! I really have to pee." She ran into the stall and slammed the door shut. The tension between Annie and Olivia was obvious, and Annie decided not to make eye contact with her as she washed her hands. Laurie was singing, shouting rather, Lady Gaga's *Poker Face.*

Annie turned to walk around Olivia to grab a paper towel when Olivia shoved the bottle in front of her. "Here." At first, Annie thought Olivia was offering her a sip, which she didn't want. But before she could get the words out, Olivia poured tequila down the front of Annie's dress.

Annie stood there, baffled, as the freezing cold liquid ran between her breasts, down into her underwear, down her leg and into a puddle on the floor.

"Oh, my God!" Annie pushed the bottle away from her. "What the hell is wrong with you?" She turned to the mirror. The whole front of her dress was soaked in liquor. The door to the stall Laurie was in swung open, and Annie caught her friend's eye in the mirror.

"What happened?" Laurie asked as she wobbled to the sink next to Annie to wash her hands.

Olivia was laughing and spoke before Annie could find her words. "I offered her a sip, and she spilled it right down her front. What an idiot!"

Annie stared defiantly at Olivia. "You know that's not what happened." Annie swung around to face Laurie. "She poured it all down my front. My dress —" She looked down at herself and reached for a few paper towels. "It's ruined."

Laurie looked between Olivia and Annie. "Now, Annie," Laurie slurred, clearly already feeling the effects of the swigs she'd taken. "Why would Olivia do that? I'm sure she was just offering you some."

"You and I both know that isn't true," Annie hissed at Laurie, who was also reaching for paper towels. Annie thought it was to help her dry off her dress, but then realized she was just drying her hands. She threw them away and reached for some more, kneeling down in front of Annie to help her clean up.

"I don't think it's ruined," she said, looking up at Annie. She wobbled on her heels.

"Of course it is," Annie said.

Olivia sucked her teeth. "Awww," she said, feigning sympathy. "See, now, Annie? That's why you can't have nice things." She snapped her fingers and sighed audibly. "Uh, Laurie? We've got to go." Laurie looked up at Annie with pleading eyes.

"Just a second," Laurie called out to Olivia as she dabbed violently at Annie's ruined dress. "We at least need to try and dry her off. She can't go out there reeking of alcohol."

"Not my problem," Olivia said flippantly. "The limo is waiting." She tapped her high-heeled foot impatiently.

Laurie grabbed the counter for support as she pulled herself up and handed Annie her paper towel.

"Seriously?" Annie didn't even try to hide the disappointment in her voice. "Don't you dare ditch me in here."

"I'm sorry," Laurie said as she pushed the bathroom door open. "I have to. The limo will leave without me if I don't." Olivia was already gone, and Laurie was standing in the doorway.

"Yeah," Annie said angrily. "You're right. You really should go. You wouldn't want your *friends* to leave without you."

"Annie, don't —"

"No," Annie stopped her. "Go. Just go."

The door fell shut behind Laurie, and Annie was left standing under the bathroom's fluorescent lights with a ruined dress and a handle of stolen Patron.

IT'S A LONG STORY

Annie emptied the paper towel dispenser trying to clean herself off. It didn't matter how much she dabbed the dress, there was a visible wet mark all down the front, and she reeked of tequila.

She threw the last of the paper towels away and sat on the counter, trying to figure out what to do. She hadn't brought her phone and she couldn't imagine walking back out to the table like this.

The door to the bathroom opened, and Amanda stood in the doorway. Upon seeing Annie, she swung the bathroom door shut and turned the latch, locking it.

"Annie, what happened?" She ran over to her and took the hem of Annie's dress in her hands. "This is absolutely ruined." She saw the bottle on the counter and looked at Annie.

"You were drinking?" Her eyes narrowed.

"No," Annie sighed. "It's —" She hopped down from the counter. "It's a long story."

"The boys sent me in here. We were worried about you. You've been in here forever. I thought maybe you had a nervous stomach. What happened?"

Annie filled Amanda in, and just as she finished, there was a faint rap on the door. Amanda glided over to it, unlocked it, and cracked it open. Annie could just barely make out Josh's face, but his voice was unmistakable. Amanda let him in.

"Dave is taking care of the check." He was holding a to-go box. "I boxed up our dessert," he said to Annie. "I saw Laurie and Olivia wobbling out of here," he said knowingly.

"They were drinking? I heard the manager talking about a missing bottle of liquor."

"Yeah," Annie sighed, "and Olivia poured it all down my front."

Amanda told her she'd be right back and to lock the door behind her. Josh collected her into a hug. "I'm so, so sorry," he breathed into her hair. "I don't know why she's like that."

"Me neither," Annie huffed. "I don't think—"

Josh pulled away and interrupted her. "No, I understand. We'll get you home." There was another rap on the door, and Annie let Amanda back in. She was carrying a coat.

"Here. Put this on and zip it up. I'm going to bring this," she grabbed the bottle, "over to the manager and tell him what happened."

Annie's stomach clenched. "Are you sure? What if he thinks you took it?"

"Well, we'll cross that bridge if we get to it. Besides, I think it makes us all look a lot more guilty if we just leave it in here." Annie nodded. "Take her to the car," she said to Josh. "Dave pulled it up front. I'll meet y'all out there."

They pulled up outside Annie's house and she unzipped the coat, slid it off, and handed it back to Amanda.

"Thank you." Annie's voice was almost inaudible. "Really, thank you so much. For everything." She felt so embarrassed. She was glad she didn't have to walk through the restaurant with people staring, but she still felt humiliated. This night hadn't gone at all like she'd hoped. Amanda waved her off.

"Not a problem." She took the coat. "Listen," she said seriously. "There are girls like that everywhere. No one is immune to them. Let it roll off your back, okay?"

"Thanks," Annie said as she reached for the door handle. She turned back to Josh. "I really am sorry. Do you think you'll still go to the dance?"

Josh scooted toward her. "Well, I was actually kind of hoping you'd be cool with me hanging out here with you for a while. You can get changed, and we could just, I don't know, listen to music or something? I was really looking forward to hanging out with you tonight. I don't really care if it's not at a dance."

Before Annie could answer, Dave piped in. "That sounds like a good idea, Josh. I wish we could all just ditch the monkey suits and go bowling or something. But I've got to make an appearance. You know — Official Class Pr —"

Josh put up air quotes, "Yeah, we know. 'Official Class President Business,'" he mocked. Everyone laughed. "Is that cool?" Josh addressed Annie again.

Her stomach was in knots. She couldn't deny that part of her really just wanted to crawl under the blankets and forget the night ever happened. But the other part? Yeah, the other part really, really wanted to spend more time with Josh.

"Sure."

They slid out of the car and slammed the door shut, shouting, "Later, dudes!" to Dave and Amanda.

Annie could feel someone staring at her. She rolled over and opened one eye. A blurry Laurie was sitting on the edge of her bed. Her hair was in a ponytail and mascara was smudged around her eyes.

"What are you doing here?" Annie mumbled through a dry mouth. She licked her lips and sat up in the bed, flattening out her ponytail with her hand.

"I'm checking on you. You never showed at the dance."

"No shit, Sherlock. Your so-called BFF ruined my dress. Did you really think I was going to show up after that?"

"Don't be so dramatic." Laurie stood up and went over to the crumpled dress on the floor. "It was hardly ruined." She examined the dress then looked up at Annie with an embarrassed expression. "Oh."

"Yeah, 'oh.'" Annie slid down into her bed and pulled the covers up to her neck. She rolled toward the wall with her back to

Laurie.

"Annie," Laurie said quietly. "I'm sorry. I didn't…"

"I really don't have anything to say to you," Annie spit.

"Please, can we just talk about this? I didn't realize it was such a big deal."

"Of course you didn't," Annie said, sitting up and flinging the covers off. She scooted to the edge of the bed and sat facing Laurie, who was sitting in the butterfly chair. "I'll be honest, I hardly recognized you last night."

"See? You say things like that and it makes everything seem so much more dramatic than it is! What are you even talking about?"

"You! I'm talking about *you*, Laurie. I'm talking about the fact that you even *want* to be friends with those people. I don't get it. I *can't* get it."

"You're so determined to hate them. You don't even know them and you *hate* them. How is that fair?"

"I've gone to school with those people my entire life. I know them way better than you think you do. Olivia has you so fooled, and the sick thing is, it's like you *like* being like her. I —" Annie hesitated. "I don't know. Never mind."

"No!" Laurie spit. "What? Say what you were gonna say."

Annie rubbed her face with both hands, then looked up at Laurie. "What if we can't be friends?"

Laurie looked hurt. "Don't be ridiculous."

"I'm *not* being ridiculous." Annie rubbed the back of her neck. "I'm totally serious. I feel like I'm losing you. Half the time I feel like I've already lost you."

"I swear you're making this into a much bigger deal than it is."

"It *is* a big deal, Laurie, because you can't have both. You can't be part of that world and still be my best friend. It just doesn't work."

"Is that an ultimatum?"

"No," Annie wrung her hands then looked Laurie directly in the eye, "it's just a fact."

Laurie sat staring at Annie for what seemed like forever. Tears collected in her eyes, but they didn't fall. It looked like she was trying to think of what to say next, but Annie knew there was nothing more to say.

"I think you should go," Annie said after a while. She felt the sting of her own words, and she knew Laurie did, too.

"Can't we fix this?" Laurie leaned forward in the chair with her hands folded.

"I think it's a little too late for that." Annie walked over to her door and opened it, a signal to Laurie to leave. Laurie stood slowly and grabbed the back of her neck as she walked toward the door. She stood in front of Annie.

"So what does this mean?" The tears that had been in Laurie's eyes were now sliding down her cheeks. "It's over? Just like that?"

Annie's throat closed, and she tried to swallow the lump. Tears stung her eyes, but she willed them not to fall. Laurie reached out to her, and Annie collected Laurie into a sad hug. "I think it has to be."

The girls stood, embracing each other as if willing time to stand still, giving them a chance to fix everything. But time did pass, and they finally released each other. Laurie walked out, closing the door behind her, both literally and figuratively.

Annie sat down on the edge of her bed and finally allowed herself to cry. After a while, she collected herself and walked outside to move the hidden key. It was more out of principle than anything else, really. She didn't necessarily *want* to keep Laurie out, but her heart hurt. She couldn't have Laurie showing up and screwing with her head anymore. She had to stick to her guns on this one.

If letting Laurie go would end the pain, she had to do it. Sometimes it just hurt less when you stopped having expectations. Laurie wasn't a bad person. Annie was sure she didn't *mean* to hurt her, but it was clear their expectations were much different. Sometimes, no matter how badly two people want something, it just doesn't work out.

She wandered into the kitchen and poured herself a cup of coffee. Her mom was gone. Again. "Working," or so she claimed. All Annie wanted to know is what kind of lawyer worked at 10 A.M. on a Saturday? The unfaithful kind, she assumed.

Her dad sauntered in with wet hair and the paper.

"Hey, kiddo." He was awfully chipper, and it made Annie's headache pound. She'd experienced far too many emotions in the previous 24 hours for her poor head to keep up. Her dad poured himself a cup of coffee and joined Annie at the table. "That Josh sure is a nice fella, huh?"

***

When Annie and Josh walked in the night before, her dad was sitting on the couch with a beer watching *Superstar.* He was surprised to see them home so soon. She left Josh downstairs with her dad so she could take a quick shower. Josh filled her dad in. When she wandered back downstairs, she was transformed back into her old self in sweats and a ponytail.

The evening was salvaged. It wasn't a dance, but she and Josh made do. They joined her dad, who seemed happy to have the company, on the couch and dug into their dessert. Josh and her dad talked about golf and football, and she could tell it had thrilled him to have another young man around the house.

When the movie ended, her dad 'went to bed.' She knew he was really just trying to give them some time alone. They played a couple rounds of Slap Jack and laughed so hard she had trouble breathing. By the time Josh left, it actually took her a moment to remember what happened earlier in the evening.

***

"Yeah," she said, taking a sip of coffee. "He is, isn't he?"

Later that afternoon, Annie was up in her room when the doorbell rang. She tensed, thinking maybe it was Laurie back for Round Two. Her dad left earlier to go scout out some locations for an engagement shoot he was doing the next day, so she went to the front door to open it. When she peered out the side pane, she couldn't believe what she saw. She unlocked the door and swung it open.

"Josh," she gasped, opening the door wide and inviting him in. She shut the door behind him. "What's up?"

He was carrying a guitar case. "Hey," he said, giving her a one-armed side hug. He indicated the guitar. "I thought maybe I could help you with the chords for that song you were telling me about last night."

Annie dabbled in music. It wasn't something she talked about much with people, because it seemed like no one understood that world unless they were in it. As it turned out, Josh wasn't just a fan of music – he was a musician, too. He hesitated when Annie didn't respond right away. "Oh." he said, seeming embarrassed. "Is this a bad time?"

"No, no," Annie assured him. "Not at all. Sorry. I just… I wasn't expecting to see you is all."

She showed him up to her bedroom. She felt a little exposed. She'd never had a boy up in her room, and she'd definitely never had a boy over when her parents weren't home.

She pulled the blankets up over her crumpled sheets in an attempt to make the bed. She was a little embarrassed at the state of her room, but Josh didn't seem to notice or care. He fell into the butterfly chair and opened his guitar case.

"Do you have any of it written down, or are you just messing with it as you go?" He wrapped the strap around his neck and strummed the guitar, tuning it. Annie grabbed her Daisy Rock from the stand in the corner and sat with it. She pulled a sheet of paper from the middle of a big stack on her messy desk and handed it to him.

"It's just a little something," she said. "I haven't decided yet if I like it or not yet." Josh took the paper from her and put it on the floor in front of him, strumming out the notes. She'd only ever heard herself play it, and for some reason, coming from Josh's guitar, it didn't even sound like her song anymore. It sounded…better, somehow.

She was entranced watching him. He was focused on the page on the floor, his bottom lip caught in his teeth and his brow furrowed. She was so mesmerized she didn't realize he'd played through all the music that was there.

"Annie?" He said, interrupting her thoughts. "That was really cool. Where'd you learn to write like that?"

She waved him off. "Oh, I don't know," she said shyly. "I

don't really know what I'm doing. I just mess around a bit."

He took his guitar off and placed it on the floor. "Don't sell yourself short. You've really got a talent." He shifted in the chair. "I'm sure I'm not the first to tell you that."

"Actually ..." Annie dropped her gaze to the floor.

"What?" Josh fidgeted in the undersized chair, his knees practically up by his ears. He got up and joined Annie on the edge of the bed. "Sorry," he laughed, "but I think that chair was made for midgets."

She playfully nudged into him. "No. You're just freakishly tall."

"Or maybe you're just freakishly short." He slipped off one of his sandals and folded his leg up onto the bed, turning to Annie. "Anyway. What were you going to say?"

"Oh," she hesitated, "nothing really. It's just... I've actually never played for anyone else before."

Josh looked at her, surprised. "You haven't played anything at all? Not even other songs?"

"Not really. I mean, my dad's heard me play, but I don't think he really counts." She laughed at herself. "It's just never come up with anyone else, I guess."

Annie fondled her guitar. "Can I hear you play it?" Josh asked, his eyes wide and excited.

"I don't know," she said, smiling down at the ground. "You saw it. It's not much."

"I don't care," he encouraged. "I'd really love to hear it. Do you have lyrics for it?"

Annie's throat closed. No, she didn't have lyrics for it, because writing lyrics would mean having to *sing* them. And she was *never* going to do that again.

Josh flipped the page over in his hand and checked the back. Nothing was there. He looked up at her. "Well, maybe we could write some together." He sounded so excited that the idea of disappointing him stung Annie's heart.

Her nerves tingled at the idea of working with Josh on anything, especially *music*. "Yeah, maybe."

"Now can I please hear you play?" Annie took the paper from him, more as a formality than anything else. She had the tune memorized. She focused on the corner of the room and started to strum out the melody.

Averting her eyes from Josh's, she removed the strap from her neck and placed the guitar next to her. Silence hung between them. Josh picked the paper back up and stared at the notes on the page.

"You know," Josh said in a low voice, finally breaking the silence, "music is sometimes the only thing I can make sense of. When the world speeds on by and we're left just hanging on and hoping for the best? Music is the one thing I can always understand."

"Yeah," Annie agreed. "I totally know what you mean." She wished she could tell him what was on her mind. She wanted to fill him in on everything that happened with Laurie that morning. But she didn't want to come across as petty and childish. Instead, she asked if he wanted a Coke.

"Absolutely!" He was back to his excited self. They left their guitars upstairs and headed into the kitchen. It had been as much exposure as she could handle for one day. Between the morning she'd had with Laurie and what just happened with Josh, she felt like her nervous system needed a break. She grabbed two Cokes from the fridge and a deck of cards from the drawer in the kitchen.

"I demand a rematch."

Yeah, maybe

October 2, 2009

Listening to: Ben Harper *Walk Away*

Things have been ... weird. It's been about a week since The Great Homecoming Disaster and my breakup with Laurie. I can't say that I don't miss her because I do. But in reality, not much has changed except my expectations. Before, back in the good old days, Laurie and I saw each other every afternoon. We used to do homework together and watch our evening shows together and, and, and ... Okay, that's sort of a lie. I would do homework — Laurie would go on and on about different things and then would panic as the evening came to an end and she hadn't touched her books. And then I'd help her with her homework. I miss that rhythm. But things have calmed down a bit in the last few days, and I'm so grateful. Olivia has basically left me alone, and I can't help but attribute that

Joey Hodges

to my lack of interaction with Laurie. It hurts to walk away from her, it does. But sometimes walking away is really the only answer. Is it sad that I could pretty much predict this? I just know Laurie. And I know me. And for some reason it works at home. But when you throw in the outside world, she and I just don't make sense. And in high school, things have to make sense. You have to fit into a category. People try desperately to find their place, and everything has to fit just so. Laurie fits. I'm okay with the fact that I don't. At least, I was. Somehow now my lack of label hurts. I guess it's because I had to lose something to keep it.

October 17, 2009

Listening to: Keri Noble *If No One Will Listen*

It's been three weeks since Laurie and I broke up. It's the longest we've ever gone without talking, but it's getting surprisingly easier. She's off doing her own thing and I get to do mine. And apparently, there's really some truth to the whole out-of-sight-out-of-mind thing because Olivia has been strangely quiet.

I say strangely mostly because of the whole Josh thing. He's been … hanging around a lot lately. More than a lot, actually. He's started sitting with me in the library, which I can't even believe. He claims it's because it's getting too cold to sit out at The Elite table (don't even get me started on why they don't move their things inside — it's almost like they're too cool for heat or something.) But I know it's because he doesn't like the idea of me sitting there alone. I told him I'm fine, really. But every day there he is. And I'm really okay with that.

He's been spending a lot of time at the house, too. We listen to music. We mess around with the chords of my song (I've held him off on the whole writing lyrics thing, thank God). Oh, and sometimes we make weird things in the kitchen. Like the other day? We had all these random ingredients and somehow we made them into a cake in the microwave. We made a huge mess in the process, and my mom was super pissed when she got home. But it was totally worth it. And the cake wasn't half bad either!

Most nights it's just Dad and us. Mom has been spending even more time away from home, which is only making me wonder where she is and who she's with. Because really, no one works that much. Not to mention the fact that I know things I wish I didn't. I wonder how long all this can really go on before my dad starts to get suspicious — maybe he already is. Who knows? Anyway, Dad always insists Josh stay for dinner, which I really don't mind. Josh says they eat a lot of takeout at his house, so he'll never turn down a home-cooked meal. That just makes me that much more curious about what happened with his mom. He hasn't mentioned her anymore, and I'm too afraid to ask.

This isn't how I saw it all going ... high school. It's not how I saw it going at all. But if I'm being honest, I'm kind of glad this is how it is. Not the torture part — I could definitely do without Olivia and the whole Laurie drama ... but honestly? I've been in this one

Yeah, maybe

little box for so long. I've been living the past 13 years in Laurie's shadow. And for once? I get to just be me. I don't like the spotlight or anything, but I don't know — it's kind of relieving and exhilarating to be forced out of my box. I'm okay.

November 30, 2009

Listening to: John Mayer *Clarity*

Okay, it's been a really freaking long time since I've written. Not much has gone on except ... OMG. Drew's engaged. ENGAGED! He asked Jamie the week before Thanksgiving. They were in town for the holiday – and that's actually when we found out. There we all were (you know, the fam: me, Mom, Dad, Drew & Jamie) just minding our own business: "can you pass the potatoes, where's the gravy, oh yum green bean casserole" and then Bam! Jamie twisted the band on her finger and there was a freaking diamond. We all went a little bonkers. The idea of a wedding is just so exciting. Plus it gives us all something to focus on together – maybe it'll drag Mom back into the house – who knows? And Jamie will officially be my sister, which is sort of kind of awesome. I've secretly always wanted a sister. I mean, I guess Laurie was like a sister, but we all know how that turned out. Jamie will be family. Real family. And, oh sweet goodness, I can't wait! They've already set the date: June 12, 2010! That's actually kind of soon. Well, soon-ish. When I think that school will already be out, it seems like a lifetime away.

Anyway, Mom and Dad wanted to host a little impromptu shindig for the happy couple. So the Saturday after Thanksgiving, our living room was bursting with people. Some of Drew's HS friends were in town for the holiday and got to come. Jamie's extended family that live in town were away for the holiday and couldn't make it. I had no idea any of her family lived here. I thought they were all in Boone. Anyway, Dad said I should invite Josh. I felt a little weird about it — but I sucked it up and called him. I was sure he'd have family stuff going on or something, but he came! We had so much fun. SO much fun. We set up the Wii, and everyone played Just Dance. We even got Mom and Dad to play. They actually seemed to have a good time together, too. It was almost as if, for just a minute, I could pretend that everything was normal. It was just a really nice night. And I'm so glad Josh got to be there. He fit right in.

Later that night, I went downstairs to get some water, and Drew was watching some late-night show on the couch. Jamie was asleep with her head in his lap, and it was just adorable. I really want that someday. Real love? But anyway, he told me he approves of Josh. I said we were just friends, but then he got all into this whole

Joey Hodges

theory of how girls and guys can't be just friends. He said something about that movie When Harry Met Sally. *I won't lie, I judged him a little for quoting a chick flick. He blamed Jamie — but I don't care, ha! Either way, it sort of reignited the hope that I've been trying so hard to squash. What if we* could *be more than just friends? That would change my whole world.*

OF ALL THE GIFTS AT CHRISTMAS...

It was Christmas Eve eve, and Annie and Josh had already spent every day of break together. They bundled up, walked the path at Misty Lake Park, and talked about how freaking embarrassing the Sex Ed program in Gym had been the last week before break.

They spent a lot of time with their guitars and different albums. So much so, that one night her dad had knocked on her door (which was ajar) at 11 p.m., saying it might be time to call it a night.

They also did their Christmas shopping together. Josh helped Annie find the perfect putter for her dad. Well, he went *with* her to find the putter. The sales associate actually helped her pick it out — but Josh tried!

Annie helped him pick out an OPI nail polish gift set for Amanda. He was freaking out because he wasn't exactly sure if he was *supposed* to buy a gift for his brother's long-term girlfriend. But Annie told him it was better to be safe than sorry. Something small was nice, and Annie noticed Amanda's manicured nails at Homecoming.

They spent an entire day baking Christmas cookies, too. Not many made the final cut, though. Practically every batch ended up consumed before she could even whip up the powdered sugar frosting. The ones that *did* make it were sort of deformed, but whatever. All along the way, they laughed. They laughed *a lot.*

The doorbell rang, and Annie heard her dad welcome Josh into the house. She smiled when she overheard her Dad telling him that maybe it was time he stopped bothering to ring the bell. Just walk in. She loved that Josh had become such a staple in her life, in her house. It was clear her dad loved having him around, too.

Josh was leaving the next day. He, his dad, and his brother were driving out to Hickory to visit his grandparents for the holiday. It was going to be the longest they'd been apart since they'd starting hanging out, and she was surprised how much she was dreading it.

It would only be a few days, but she'd just gotten so used to him being around. She *liked* having him around. Part of her was a little worried that, in his absence, the screeching silence of her loneliness would break her. He'd been a good distraction from the whole Laurie thing.

The day before, while they were up in Annie's room listening to *Only by the Night*, the new Kings of Leon album, Josh grabbed her guitar and strummed a melody. She quickly clicked down the volume on her MacBook. He grinned like a giddy schoolboy and belted out freestyle lyrics:

"Miss Annie Kate

Homecoming was a tragic date

You deserve a night that's great!

You to West End I'd like to take.

Tomorrow night, okay?"

Annie burst out laughing, but her heart filled with gleeful anxiety and anticipation. Date? Friends? What? Either way, she accepted.

Annie scanned her closet and settled on a pair of her nicer dark jeans and a black top. The dress she'd worn to Homecoming was completely ruined, but it was still hanging in her closet. She didn't have the heart to throw it out.

West End was a fancy place, but she was sure she could get away with not overdoing it. How embarrassing would it be if she walked down the stairs in a party dress and Josh was dressed for a regular evening?

She took some time before he got there to run her mom's flat iron through her hair and apply some makeup. Even though Josh had no objection to her casual style, she figured it would be nice to dress up a little. She convinced herself it wasn't a date, despite her hopes, but better to be prepared.

Lastly, she grabbed a pair of black boot heels from her mother's closet. She glanced in the full-length mirror that hung on the back of the door: nice enough. She looked like herself, but sharper. Like she'd come into focus.

She descended the stairs and found Josh sitting on the couch in the living room with her dad, watching TV. He turned to greet her and surprise covered his face. Her heart dropped, and she silently freaked out. Was it completely obvious she was hoping this was a date?

"You look," Josh smiled, "fantastic." He enveloped her into a hug, and she quickly scanned his outfit – a button-down Polo shirt tucked into khakis. Her heart rate slowed a little. They seemed to be on the same page, whatever that might be.

"Thank you," she said as her cheeks flushed. "All set?"

"You kids want me to give you a ride?" Annie's dad stood from the couch. Annie and Josh exchanged a glance.

"Well," Josh said, "it's pretty mild tonight. I was thinking maybe we could walk." He glanced to Annie. "Alright?"

Annie nodded eagerly and thanked her dad before they headed out the front door. Josh was right. The weather was fairly mild considering it was December, mid 50s or so?

They chatted about basically nothing as they walked into town, but Josh kept his hands in his pockets. *Not a date.* West End was just down the street from Storie Thyme. As they walked past, her mind flashed back to that night. Her stomach dropped into her shoes.

It all seemed so stupid to her now. But maybe that was just life. Things happen that make it seem like your life is spiraling out of control when, in reality, everything is just sorting itself out.

They arrived at the restaurant, which was dimly lit and warm. There were several groups of people waiting, but Josh walked right up to the podium and let the Maître D know they were there for the Watson reservation. Huh. Reservations. *Date.*

They settled into the small booth and the waiter ran down the specials. When he walked away to get their drinks, Josh asked Annie if anything was jumping out at her on the menu.

"Oh, I don't know," she said, glancing at it. "The shrimp linguine sounds good."

When the waiter returned, Josh ordered for both of them. Huh. Pretty date-ish. He settled on the dinner portion of the crab cakes. That boy and his crab cakes, seriously.

When their food arrived, they were mid-conversation.

"You really think he'd want to go?" Josh asked.

"Of course! My dad loves golf."

"I know, but you sure he would want to go with *me*? I'm terrible."

"He doesn't care about that. I'm sure he'd love to go." Annie loved how close Josh was getting with her dad. "Plus, I'm sure he'd love an excuse to test out the new putter we got him." Annie smirked and tried to wink but failed. Josh laughed.

"Well, I guess I'll have to ask him."

"Yeah," Annie said as she watched Josh savor a bite. "He'd seriously love that."

"These are so awesome," he said with his mouth half full. He offered some to Annie by holding out his fork. *Date*. And yeah, they were seriously good crab cakes.

They finished their meal. "We need dessert," he said decisively. "I've heard their banana pudding is unbelievable." She watched as he flicked his shaggy curls from his eyes, a habit of his she'd grown so accustomed to but still found completely endearing.

"Let's do it!"

They were sharing their dessert. When the waiter brought it to the table, Annie's eyes grew huge. It was massive!

"Brandon called again today," Josh said casually. Apparently, Brandon had been trying to get Josh to hang out for weeks. Since Brandon and Olivia had gotten "together," it was rare to find either of them alone. Annie hesitated to actually say they were *together* because she couldn't see them having a relationship. "I told him we'd catch up another time. There's a party or something tonight."

Annie felt bad. Josh had been avoiding Brandon for weeks, and though he denied it, she knew it was because of her. She hadn't quite figured out their friendship, but Josh definitely had some kind of loyalty Brandon. And she could tell it wasn't easy for Josh to ditch him. "Did you want to go?" Annie asked, dreading the answer.

Josh laughed as he shoved another spoonful of pudding into his mouth. "Not even a little bit." Relief flooded over her.

"You guys normally spend a lot of time together, huh?" Annie dipped her spoon into the pudding.

"Yeah, sort of. I guess." Josh leaned back in his chair and put his spoon down. "We've been friends a long time."

Annie sat quietly, hoping Josh would continue. There *had* to be some kind of story there. From what she'd gathered, Brandon and Josh didn't really have anything in common. Sort of like herself and Laurie, actually. Brandon just seemed troubled.

"Brandon hasn't exactly had it all that easy, I guess." Josh offered. "He's an only kid. His dad is sort of— well he's not really a great guy. His parents divorced," Josh reached up and scratches his head, "oh, man, I don't know, years ago. We were kids. Little kids. And his mom has just kind of gone from job to job and guy to guy. There hasn't been a whole lot of stability in his life."

Annie nodded and took her last bite of pudding. She was stuffed, but it was so dang good.

"That sucks." She meant it. Laurie's parents weren't awful, but she definitely didn't have the kind of guidance she should. Seemed like she and Josh had another thing in common. No wonder they got along so well.

"Yeah, so anyway. I guess we just sort of adopted him. My dad is pretty much his only father figure. I guess he hangs with Olivia mostly now, though." Josh contemplated that for a moment and then shook it off. "Anyway, that pudding was amazing," he said, changing the subject. "I don't think I can eat another bite." He patted his stomach and stretched back in the chair. "You gonna be able to man up on the rest of that?"

"Not a chance," Annie laughed. "Totally stuffed."

The waiter came over to make sure they didn't need anything else, code for *Are you ready for your check?* Cue the awkward. But before real panic could set in, Josh said he was.

"Together, or –" the waiter asked. Annie's heart pounded. *Date or not a date?*

"Together," Josh said.

Oh, gosh. She suddenly grew warm. *Date.* Absolutely a date! She tried to swallow the smile that threatened.

"Merry Christmas, Annie," Josh said as he pulled his wallet from his back pocket. "I just wanted to make things up to you after Homecoming. I felt so bad."

Drat. *Not a date.* "Merry Christmas, Josh."

They walked back to Annie's house slowly. They talked about Josh's family and his grandparents and their Christmas traditions. Annie just wished he'd grab her hand.

"Christmas morning," he was saying, "is more like a scavenger hunt. It doesn't matter how old my brother and I get, I think my grandparents will always see us as three and seven. We wake up on Christmas morning, and we each find an envelope with our names on it underneath the tree. From there, we're sent on a hunt for each present. They still even sign them '*From: Santa*'."

"That sounds like a lot of fun," Annie said as she imagined Josh in his pajamas, hunting throughout his grandparent's house, appeasing them for their joy.

"Yeah," Josh said. "I guess it is."

When they arrived at Annie's house, they stopped on the doorstep. "I can't stay," Josh said. "I have to get home to finish packing. We're leaving first thing in the morning."

"I figured," Annie said with a sad smile. "But I do have something for you. Come in for just a minute. I just have to grab it from my room."

"Annie, you didn't have to –"

"I know. I *wanted* to."

Josh followed her through the front door and waited at the bottom of the stairs while she ran up to her room.

Annie walked back down with a small package. "It isn't much," she said, "but I thought you'd like it."

Josh took the package, carefully removed the shiny red wrapping paper, and flipped the CD over in his hands.

"I burned that new Avett Brothers album for you —*I and Love and You*. It's inexcusable that you call yourself a music lover but don't have it," she teased.

Josh smiled and gave Annie a big hug. "It's great, thank you. I'll listen to it on the drive up tomorrow."

"Yeah," Annie said. "Exactly."

"Well, I really should get going."

"Yeah, okay."

Josh hesitated before he turned toward the door. "Merry Christmas, Annie. Oh, and thanks for the CD."

"Of course." She watched Josh leave with conflicting feelings. She felt electrically charged from the whole night, but part of her felt … disappointed. She really wanted something, *anything* to let her know that Josh felt the same way about her. And if he didn't … she wished he would make that absolutely clear. She stood, staring at the closed door. She still had no idea if their evening had been a date or not.

As she turned to head back upstairs, there was a light rapping on the door. Annie opened it and found Josh.

"Wha –" she started.

"Annie," Josh cut her off. "There's something I want to ask you. In fact, this is something I've wanted to ask you for a pretty long time now."

"Yeah?" Annie felt a nervous lump form in her throat.

"Would you," Josh began. "Would you like to, um …" He flicked his hair out of his eyes. "Will you be my girlfriend?"

Annie's cheeks burned, and excitement boiled inside her. "Absolutely!" she beamed.

Josh leaned forward and kissed her on the cheek.

"Okay, good," Josh smiled. "Now that that's settled," he joked as he started to pull the door closed. "Merry Christmas, Annie. See ya when I get home."

Definitely a date!

*****

Annie was beside herself the next day. She and her dad were alone Christmas Eve morning. They sat together at the table sipping coffee while her mother worked. Yeah, even on Christmas Eve. Her brother was in Boone with Jamie until Christmas afternoon.

Annie couldn't stop smiling. Things had been so out of sorts for so long that it had been a while since she felt genuinely happy. She filled her dad in on everything from the night before. "I like that guy," he said casually as he took a sip of his coffee.

"Ha," Annie laughed. "Yeah, I know."

Later that night, she and her dad were watching *Christmas Vacation*. Her mom should have been home hours before, but there'd been no word from her. The fact that her mom seemed to want to be anywhere but home on Christmas Eve pissed Annie off. But she tried not to focus on it.

As the movie was ending, Annie heard someone walk up the front porch, but there was no knock. For a second, she thought it might finally be her mom. But there was no sound of a key turning in the lock.

Her heart raced. She hoped maybe it was Josh.

Still curious, Annie peeked out the window. No one. So she opened the door. An envelope fell from the crease of the door. She picked it up and flipped it over.

Joey Hodges

To: Annie

She tore it open with a heavy heart. She knew the handwriting. She knew it well.

Dear Annie,

I know the hurt I've caused you over the last few months is probably irreparable, but I have to try.

I miss you, and I hope you know that. I don't expect you to forgive me so easy, but I just needed you to know that I miss our friendship, and I won't ever take it for granted ever again.

Of all the gifts at Christmas, I am most thankful for the years of friendship you've given me.

I hope we can be friends again.

Merry Christmas, Annie.

Friends Always

& Always,

Laurie

Annie finished reading and her dad called from the living room, "Who's at the door, Sweet?"

Annie shoved the letter back into its envelope and closed the door.

     "No one, Dad." *No one*, she muttered to herself.

December 26, 2009

Listening to: Mairi Campbell *Auld Lang Syne*

I'm ignoring Laurie's letter for now. Drew and Jamie came in around noon on Christmas Day, and I really just wanted to enjoy what little time they had here. It was really awesome to have them home!

Oh! Jamie asked me to be a bridesmaid! I'm so freaking excited!!

SO I'M SUPPOSED TO JUST CUT MY LOSSES?

"So what do you think?" Annie asked Josh as she pulled her hair back into a low ponytail.

Josh fiddled with the letter then looked up at Annie. "I think you should do what you want."

He'd gotten back from Hickory on New Year's Day.

***

Annie spent New Year's Eve watching *Dick Clark's New Year's Rockin' Eve* with her dad. Knowing that most of her classmates were out partying made her feel pretty pathetic. But her night ended up being pretty awesome.

She and her dad spent the day together. They made a bunch of appetizers just for the two of them. Early in the day, Annie baked brownies and chocolate chip cookies. Her dad *tried* to help but kept getting in the way. So Annie banished him to the kitchen table, where he kept her laughing. Then the two of them pigged out. Pathetic or not, it had been perfect.

Normally, she spent New Year's Eve with Laurie, but she hadn't been able to bring herself to do anything with the letter. She didn't even tell her dad about it. She was afraid he'd tell her to stop being selfish and to fix the friendship.

She wanted to feel relieved. She wanted to believe that the letter had been sincere and genuine. But lately, she'd been wrong about Laurie more than she'd been right. As much as she missed Laurie, things had been so much easier (and quieter) since they'd "broken up." She really didn't know what to do, or what she even *wanted* to do.

***

"I do –" Annie cut herself off and walked over to Josh, who was sitting on her bed. She sat next to him and pulled the letter from his hands.

"You do what?" Josh asked. He put his hands behind his head and leaned back against the husband pillow propped up against the wall.

"I guess I miss her," Annie said. "But –" Annie turned to look at Josh. "But I just don't know if that friend I miss is there anymore. You know?"

"Then I wouldn't bother," Josh said casually. "If the friend you miss is gone, why bother adjusting to someone you just don't like?"

"I do like her!" Annie defended. "Well, I *used* to. If that person existed once, she's got to be in there somewhere."

"People change, Annie."

"So I'm supposed to just cut my losses?" Annie asked with a heavy heart. Maybe Josh was right. Maybe she really was better off without Laurie. Things had changed for sure, but maybe the changes were for the better.

"You lose some, you win some," Josh said, grinning sadly and pulling Annie next to him. He cuddled her into a hug. "Man, I missed you."

Annie pushed Laurie to the back of her mind, underneath all the other things she'd learned to forget. Despite everything, she was happy.

*****

Joey Hodges

After two weeks off from school, it was hard for Annie to respond to the alarm clock when it sang out at 6:00 a.m. her first day back. Her dad smiled at her when she made her way downstairs. She'd put a little more effort into her appearance — she was Josh's girlfriend now and wanted to look the part.

Her hair was carefully straightened and tucked behind her ears. Her Abercrombie sweater was a Christmas gift from under the tree. Her jeans, which she pulled from the unworn side of her closet, hugged her hips, accentuating her tiny tush. And she'd swiped on some mascara and lip-gloss. *Understated*, she thought when she looked in the mirror before going downstairs, *but in focus*.

Josh met Annie at the end of her driveway when she left for school. He hugged her. "You look different," he said. Annie brushed it off.

"Good, but different," he backpedaled. They could see Laurie walking way ahead of them, and Annie stiffened a little.

"You okay?" Josh asked.

"Yeah," Annie said, looking up at him and smiling. "Perfect."

Josh slipped his hand into hers, and Annie felt an electric shock surge through her body.

Laurie stopped in the schoolyard where she met Olivia and Maddie. When Annie and Josh passed, hand-in-hand, Annie felt Olivia's stare pierce through her.

Out of the corner of her eye, she could see Laurie staring, too. Laurie didn't look shocked, like Olivia, she just looked sad. A wave of pain gushed through Annie, but she shook it off. She made up her mind; her friendship with Laurie was over. One little note couldn't fix that damage.

She was on autopilot through her morning classes. She couldn't bring herself to focus for some reason. Christmas break was on repeat in her mind. It had been perfect. The most perfect Christmas break there ever was. It was ridiculous – she couldn't stop thinking about Josh.

When the lunch bell rang, she practically ran through the hallway to meet him. She'd always been excited to see him before, but now she had a sort of claim to him. Her feelings had been validated. She wasn't some pathetic girl hoping for his attention. She was his *girlfriend.* The thought made her heart race.

She spotted Josh, but he was walking with Brandon and didn't see her. She figured they'd head to the library for lunch like they had been, but Josh followed Brandon into the cafeteria.

There she found him leaning against the wall talking to Brandon. She scanned the perimeter and for the first time in a long time, Olivia was not at Brandon's side. Annie hoped that having a boyfriend would change Olivia; make her less cold. But it quickly became obvious that Brandon was more like an accessory than anything else.

Annie approached the boys, suddenly feeling nervous. Ridiculous! They'd been spending all their time together for months. Nothing was different now, she reminded herself. He was still just Josh, and she was still just Annie.

"So Annie," Brandon said as she approached. "I hear you and this guy here are like a thing now." Brandon nudged Josh, who playfully punched Brandon in the arm. "Couldn't say I didn't see that one coming."

"Oh yeah?" Annie said with an uncharacteristic surge of confidence.

"So tell me. Y'all gonna be antisocial forever or are you finally gonna sit with us again?"

Annie felt like she might throw up. She had no desire to ever sit with any of them again. She hadn't even talked with Laurie yet about her letter. And she really didn't want to do that at school, if at all.

"Sure," Josh said casually, without considering Annie's feelings at all. She shot him a look. He wrapped his arm around her shoulders as they neared the picnic table.

"It won't be so bad," he whispered. "I promise."

Annie sat at the end of the table. She was freezing, and her foul mood was growing. It was January for crying out loud! The Elite were the only idiots still occupying the picnic table field. Everyone else had been smart enough to move inside back in October.

Olivia's eyes were on her as she took her seat at the opposite end of the table. Maddie and Laurie were glued to her side, like good little lemmings. Annie tried to ignore her and waited for her gaze to lift, but it didn't. Annie felt as if her skin were burning off.

She finally looked up and made eye contact with Olivia, probably for the first time since Homecoming.

They sat, staring at each other for what seemed like forever. Who would turn away first? Who would surrender?

Annie's heart was racing. She was terrified of the girl – but no. That wasn't it. Annie felt something swirl around in her mouth, words on the tip of her tongue. She willed herself to keep her mouth shut, to keep the words trapped. But the urge became uncontrollable, and she couldn't help it anymore.

"What?" Annie spit. "Can I help you with something?"

Olivia's eyes widened in surprise then narrowed.

"What's with you?" Olivia shot back. "Are you confused?"

Annie's throat constricted. *What was she doing?* This was a mistake. But no. Who the heck was Olivia to decide what everyone was allowed to do?

"Nope, don't think so," Annie said flippantly, looking around the table. All eyes were on her. Josh reached his hand under the table and squeezed her knee. Olivia looked affronted.

"Who do you think you're kidding here, huh? So you change your clothes and straighten your hair and suddenly you think it's okay to sit here and love up on *him?*" Laurie's eyes were wide like she wanted to jump in and save Annie. But Annie didn't need her help. She didn't need any help at all.

"Well, who the hell do you think *you* are to dictate who can and can't sit here? I have news for you, Olivia. You're not as badass as you think you are. I promise you the only reason no one else has said anything to you is because they're *afraid* of you—not because they *like* you. For real, woman. You need a reality check."

Annie stood and stormed off. She instantly felt relief and guilt. The adrenaline pumped through her veins, numbing her. Before she could think clearly, she was on her front porch.

Uh. So, apparently, she was skipping school now? For the first time, she'd finally said exactly what she was feeling *the moment* she was feeling it, and she didn't even have the balls to stand and take the backlash. What exactly did *that* say about her?

After about 30 minutes and a turkey sandwich, she realized Josh wasn't coming after her. Of course he wasn't. Why would he skip school because she freaked out? She was new to the whole boyfriend thing, but she was *pretty* sure that wasn't in the rulebook. *Whatever.* Either way, she was annoyed.

She docked her iPod, selected The Avett Brothers' playlist, and picked up her guitar to play along.

About an hour later, she didn't hear her cell phone, but she saw it light up in the mesh pocket of her backpack. She turned down the music. She expected it to be Josh, but instead, she saw Laurie's name dancing across the screen. She hesitated and then pushed "ignore."

She tossed the phone onto her bed then lay down next to it. Just as she was wondering what Laurie could possibly have to say to her, her phone rang again. Missy Higgins' *Any Day Now* filled the room, and she saw Laurie's name flash across the screen. Again.

She mashed ignore again then threw the phone across the room in frustration. It smashed into the wall, and the case snapped off. She didn't have the energy to care.

A knock at her bedroom door interrupted her thoughts.

"Annie?" her mother called from the other side of the door.

Crap. What was her mother doing home? It was only 1 p.m. Annie thought and then coughed. She cleared her throat and disguised her voice. "Yeah?" she croaked.

"You're sick?" Her mom actually sounded concerned. That was a first.

"Yeah," Annie croaked again. "I started feeling bad at lunch, so I just walked home."

"Open the door."

Annie pulled tissues from the box on her nightstand and scrunched them up, tossing them around her bed and the floor. She pulled the blanket from the back of her desk chair and wrapped it around herself. She opened the door just a crack.

"Oh," her mom gasped. "You look awful." *Gee, thanks.*

Lisa put the back of her hand to Annie's forehead. "Well,

you don't feel feverish, but you should get some rest."

"Yeah." Annie coughed again and started to shut her door.

"But Annie?" Lisa called out. Annie opened the door back up.

"Yeah?"

"You really ought to follow school procedure when you leave sick. I got a call on my cell explaining your absence from Science." Oh, she'd forgotten about the automatic attendance call system. Oh well, she'd already gotten away with it. Some system.

"Yeah, sorry. Noted." Annie shut the door and leaned against it.

She crawled in between her sheets and pushed her face into her pillow. She felt alone, and maybe she was.

Maybe she *was* fooling herself with the whole Josh thing. They were fine in their little bubble, but the second they reentered The Elite world, everything got screwed up, just like with Laurie. That was Olivia's power– she could screw up anything and everything

Annie must have fallen asleep because the vibration of her cell phone against the broken case across the room woke her up with a jolt. She looked at the time on her clock: 3:30 p.m. School was out.

She stumbled across the room and picked up the phone. She instantly felt excited when she saw Josh's name, but then she remembered that he hadn't even bothered to call or text her after lunch. She swallowed her disappointment, clicked accept, and brought the phone to her ear.

"Hey," Annie said quietly.

"Are you okay?"

"Yeah, I'm fine." Annie felt nerves growing in the pit of her stomach.

"Well, dang. I can't believe what you said." He was quiet for a moment and Annie worried.

"You were freaking *awesome*." He was gushing.

"What happened after I left?"

"Oh, nothing really. Olivia left the table, I assume to go cry in the bathroom. Laurie and Maddie, of course, jumped up after her and disappeared from the table. It was pretty uneventful."

"Oh." Annie was sort of disappointed. "Laurie called me a few times not long after lunch. I thought maybe something happened."

"Not that I know of. Anyway, I just wanted to check on you. Is it okay if I come by?"

She quickly forgot about Laurie and Olivia and, well, pretty much everything. "Of course."

January 4, 2010

Listening to: Missy Higgins *Blind Winter*

I went off on Olivia! Part of me feels so freaking guilty, but the other part is really kind of excited. I'm so tired of her and her stupid mouth. She doesn't run everything and she totally thinks she does! I'm allowed to do me. And I guess, she's allowed to do her, but if she could leave me alone in the process that'd be great.

I still haven't talked to Laurie and I don't think I'm going to. It seems kind of pointless, really. Anyway! Gotta go! Josh just got here. <3

PLEASE CALL ME

The entire week had been so weird. After all the drama on Monday, Josh and Annie decided it was best to take their lunches back to the library. Thankfully, things had been pretty peaceful since then. Any time Olivia spotted Annie, she practically glared through her soul. But Olivia was only as powerful as Annie allowed her to be. So Annie decided she didn't care.

Laurie was another story. She'd been calling and texting all week. Annie avoided her calls, but she couldn't ignore the texts. Apparently, Laurie desperately needed to talk with her about something. Annie didn't responded, but she was a *little* interested in what Laurie had to tell her.

She always thought better of it. Annie just didn't have the energy for any more drama. Laurie stopped at Annie's desk on

Wednesday before Science, but didn't get farther than, "I need to talk to you," before Mrs. Swanson asked everyone to be seated.

When the final bell rang on Friday, marking the end of yet another week, Josh told Annie he'd meet her at her house later. He had some chores to do before their midnight bowling date.

Annie and Laurie used to go midnight bowling all the time. It actually started at 10 p.m., not midnight. And Annie *loved* it. It might sound kind of lame, but it was one of the few fun things to do in town. Midnight bowling featured karaoke, too. But Annie never, *ever* sang. Still, it was fun to watch.

Annie was stepping out of the shower when the doorbell rang. It was only 7. She didn't expect Josh until 9. And he would have used the hidden key her dad showed him over Christmas break.

So Annie ignored it. She looked down through her window in time to see Laurie walking across the front lawn, back to her own house. Huh. Annie checked her phone. Nothing.

She scanned her closet and settled on a pair of lighter jeans and a navy long-sleeved top. She pulled out her song and let her hair air dry while she worked on some of the chords. Her phone chirped.

Laurie: **I get that you're ignoring me and that's okay I guess. But there's something we really need to talk about. Please**

call me.

She almost felt bad, but whatever Laurie needed to talk about really didn't interest her. Annie was almost surprised at how much she'd moved on.

She and Josh arrived at Burgette's and sat in a small booth in the back of the diner.

"May I have the American burger with just pickles and cheese?" Annie handed the menu back to the waitress, who she recognized as a pretty girl from Drew's grade.

"How do you want your burger cooked?"

"Um, medium-well is fine."

"And for you?" The waitress smiled at Josh, and Annie felt a flicker of both jealousy and pride. No one could deny that Josh was good-looking. She knew people must wonder what he saw in her. It took all she had not to let herself worry that someday he'd wonder the same thing.

"I'll just have the same." Josh smiled at Annie and handed the menu back to the waitress, whom he barely noticed. Annie smiled back at him.

"So I've never done this whole midnight bowling thing," he said. "Tell me about it."

"Well, you see, you get these special shoes and these really heavy balls and you roll them down these things called lanes and try to knock down these things called pins." Annie took a sip of her soda.

"Oh shut up," Josh said and tossed Annie's balled up straw wrapper at her.

"No, really though," Annie said, "it's really not any different than regular bowling except they keep all the overhead lights off and they have these different multi-colored lights on. And there's karaoke."

"You gonna sing?" Josh asked even though he *knew* the answer. He'd been bugging her about singing ever since she showed him her song. She told him then that she wasn't any good, but it seemed like maybe he didn't believe her.

"You know that I'm not," she said, annoyed. She glared at him, hoping he'd get the point and leave it alone. "I told you—I can't carry a tune in a bucket."

"For some reason, I don't think that's true." He stared at her, and his eyes crinkled into a smile.

"Well, it is," she spit. "Are *you* going to sing?" she asked pointedly.

"Nah," he said casually. "Karaoke isn't really my thing."

"You see how I'm just going to let that be your answer?" She took another sip of her soda. "You really could learn a thing or two from me," she said flirtatiously.

Their food arrived, and she told him about Laurie stopping by. He agreed it was probably best just to ignore the drama.

"I know all of this hasn't been easy for you," he said somberly. "It wouldn't be easy for anybody. But you're handling everything with such grace."

"Ha!" Annie wiped her mouth with a napkin. "I wouldn't exactly say that. I'm not sure there even *is* a graceful way to handle any of this."

"Yeah, you're probably right." He was quiet for a while as he finished his burger and drained his soda. The waitress came over to check on them. He ordered two chocolate shakes.

"Are you *insane?*" Annie laughed. "I feel like I just ate a whole cow. No way I can finish an entire shake on my own."

"No worries." His eyes crinkled. "I'll finish what you can't."

He's such a bottomless pit.

Their shakes arrived. He was practically finished when he put his cup down and stared at Annie, his arms resting folded on the table.

"What?" she questioned, self-conscious.

"Don't get mad, okay?"

"*What*? Now she was paranoid.

"Okay, it's just. Well, I know you're lying about the singing thing."

Annie's pulse quickened and her throat went dry. "And why do you think that?"

"I don't think it," Josh corrected. "I *know* it." He slurped the remainder of his milkshake. "Sometimes, when we're listening to music, you hum along."

"So?" she asked, not really sure where he was going with this. "A lot of people hum when they listen to music."

"Sure, but not everyone sounds like you when they do."

"What are you getting at?"

He leaned forward and took Annie's hands in his. They were cold from holding her milkshake, which she'd only half finished.

"When you hum, there's this, I don't know, flare or something. It seems effortless, and it's beautiful. And it really just makes me wonder why you won't sing. You obviously can."

Annie stared at him for a minute then took her hands out of his. She ran them through her hair, which she hadn't bothered to straighten after it air-dried. She'd been caught.

"Okay," she admitted quietly. "Maybe I *can* sing. But it doesn't matter because I *don't* sing."

"Why not?" He leaned back into the booth and rested his head against it.

"Maybe it's not something I talk about."

He was quiet for a minute as if chewing on what she'd said. "I guess that's fair," he said, his tone full of disappointment. "But for what it's worth? I really think that you *should* sing. I see your face when you're immersed in music. I can tell that you *want* to sing. And I hope someday you can break free from whatever is holding you back."

"Yeah," she said quietly. "Maybe." She slid her shake toward him, and he happily took it.

The bowling alley was fairly empty. There were a few kids from school, but they seemed more interested in making out with each other than bowling. And the usual drunk alley rats. Annie was a little bummed. There wouldn't be much of a karaoke show. Well, except for the drunkards who murdered the songs. Oh, well. That could be entertaining, too.

Josh picked up their shoes while Annie set up their names in the computer at their lane.

"That guy working the shoe rental counter? His dad works for my dad, so he gave us our shoes for free. Cool, huh?"

Annie loved how sweet Josh was. And so easy to please.

"Great! Well, let's get started. Are you ready to get your butt kicked?"

"Go easy on me, pal. I'm a rookie."

"Sure," Annie said with a sarcastic smile.

Annie killed Josh in their first game. Just as they were deciding whether to play again, the DJ announced the start of the karaoke.

"Let's go watch," Josh said.

Annie and Josh changed their shoes and headed to the bar. Josh grabbed two sodas and some popcorn.

"How can you possibly still be hungry?" Josh flashed her a wide, sincere smile. Annie's stomach filled with butterflies.

The first drunk to grace the stage was a middle-aged lady that

Annie recognized from her mother's office. She snatched the microphone from the DJ's hands and called out to the small crowd.

"Be prepared to be blown away, y'all!" Her words were slurred. Josh and Annie laughed and leaned back in their seats, preparing themselves.

The woman belted out the first two lines of *Pour Some Sugar on Me* before she literally fell off the stage. The DJ jumped up and ran over to her. At first, Annie thought he was going to help her, but he just snatched the microphone.

"Next? Someone? Anyone?"

Josh nudged Annie, who glared at him. "Not a chance," she growled.

Josh kept nudging her with a giant smile on his face. The DJ noticed them.

"Knock it off, Josh. Stop," she hissed, feeling the eyes of the DJ on her. "This isn't funny." She actually felt rage in her heart.

"You!" The DJ pointed at Annie. "Young lady. Get on up here." The DJ held the microphone out toward her.

Annie blushed and slouched down. "Oh, um, no thanks."

"Aw, c'mon pretty girl. Help me out here."

"Really, I'd rather not," Annie felt her cheeks burning.

The DJ approached her and pulled her out of her chair by her small wrist.

"I'm sure you've got a voice like an angel. And well, if not, the crowd is too drunk to care."

As the DJ dragged Annie onstage, she turned back to Josh and mouthed, "I hate you." Josh's smile spread across his entire face. She mirrored his smile unconsciously.

The DJ started *Landslide,* by Fleetwood Mac. Her heart clenched when she saw the title on the screen in front of her. It was a little too fitting for her life at that moment. The guitar track filled the alley. She stared at the blue screen with such intensity that it started to blur.

The words began to scroll, and she let herself go, pushing the memories of the last time she'd held a microphone from her mind. The lyrics poured from her soul as she stood like a stone, clutching the microphone with both hands.

She couldn't hear anything but the music. She couldn't see anything but the scrolling words. Electricity surged through her.

Little by little she loosened up. Her knees unlocked as she hit the chorus. Her nerves began shedding their layers. Then she spotted Josh in the small crowd. She could see his smile and she mirrored it.

He had such a way of making her smile when she wasn't prepared to.

She saw that the crowd was swaying and smiling. No one was talking. The bartender stood, mesmerized. Bowlers paused their games to watch. The kids making out came up for air and watched, too. Every eye in the place was on her. She was doing it, and it felt … *good.*

When the song ended, she handed the microphone back to the DJ and walked quietly back to Josh. Then the crowd erupted into applause. Josh threw his arms around her, and she whispered into his ear, "Let's go."

"Whatever you want, rock star."

When they finally made their way outside, Josh squeezed her hand.

"I'm so proud of you." He said this calmlyi as if he knew that performance was inside of her all this time.

"I hate you for that, you know."

"I know," he said. "But tell me you didn't love it."

She knew she couldn't.

"I hate to even admit this," she said, looking at the ground as they walked. "But it was Olivia."

Josh stopped her and looked down at her, puzzled. "What was Olivia?"

She took her hand from his and nervously ran it through her hair. "It was years ago," she said, "sixth grade, actually. Remember that talent show they used to force everyone to participate in?"

"Yeah."

"I'd never sung in front of anyone except my family and Laurie. She insisted I do it. Obviously, she didn't know our school or the people in it. But she assured me it would earn me cool points, not that I really wanted any of those."

She took Josh's hand and began walking again. She would rather he not look at her while she explained.

"Everyone was allowed to use the auditorium to practice, but we had to sign up. So I signed up for the last possible slot. I was so nervous, and I really didn't want any of the other students hanging around when I practiced."

"Makes sense," Josh said. "That's actually kind of smart." He laughed.

"Well, it was just me and Mrs. Abrahams. Everyone else had left or so I thought. Well, anyway. I started practicing. I was nervous so my voice was shaky, but I was trying. Olivia busted into the auditorium with some of her friends. Remember that girl she used to hang out with? Oh, what was her name? Samantha? The one who got sent to reform school?

"Anyway, the two of them busted in and just laid into me. Mrs. Abrahams ordered them out, but it was too late. Their words were already implanted in my mind. They said I sounded like someone swinging a bag of cats against a wall. I pulled out of the talent show. I told my dad about what happened and he let me stay home sick."

Josh was quiet for a while as they walked. "No wonder you hate her so much."

"I didn't hate her. I really didn't think of her at all. I just felt foolish for even thinking that singing would be a good idea. I never sang in front of people again."

"Well," he said, squeezing her hand, "she's an idiot and *wrong*. But I'm glad you told me." He paused. "And I'm glad you sang tonight, even if you hate me for it. You were amazing. I mean that," he took his hand from hers and gestured wildly. "Actually, I don't think there are words for what that was. Unbelievable, really."

She blushed. "Stop. You're going to give me a big head."

"I hope so!" he teased. "Maybe you'll sing again, then!" He

looked at her. "Can we *please* write lyrics for your song now?" he begged.

"One step at a time, buddy," she giggled.

Just before they turned the corner onto Annie's street, Josh stopped her. He stood facing her beneath the stars. The moon hung high in the sky, and Annie yawned.

"Sorry, it's past my bedtime," she joked. She glanced at her watch: 12:37 a.m.

Josh took Annie's hands. She looked up at him and half smiled. "What's up?" she asked, almost nervous. She waited a moment. "Josh, you okay?"

Josh looked from left to right, then back at Annie. The street in the early morning hour was empty. He smiled, closed his eyes and leaned in. To Annie, it was as if he were moving in slow motion.

She closed her eyes and took a deep breath. She tilted her head to the right and stretched her neck. She pushed herself onto her tippy toes and received Josh's kiss.

Her knees loosened. Ha! She was *literally* weak in the knees.

His kiss was soft and strong at the same time. Perfect. Exactly what every girl's first kiss should be. It took all of her willpower not to go in for another the moment it was over. He didn't say anything. He just grabbed her hand and started walking again.

Annie twisted her key in the front door and was surprised it had been left unlocked. She pushed the door open and the light caught her by surprise.

Annie and Josh found her mom at the kitchen table. Her makeup had been removed, and she was wearing a robe over her pajamas. Next to her was a swollen-eyed, tear-soaked Laurie.

"Mom?" Annie asked, surprised. "Laurie? What are you doing here? What's going on?"

Lisa stared at Annie.

"Mom?" Annie's voice was shaking. Laurie wiped at her tears. "Is everything okay?" Laurie was visibly shaking.

Lisa turned her gaze to Josh. "Go home." Her tone was harsh.

"Mom!"

"Annie, trust me when I say you want him to leave. Josh. Go home *now*." Lisa spoke through gritted teeth.

Josh leaned forward and kissed Annie's cheek softly and whispered that he had a great night. She nodded slowly. "Good night, Annie. Good night, Mrs. Mackey." He left Laurie out.

Annie turned to the table, confused and angry. "What the heck is going on?"

"Annette Mackey. You will let me speak and then you will go to your room. Laurie here was kind enough to pay me a visit this evening. She tells me you two have had quite a falling out. Is this true?" Lisa didn't look amused.

"Well …" Annie stared right at Laurie. She shifted her weight from one foot to another and crossed her arms defensively. "Yeah. We have."

"I see," she said. "It seems *keeping* things from me is a growing trend."

Annie felt rage boiling. Keeping things from her mother? Ha! She could be on *fire* and her mother wouldn't notice.

"Why, Annette? You're a smart girl. At least I *thought* you were. You had dreams. You had goals! I thought you were better than all those," she waved her hand, "those angsty teenage screw-ups."

"Mom! What are you talking about?"

"When?" Lisa asked with poison in her tone. "When were you going to tell me you were having sex with that boy? And *when,* exactly, were you going to tell me that you, my 15-year-old daughter, are pregnant?"

Annie blinked, stunned. *What?* She couldn't find her voice, and her fingertips felt numb. Rage boiled inside her stomach, and she glared at Laurie who was still violently shaking and now sobbing.

Laurie got up from the table quickly, knocking the chair backwards in the process. "I'm sorry," Laurie said to Mrs. Mackey. She glanced at Annie with despair and mouthed, "I'm sorry" as she turned and ran out the front door, leaving Annie standing in the kitchen facing her seething mother.

What the hell just happened?

January 8/technically 9ᵗʰ 2010

Listening to: nothing because it's the middle of the night and
everyone is sleeping and I just don't care.

*Why is it that every time something amazing happens,
something awful has to come along and trump it all? Josh* kissed *me!
He FINALLY kissed me, and I can't even focus on that right now. I
don't even know if I can remember what it felt like and it was only a
few hours ago. But it feels like it was ages ago. I'm exhausted and
mentally and emotionally drained.*

*I can't even begin to understand all that happened tonight or
why.*

*Oh. And not that anyone cares or that it even matters at this
point because I can pretty much guarantee I'm grounded for life and
I'll never see humans ever again…but I sang tonight. And it felt
awesome.*

*Whatever. Everything sucks. Seeing Laurie sitting at the table
when I walked in freaked me out. She looked awful and I was really*

Yeah, maybe

scared that something terrible happened to her. Can you believe it? I

actually felt bad *for her when I first saw her. And she was here*

ruining *my life!*

JUST PLACE ONE FOOT IN EACH STIRRUP

"Mom, this is ridiculous," Annie whispered as she peered around the waiting room of the doctor's office. "You know I'm not pregnant."

Annie felt as if all the other patients were staring at her, judging.

***

Her mom drove her to the corner 24-hour drug store Friday night and forced her to buy five pregnancy tests with her own money while Lisa waited in the car. Five! Those suckers were *expensive.* She was mortified as she placed them down on the counter in front of Janelle.

Janelle worked the night shift at the pharmacy for as long as Annie could remember. She tried her best to make small talk as she quickly rang up the items. Seventy-five freaking dollars. For a rumor. Annie had been considering that maybe she'd made a mistake cutting Laurie out of her life. *Not anymore.*

     ***

"Knock it off," Lisa grunted as she flipped through a *Better Homes and Gardens* magazine she'd picked up from the table in the center of the room.

Annie stared at the clock. She'd already missed all of first period and half of second for a bogus doctor's appointment. Her mom hadn't been swayed by the *five* negative test results. Or the hysterical tears. Or Annie's pleas. It was like her mom *hoped* she was pregnant so she'd have another excuse to hate her.

Either way, Lisa's mind was set. "Why would your best friend in the whole world come over in the middle of the night to spread *lies*? Huh, Annie? Does that make any sense to you?"

Well, no, she thought. *None* of this made any sense to her. She was exhausted and her head was swimming. The weekend had been brutal as she awaited the dreadful Monday appointment her mother insisted on.

Annie toyed with the idea of calling Laurie, texting her, showing up at her house, *something*. But the more she thought about it, the more she realized it was useless. There was no making sense of the person Laurie had become.

"Annette Mackey," the nurse standing in the doorway called. Annie's cheeks burned as she walked toward the nurse with her angry mother in tow. The nurse led them down a long, white hallway and opened the door to an empty exam room.

Annie sat on the table, her legs swinging over the edge. The white paper covering the leather table crinkled with each swing of her legs. Lisa sat on a plastic chair positioned against the opposite wall. The nurse snapped on a pair of latex gloves and prepared the instruments lined up on a blue napkin. Annie examined them. They were all long and sharp. She cringed and hoped they wouldn't come near her.

"Now, Annette, I'm just going to take some blood." The nurse pulled Annie's arm straight and positioned the needle over the crease of her elbow. "Okay, just a little stick."

Annie winced at the prick and kept her eyes forward. Saying she didn't like blood seemed useless—who did, really?

"So, you go to Willow Point High?" the nurse asked in an attempt to keep Annie's attention off the fact that blood was being pulled from her veins. "I went there quite some time ago."

"Yeah, it's probably still the same though," Annie said. "They haven't renovated it, but they should."

"Yeah. Alrighty then. All done." The nurse disposed of the needle and threw her gloves away. She wrote something on the tube of Annie's blood.

"Dr. Slack will be with you in just a bit to discuss the results." The nurse smiled brightly, a harsh contrast to the tension in the room. Annie and Lisa sat in silence for several minutes.

"This is a waste of time." Annie exhaled.

Lisa said nothing and glared toward the closed door with an anxious look. She silenced her cell phone that was ringing for the millionth time.

"I hope you realize how much your irresponsibility inconveniences this entire family."

Annie had had enough. "We don't *have* to be here, Mom! Go back to your precious job and ..." Annie hesitated, "and whatever else it is that sucks up all your time." Annie watched fury contort her mother's face. Before Lisa could respond, there was a soft rap on the exam room door, and it swung open.

Dr. Slack glided through the door with a cheerful smile and a perky blonde ponytail swinging in her wake. She couldn't have been older than 35. She quickly introduced herself to Annie and shook

both Annie and her mother's hands. She flipped through the papers

on the clipboard she was holding and sat on the wheelie stool,

scooting close to Annie.

"Alright, now. Annette, you took an at home pregnancy test

that was negative?"

"Yes," Annie said. "Oh, God." She looked up at the ceiling,

willing back tears. "This is so embarrassing. I swear I'm not

pregnant. We're only here because I have a deranged ex-best friend.

I've never even had sex."

Lisa scoffed in the corner. "Dr. Slack, can we just get to the

results?" Lisa asked sternly. "I really have to get to work."

"Alright. Well, Annette –"

A lump formed in Annie's throat. She swallowed it. This was

ridiculous. She *knew* she wasn't pregnant.

"You are certainly not pregnant," Dr. Slack said. A smug

smile danced across Annie's face. She looked at her mother, who

was looking at Dr. Slack in shock.

Dr. Slack smiled at Annie brightly. "But what I do think is

that I should just take a look and make sure everything is alright.

Having unprotected sex can lead to complications other than

pregnancy."

Annie looked back at Dr. Slack horrified. "B-but I haven't had sex. Seriously. This is all just a stupid rumor."

"She's lying," Lisa said. "Please proceed."

"Now, Annie. I know it can be quite awkward to talk about this in front of your mother, but this is a safe space. There's no need for stories. Now I'm going to excuse myself for a moment." Dr. Slack headed for the door. "Please remove your pants and undergarment. You can drape this sheet over yourself." Dr. Slack handed Annie a stark white sheet.

"And Annie? Maybe you would feel a little more comfortable if Mom waits in the waiting room." She looked expectantly at Lisa, leaving no room for argument. Lisa followed Dr. Slack out of the room in a huff.

This was so unfair. How did she end up here? Why didn't anyone believe her? Annie removed her pants grudgingly and sat on the examination table with the white sheet draped over her lower half. Dr. Slack returned moments later.

"Ok, Annette. Just lie back for me." Dr. Slack pulled the stirrups out from the examination table. "Just place one foot in each stirrup. And relax."

Annie was mortified. *Completely* mortified. She closed her eyes and tears crept down the sides of her face and dropped back behind her ears. She sniffled.

This isn't happening, this isn't happening, this isn't happening, she chanted inside her head.

"I'm sorry," Annie squeaked out, sitting up on the table. "I just, I can't do this!" She was openly sobbing. "This isn't fair. I promise you I haven't done anything. My mom, she just doesn't get it! And my best friend? Or ex-best friend? She's mad at me, so she's spreading this rumor. I don't even know why!"

Annie looked at Dr. Slack through her ugly cry. "You have to believe me! Please don't —" She hiccupped. "Please don't do this. Please."

She told Dr. Slack everything. She tried to be as open and honest as possible. Yes, she had a boyfriend, but they'd only kissed! They hadn't even had their *first* kiss until the night everything erupted!

She told Dr. Slack how she felt. She told her honestly that she didn't think she could handle the responsibility of sex, that it would probably change everything.

Dr. Slack commended her on her perspective.

"I think you're telling the truth. And in that case, I really don't think we should do this exam. It's pretty invasive, and can be painful."

Annie was flooded with relief.

"But listen. Keep that head about you, okay? Because you're right. Sex *does* change everything."

Annie met Lisa in the waiting room.

"Well?" her mom exhaled obviously annoyed she had been kicked out of the room.

"Mom." Annie looked around her. "Can we *not* right here?" She asked, scanning the room of judgmental eyes. They exited into the main part of the office building. Despite the cool temperature outside, the sun had baked the tiny room between the two sets of doors. "She didn't do the exam," Annie told her mother.

"And why the hell not?"

"Because, Mom! Don't you freaking get it? I was telling the truth. I *am* telling the truth! I'm not having sex. I'm not that dumb. You *know* I'm not that dumb." The tears returned and Annie's voice softened. "At least you *used* to." Annie looked at her mother, and the tears in Lisa's eyes shocked her. She'd almost forgotten that Lisa was capable of any emotion besides anger or annoyance.

Lisa cleared her throat, and Annie was sure an apology was coming her way.

"You know what?" Lisa said harshly. "I think a walk would do you some good." Lisa spun on her heel and stormed out into the cool morning.

Annie stood there shocked. Baffled. Then she chased after her mom into the parking lot.

"Mom!" Annie screamed as she caught up. "Mom! Stop!" Lisa twirled around still with tears in her eyes. She said nothing.

"Why are *you* crying? I was telling the truth. This is good news!" Annie stopped a few feet away from her mother, afraid to get too close.

"Who *are* you, Annie?" Lisa growled. She wiped angrily at a tear that fell. "I look at you and feel like I don't even know you."

"I'm the same girl I've always been, Mom. I am." Annie took a step closer. Lisa held up her hands in protest.

"No. No, you're not." She shook her head. "You've let your friendship with Laurie dissolve and you're spending way too much time with that boy, getting into God only knows what. I don't like who you're becoming at all, Annie. Not one bit."

"*Mom.*" Tears stung her eyes. Frustration burned in her

throat. *She* wasn't the one changing. She was simply making do with the changes happening around her. "You can't mean that."

"I do," Lisa said, turning back around. She walked to her car.

She stopped and turned back to face Annie. "Those results don't change anything. You're still grounded."

Annie stomped her foot. "Mom! Seriously? What for? Because Laurie's a bitch?"

Lisa winced at her daughter's dramatics. "Because I said so. And you know what? I don't want you seeing that boy anymore, either. I mean it, Annie. End it."

Lisa got into her car. Annie stood still, tears flowing, as she watched her mother drive away.

*****

Annie walked the whole way from one side of town to the other, probably a good 5 miles. *Ill with Want* groaned through her headphones and rattled her brain. If anyone could speak to her soul at that moment, it was The Avett Brothers.

Annie got to school just as the lunch bell rang. But she just couldn't do it that day. Any of it. The pretending. She was gutted. She didn't have the energy to be any version of herself right then.

She sat on the front steps of the school, her eyes puffy and stinging. She'd cried the entire walk, not even caring what the passersby thought. She rested her elbows on her knees and buried her face in her hands.

"Annie?" a small voice called out. Annie jumped, startled. "You okay?"

Maddie approached the steps with an armful of books. She stopped and turned toward the car sitting idly at the curb. She waved, and the car drove off. Annie didn't speak but looked at Maddie quizzically.

"My mom. I had a dentist appointment."

Annie nodded. "I'm fine," she said quietly, dropping her eyes to the sidewalk. Maddie climbed up to meet Annie and sat down next to her.

"You don't look fine," Maddie said with concern.

Annie shrugged.

"Okay," Maddie said. She hesitated. "I, like, have to tell you something. But you have to promise you won't, like, kill me, K?"

Though they hadn't spent much time together, Annie and Maddie had become sort of... friends, despite the chaos around them.

Annie's eyes narrowed. "Spill."

"I know what happened."

Annie opened her mouth to interrupt, but Maddie stopped her. "Listen," she said sternly. "I know you must be, like, so pissed at Laurie right now."

"Well, duh," Annie said. "I don't eve—"

Maddie cut her off. "I really need you to just trust me when I tell you she did it for a good reason."

"Um, no?" Annie said, affronted. "I can't just believe that. What kind of reason could Laurie *possibly* have for that, huh?" Annie was actually asking. She glared at Maddie hoping for, no, *demanding* an answer.

"I —" Maddie hesitated. "I really can't tell you. I'm sorry — "

Annie started to go off, but Maddie interrupted her. "I know you must hate her. You must hate all of us, really. I know all of this totally sucks. And I'm so, so sorry. Just try to keep an open mind, okay? Be mad at me if you have to, but I promise you, Laurie was really just trying to protect you from something bigger."

Annie couldn't make sense of anything Maddie was saying. The bell rang, and Maddie hesitantly stood. She muttered that she was sorry again and left Annie on the steps.

As Annie took her seat in Science, her chest felt tight. Laurie wasn't there yet – she was probably still gossiping in the hallway with Olivia.

Annie pulled her notebook from her backpack. As she started writing the header in the top corner, she saw Laurie out of the corner of her eye. Annie looked up and glared at her.

Laurie held Annie's gaze as she walked passed Annie's desk. Her eyes were apologetic. Laurie sat at the table directly behind her, and Annie kept her eyes forward, trying to make sense of the expression she'd seen on Laurie's face.

Annie felt a jab in her back. She swung around to see Laurie leaning over the table toward her with a pencil extended.

"What?" Annie whispered sharply.

"I didn't have a choice," Laurie said. "I'm so, so sorry." Tears filled Laurie's giant green eyes. "Really," she said. "You know I'd never do something like that otherwise."

"Oh, please. The victim act is getting *so* old. No one is making you do *anything*. You're *choosing* to be this way!" Annie yell-whispered as the teacher entered the room. "You know what? Don't talk to me ever again. I mean it, Laurie. You've gone way too far this time. We're done."

Class started, and Annie turned her back on Laurie. But no matter how hard she tried, she couldn't focus. Her mind kept drifting back to the doctor's parking lot, to her mom's hurt expression, to Josh and the idea of never seeing him again. The bell rang before she'd taken a single note.

She caught up to Josh just as he was approaching the locker room. Her heart ached. She pulled on his backpack, and he spun around.

"Ann! There you are! Dude, what happened? I didn't hear from you the rest of the weekend!"

"Grounded."

"Ah, that explains it," Josh said. "Everything work out?"

"Well, if by 'work out,' you mean 'me half naked on an exam table with a perfect stranger staring at my lady business,' then sure. Worked out just fine."

Josh stared, mortified. "*What?*"

"Laurie told my mom I was pregnant." She watched his eyes widen in shock, and she filled him in. She adjusted the strap of her backpack. "Sorry I missed lunch. In fact, I'm sorry for everything. This morning was such a complete waste. All for nothing, and I'm still grounded."

"Bummer," Josh said uncomfortably.

"But listen, there's something we kind of need to talk about. Skip with me?"

"Sure." Josh looked around the swarming hallway, and they ducked out the side door into the courtyard. They were halfway down the street toward Misty Lake Park before she couldn't hold it in any longer. The thought of having to walk away from him was just too much. He'd been her only ally, the only one who had been remotely consistent through everything. She burst into tears.

Josh stopped. "Whoa, whoa! What is it?" He pulled her into a tight hug and stroked her hair. "Shhhh," he whispered into her hair. "It's okay. It's okay."

She was blubbering. The gravity of the entire situation really hadn't hit her until that second, and she couldn't find any words that made sense. Even if she could, she wouldn't have been able to get them out through her hysterics.

"Annie." Josh held her at arm's length and tried to look her in the eye. "Annie, look at me. You need to calm down." His expression was panicked. "Tell me what's going on."

Annie sniffed and wiped her nose with her arm. She tried to

take in a few deep breaths, but then she heard her mom's words in her head all over again, and she lost it again. She pulled her arms up to her chest and burrowed her face into Josh's chest.

In that moment, everything could still be the same. The second she said the words, everything was going to change. He would have to walk away from her, and her world would officially be empty. She'd have nothing left.

"Baby," Josh crooned into her hair. "Please tell me what's wrong. You're scaring me."

"It has to be over," she hiccupped into his shirt. "You and me. She said we have to end it." Her heart broke in two. "God, I hate Laurie so much. This is all her fault." She pulled away from him and wiped at her eyes as she looked up at him. "I know we'll see each other at school and stuff," she sniffled. "But it won't be the same."

"What about your dad? Can't he loosen her up a bit? He likes me, right?"

"Yeah, but he's powerless when it comes to my mom. She's a monster, Josh. It's sickening." Her heart tightened as she remembered her dad's sad glance when he left for work early that morning. She still didn't even know what he thought about the whole thing. It was all so messed up.

"Well," Josh sighed, "I can tell you one thing. I'm not going to just sit back and not see you. We'll work this out. Promise." Josh flashed his perfectly white smile and shook his hair from his eyes. He had a way of making anything seem possible, and he made her feel like she was worth the effort.

"But how?" Annie asked. "I don't think you realize how crazy my mom can be when she puts her mind to something. One time Drew got grounded for being 3 minutes past curfew. *Three minutes*. She's isn't going to let this go easily."

"I'll see you. Trust me." Josh wrapped his arms around Annie and pulled her closer. He kissed the top of her head.

She was just going to have to trust him.

February 10, 2010

Listening to: Pearl Jam *Just Breathe*

It's been ages since I've written. But in all honesty nothing has happened. That's what happens when you're grounded for life. I've hardly talked to anyone and I feel so alone. It's given me a lot of time to think about things with Laurie. My heart feels so torn because I do miss her. But I miss the girl she used to be. Sometimes I sit at my window and look at her house just to see when her light goes on and off. I feel so disconnected from her life, and she's so disconnected from mine. She said she had a good reason—and so did Maddie, but that's crap. There's no way she could have a good reason for what she did. She ruined my life.

I miss Josh most of all. I miss him so much I can't stand it. I'd gotten so used to having him around. I tried talking to my dad like he asked, but I knew there wasn't anything he could do. Seeing Josh at school is just not the same. I miss playing guitar with him and laughing until my sides hurt with him.

I miss laughing in general.

HAPPY VALENTINE'S DAY

"Are you crazy?" Annie laughed as she reached for the hand Josh extended to help her out of the tree. "This is so cliché."

Annie jumped, and her knees buckled. She crumbled into the grass.

"Alright, klutz. This isn't exactly how I pictured it," Josh said, pulling Annie up as she brushed herself off. The moon, accompanied by a sprinkle of stars, was huge and bright in the night sky. The February air was crisp, and Annie's breath puffed in white clouds. She remembered how she and Laurie would pretend to smoke when they were kids, laughing as they exhaled. She quickly shook the memory away.

Annie had been grounded for four weeks with no end in

sight. She went to and from school and straight to her room for approximately 24 days. She spent her weekends scribbling lyrics then scratching them out while music seeped from her speakers. She had nothing to show for her time.

"So, Romeo, what's so important that you had to toss rocks at my window?"

"I needed to spend time with you. You know, away from school." Josh clasped Annie's hand. They walked to the end of Annie's driveway and turned left. The street was so empty, ghostly. The orange glow from the street lamp painted their path.

"I've really missed you, you know?" Josh squeezed Annie's hand, and the feeling went straight to her heart. *Yeah. She knew.*

It was Thursday night, and while Annie was excited to spend some stolen time with Josh, she couldn't help but worry about her early morning Algebra I exam. She'd gotten no better than a D on her last two. To say she'd been a little distracted the last few months would be an epic understatement.

She was taking advantage of her grounding to focus on school, math in particular. Heck, if she was going to be grounded, something might as well come out of it.

Stop, she told herself. *Enjoy this time with Josh.*

All the studying that could have possibly been done had been. She'd been asleep for two hours when the pebble smacked against her window, waking her.

"The park?" Annie asked, breaking the silence as they walked.

"Mm," Josh grunted. He looked great in his break-away athletic pants and long-sleeved Abercrombie T-shirt. She felt self-conscience in her black leggings, oversized T-shirt and puffy blue coat. When they reached the end of the street and made another left, Annie was confused.

"I thought you said we were going to the park?"

"I said nothing. I grunted." He smiled coyly.

"But then —" Annie suddenly remembered what Josh had said during Gym earlier in the day. *My dad took my brother to look at the University of South Carolina. They won't be back until late Sunday.*

"Your house?" Annie asked with butterflies in her stomach. She couldn't tell if she was excited or nervous. Maybe both. She hadn't been to his house since the night of the party.

That night she hadn't noticed the family photos on almost every surface. Toothy smiles from Josh and Dave as kids, arms slung around each other. Camping photos. Photos with giant fish. Photos of their dad with an arm over each of them, grinning hard outside what looked like a church. They were all in suits, a wedding maybe?

She scanned the walls for any trace of his mother. She'd wanted to ask —especially because he was well aware of her family dysfunction. He was the only person besides Laurie who knew her suspicions about her mom. But she hadn't found the right moment.

Just as they were about to reach the stairs to the basement, she spotted it. His mother's bridal portrait was hanging just left of the TV in the living room. God, she looked so young. She couldn't have been more than 22? 23? in the photo. Her golden-brown hair, eerily similar to Josh's, was in a short, cropped bob. Her veil was a simple headband that tucked her hair behind her ears. Her face was radiant. Flawless. There was a sparkle in her eye that intrigued Annie.

Something must have happened to that woman. The thought made Annie's stomach twist.

Josh led Annie down to the basement. She flashed back to the night of the party — seeing him with Laurie. She shook the memory away. Tonight he was with her, and only her. He brought *her* here. He chose *her*. He opened the door to his bedroom and Annie gasped.

"Happy Valentine's Day, Annie."

She took in the view. Flickering votive candles made the entire room glow. His full-sized bed was covered in rose petals. Annie could make out the shape of a heart in the center.

There was something written in candy hearts in the center. She had to walk closer to read it. When she did, she turned to Josh. He held his hands up in defense.

"I don't want you to feel like you have to say anything just because I did."

"Well." Annie swallowed, her mouth suddenly very dry. "Technically, you didn't *say* anything." She felt a pull at the corners of her mouth. Josh walked toward her and wrapped his arms around her waist.

"I've actually felt this way for a while. But I couldn't hold it in anymore. I love you, Annie." He leaned into her and she felt his kiss overwhelm her. They fell onto the bed and before Annie could think of a reason not to, she was laying beside him, kissing him on top of all the rose petals.

"You know," she said, pulling her lips from his, "those will stain your comforter." Josh pushed his mouth firmly onto hers.

"Who cares?"

Yeah, Annie thought, letting go. *Who cares?* He entwined his fingers in her messy bedhead hair, and it felt so good.

"I – " she started but continued kissing him. "I, you know," she was struggling for breath. "I do, too. *You* know."

"Wha —" Josh started to pull away but she smothered his words with her kiss.

"Love you," she said. She pushed herself up onto her knees and removed her coat and threw it next to them on the bed. A cloud of petals floated up then fell. She leaned back into him.

She could feel Josh's smile on her lips. She'd let herself fall. She'd let herself be *vulnerable* for the very first time. There was a little pang of fear that bubbled in her stomach – the fear of getting hurt.

Josh accepted her exactly as she was. There had been no pretending with him. She'd never had the chance to pretend, really. He came into her world when everything in it was crashing down. He'd seen her at her worst. He had encouraged her to be her best. He'd challenged her, counseled her, and been there for her.

She'd never let anyone in like this besides Laurie. And that had been less of a choice. That had been the typical childhood friendship forged by proximity.

She felt so assured. It was okay to be *herself.* It was okay if The Elite didn't like her. It was okay if she was the target of every rumor and prank. Because she was being true to *herself.* And for the first time in a *long* time, she was completely okay with that.

Josh's hand wandered down to her waist, inching her T-shirt up to the elastic band of her leggings. She continued kissing him, but her nerves started dancing. She was paying careful attention to where his hand would go next.

Relief flooded over her when Josh lifted her shirt and pinched her side causing Annie to squeal with laughter. She smacked his hand down and pushed herself up onto her elbows.

"You're such a jer—"

A vibration buzzed through the otherwise quiet room, interrupting her. She and Josh sat straight up, patting around the bed. Annie's heart dropped when she realized it was her phone in her coat pocket.

She frantically grabbed it, and her nerves settled when she saw who it was. She flashed the screen at Josh and laughed in relief.

"It's just Laurie. *Again.*"

She mashed ignore and put the phone down beside her.

"Again?" Josh asked. "She's been calling?"

"Practically non-stop. It's getting *so* annoying!"

Josh leaned into her and kissed her lightly. "Let's please not talk about Laurie." The words weren't out of his mouth before Annie's phone rang again. She immediately mashed ignore and rolled her eyes.

"Sorry," Annie said. Her phone chimed in her hand. A text message.

Laurie: URGENT!! Call me immediately!

Annie showed Josh the message. "I'm just going to turn my phone off." She went to press the power button when Josh stopped her.

"Maybe you should call her."

"What?" No! I'm not letting her ruin this. She's ruined everything else!"

"But it seems important, doesn't it? Just call her, please. If it's nothing, then it's nothing. But maybe you should find that out."

She was ready to argue, but before she could, her phone rang again. She exhaled in annoyance but answered.

"God! What is it?"

Laurie was panicked on the other end. It sounded like she was crying or hyperventilating or both.

"You need to meet me at the end of our street right this freaking second! I saw you leave with Josh. And I'm so sorry to interrupt, but this is important!"

Annie sighed. "I really don't have time for your drama, Laurie. I'm hanging up." Annie pulled the phone from her ear.

"Annie! No!" Laurie sobbed. "You *have* to come! It's our parents!" Annie's blood ran cold. Laurie was screaming, so she knew Josh could hear. Before she said anything, before she could *do* anything, Josh took the phone from her hand and told Laurie they'd be right there.

Annie's heart was pounding. Josh handed her her coat, and they took off running down the street. Annie's mind was racing. She'd never heard that kind of panic in Laurie's voice before.

They reached the intersection of her street and Annie saw Laurie sitting with her knees up to her chest rocking back and forth. There was yelling. *Lots* of yelling. But she couldn't make out what anyone was saying or to whom the voices belonged.

Laurie spotted them and sprung up to meet them. Annie broke away from Josh, and Laurie threw herself into her friend.

"I'm so sorry!" Laurie wailed.

She was hysterical. Annie immediately felt panicked, worried that something awful happened to her dad. Her thoughts were interrupted by more yelling.

"I've been trying to tell you for weeks. And I —" Laurie hiccupped a sob. "Oh, gosh Annie, it's just *so* awful."

Annie pulled away, forcing Laurie to calm down and look her in the eye. "What are you talking about?"

Laurie broke down again. The yelling was getting more intense, and Annie tried to quiet Laurie down so she could hear what was happening.

"I found out a few weeks ago. And I've been trying to tell you. I've been trying to figure out *what* to do about it. Your mom and my dad!"

Annie couldn't make sense of what she'd just heard. "What?"

"My dad. He's the guy, Annie. He's the one your mom has been sneaking around with."

The words coming from Laurie's mouth seemed foreign to Annie. Josh put his arm around her again and pulled her close.

"I saw them come home one night. I saw headlights pull in, so I went to look out my window and your mom was pulling in your driveway the same time my dad was pulling into ours. I didn't think anything of it and was about to head back to bed when they met in

the street after they got out of their cars. Curious," she sniffled,
calming herself, "I cracked my window to try and hear them. I
couldn't imagine what they had to talk about…you know, since the
falling out."

She was referring to the Beach House Incident. The
Wentworths and the Mackeys owned a beach house on Wrightsville
Beach, and they rented it out when they weren't using it.

Two summers ago, they had a *huge* fight about it. That was
why the families didn't speak anymore. Annie wasn't supposed to
know what happened, but one night, she heard Mrs. Wentworth and
her mom talking on their front porch. Mrs. Wentworth was pissed.
Seething mad.

One weekend, Lisa reserved the house under a false name.
Mrs. Wentworth found out when the housekeepers mentioned seeing
her. And, apparently, Lisa hadn't been alone. Mrs. Wentworth was
disgusted with Lisa's behavior. She dissolved the partnership with
the house *and* their friendship in the process.

That night that Annie realized something was off with her
mom. But it hadn't been until she'd overheard Lisa on the phone that
Annie assumed her mom was having an affair. Annie hadn't told
Laurie about the beach house drama. She'd been too ashamed.

"Annie, I couldn't believe what I was seeing. They *kissed*! Right there! In the middle of the street! It wasn't anything passionate or anything; it was more of an 'okay well, good night' sort of kiss. But still! Our parents, Ans. My dad and your mom!" she groaned in disgust.

Annie was dumbfounded. "I wish you'd told me sooner."

The screaming escalated. Annie walked away from Josh and Laurie toward the sound. She rounded the corner and squatted behind the neighbor's bush. All four parents were in the street, shouting. Annie couldn't believe it.

Her dad looked *so* hurt. Her mom looked indignant. Chaos swirled around in Annie's mind, and suddenly she felt lightheaded. Josh and Laurie joined her behind the bush, but Annie couldn't ignore the rage boiling in her heart. She turned to Laurie and slapped her across the face.

Laurie fell backward onto her butt. She brought her palm to her cheek. Before she could say anything, Annie scream-whispered, "how could you know about this for *weeks* and not *say* anything to me!?"

"Annie!" Josh whispered, trying to reel her in, but Laurie interrupted.

"I've been *trying* to tell you," Laurie hissed. "You've been ignoring me!"

"Because you *told my mom I was pregnant*!" Annie lunged at Laurie again, but Josh stood, pulling her up and away from Laurie. Laurie stood and stepped toward Annie, her head down, still rubbing her cheek. Josh held Annie by the shoulders and tightened his grip as Laurie came closer.

"I made a mistake," Laurie said quietly.

Annie interrupted. "You could say that agai —"

"Would you let me talk?" Laurie hissed. "I made a mistake! When you stood up to Olivia that day, I really needed to talk, but you ditched.

"I tried to talk to you during Science. I thought maybe we could walk home together. But you started ignoring me. I really needed to talk to you! You're my *best* friend! At least you *used* to be. And this was the biggest thing I'd ever gone through! And you weren't *there!* I had all these thoughts swirling around in my head, and I was so confused. So that evening when Olivia invited me over, I let it slip."

"*Olivia* knew about this before *I* did?" Annie's throat closed up and she felt the urge to just walk away. But Josh was still holding on to her.

"Well, she was so angry with you, Annie. For what happened at lunch? So she blackmailed me. She told me if I didn't tell your mom that you were pregnant, she was going to tell your dad about your mom. I felt trapped!"

Laurie began to cry again. "I didn't know what to do! I just figured I'd rather have you hate me than break your dad's heart. I *love* your dad."

Annie's shoulders relaxed, and she felt like she'd been kicked in the stomach. The yelling had died down. Annie's dad was walking into the house while Mrs. Wentworth got into her car.

Annie, Laurie, and Josh stood and watched as Lisa ran to the front door and Mr. Wentworth followed Mrs. Wentworth's car down the street on foot. Soon, the street was empty, except for the three left standing in the wake of the chaos.

Suddenly, Annie was exhausted. "I –" she started to walk away. "I just need to go to sleep." She couldn't make sense of what just happened, and she didn't have the energy for anything. The downstairs lights were on, and she could see her parents' shadows in the window. They were still arguing.

"Annie, I'm so sorry. But what are we going to do?" Laurie

asked. Annie looked at her, a shell of a girl with tears soaking her face, and for the first time in months, Annie saw her best friend. She looked as tortured as Annie felt.

"I really need you right now," Laurie hiccupped. "I—I can't do this alone."

Annie laced her arm through Laurie's, and Laurie rested her head on Annie's shoulder.

"Come on," Josh said, draping his arm around Annie. "Let's get y'all out of here."

In a zombie-like state, Annie, Josh, and Laurie walked back to Josh's house. He told them they could crash with him to avoid the parental drama. Annie just wanted a good night's sleep. They'd figure everything out in the morning. Josh made up the sofa in his mini-living room for Laurie and offered her some gym shorts and a T-shirt. She disappeared into the bathroom to change.

Annie crawled under the covers in Josh's bed, joining him. Her heart would be racing, but it was numb. She cuddled into him, laying her head on his chest. The last thing she remembered was Josh stroking her hair as tears slid down her face and dripped onto his shirt.

The next morning, she gently untangled herself from Josh's arms, trying not to wake him. She found a piece of paper on his desk and left a note thanking him, and letting him know that she'd gone home to change.

She was terrified of what she would find when she got there. What did this mean for her family? And, oh, her dad. He must feel so hollow. Her thoughts were interrupted by the sound of a door closing and footsteps behind her.

"Annie!" Laurie yelled as she ran. "Wait up."

Annie slowed down, allowing Laurie to catch up. They walked in silence together. They stopped in the road between their houses, exactly where all the madness had taken place the night before.

When Annie headed for her front door, Laurie called after her, "Ans!" She looked so broken standing alone in the street. "What does all of this mean?"

"It means everything is royally screwed up."

"No," Laurie said, stopping Annie from walking inside. "I mean for us."

"I have no idea," Annie admitted as she turned and walked inside. It was 5 a.m., so when her dad greeted her from the darkened kitchen, it startled her half to death.

"Dad!" She hesitated. *Busted.* "Sorry. I — I can explain." She turned the light on. He winced. In front of him were a fifth of Jack Daniels and a glass. He drained the glass and poured another.

"It doesn't matter," he said mechanically.

She noticed when she walked up to the house that her mom's Prius wasn't in the driveway. But she couldn't tell whether Mr. Wentworth's car was in his garage.

"Where's Mom?" Annie's dad had no idea she witnessed what happened the night before. For some reason, that broke her heart all over again.

"Who knows?" He was staring straight ahead at the wall. She had no idea how long he'd been sitting there or how much he'd had to drink. He drained his glass again and poured another.

She walked over to him and took the bottle away, replacing the cap. She returned it to the freezer and took his glass, dumping it into the sink.

"Get up," she said forcefully as she walked to him. He stayed put. "Dad." She crouched down in front of him and forced him to look at her. "You need to get up. Let's get you to bed."

He complied without saying a word, wobbling as she directed him up the stairs and into his room. He dove into his bed, which was still made from the day before.

"Sweet?" he slurred as she exited the room. She poked her head back in.

"Yeah, Dad?"

"She left."

WE'VE NEVER ACTUALLY SPOKEN

Annie blinked and stared at the exam Mr. Peterson placed face down on her desk. *Crap.* That was never a good sign.

She took a deep breath and turned it over. The grade was a first for her; not only was it an F, but it was an F so low she probably could have saved herself some time by not even turning it in.

She pushed her shame down into the pit of her stomach, where she carried all of her uneasy feelings. It had been one week since the morning after, and her mother was still missing in action. She shoved the test into the front pocket of her backpack and walked out of the room.

Maddie met her on the way to her next class. Annie half-listened to her go on about Simon. At least that's what Annie *thought* she heard Maddie say his name was.

Apparently, Maddie stared at the back of his head all first period every day and had fallen deeply in love with him. Annie was preoccupied and didn't care. When Maddie asked her opinion, she failed to respond. Maddie huffed, "Are you even listening to me?"

Annie shifted her backpack's strap on her right shoulder and stopped walking.

"Uh. Yeah. Sorry, I've just got a lo—"

"Yeah, we all know," Maddie snapped. "I understand you've, like, got some stuff going on at home and all, but you can't just totally ignore your friends."

Crap. She had a point. "You're right, I'm sorry," Annie said. "So, Simon huh?"

"Well, yeah. I think he might like me too!"

"Oh, really? Did he tell you?" Annie was doing her best to feign interest. She really couldn't have cared less.

"Well, we've never actually spoken directly, but he always smiles when he hands papers back to me."

"Yeah, he *must* like you," Annie said sarcastically, but Maddie failed to sense it.

They parted ways when they reached Maddie's classroom. Annie nearly ran into a girl struggling with a giant pile of books.

"Watch it!" Annie shouted.

"Sorry," the girl squeaked out.

"Laurie?" Annie asked, peering around the book tower. "What are you doing?"

"Extra credit. I'm helping Mr. Sayster around the classroom and stuff. I'm not doing so great in his class." The two hadn't spoken since the morning after. Annie didn't know what to say or how to make sense of everything. Nothing was black and white. And she didn't know how to handle any of it.

Her best coping mechanism had been pretending nothing happened at all.

"Oh." Annie was tempted to just walk away, but Laurie's anxious expression stopped her.

"Here," Annie said, taking some of the books off of the pile. "Show me the way."

"Thank you," Laurie said once they unloaded the books. "Go, go!" She shooed Annie toward the door. "You're going to be late."

Annie nodded and walked out. She was still angry with Laurie. *So* angry. She had been so hurt by her. But she was still *Laurie*. And no matter what happened, Annie couldn't stand to watch her suffer. It was complicated. It wasn't Annie's nature to completely cut someone out, no matter how messed up things had gotten.

Maybe that was weakness. Or maybe it was loyalty. But either way, it sure screwed with Annie's head. *And* her heart.

When Annie got home that afternoon, Josh was waiting for her on the front porch.

"Grounded," was all she said as she walked past him.

"Ans," he said, standing up and reaching for her arm. She shrugged him off.

"I'm still grounded, Josh," she snapped. She was a little surprised at how angry she sounded. "You need to get out of here." She watched his face morph from concerned to wounded.

"I've hardly seen you. What's up? Did I do something?"

"No," she said, reaching for the front door. "You didn't do anything. But just go!" When he didn't move, she quietly added, "Please."

"I don't understand," he said with sad eyes. "Don't you even want to talk about it? No one's here. How will anyone ever know?"

"That's just it, Josh! No one is here! So what? I'm just grounded for life? It's not like she's *here* to un-ground me!"

Josh stared at her. "I get it. I do. I know what this feels like."

"You can't possibly —" Annie started. Josh held up his hands.

"Annie, I do. I get it. It feels like your world is over. And it doesn't matter how things have been the last few years, it doesn't matter how much y'all have clashed. She's your mom. And you miss her."

"Josh, stop."

"And you're snapping at me because you're angry with her. You're pushing me away because she's being selfish. Does that seem fair?"

Annie said nothing.

"At least you know where your mom is!" Josh exclaimed. Annie found out that her mom was staying at a hotel just outside of town. As far as she knew, her mom was alone. She couldn't stomach the idea of Mr. Wentworth staying with her. And Annie hadn't been brave enough to ask Laurie if her dad was home. It was all *so* messed up.

"Even if you don't like it, at least you know what's going on," Josh added.

"And what the hell is that supposed to mean?"

"I'm just saying … I don't know." He dropped his gaze to

the ground. "It's been 5 years for me, Annie. And I still don't have any answers about what happened with *my* mom. It all happened so fast. One minute she was there, happy and singing as she put the dishes away. And the next my dad's sitting at the kitchen table with his head in his hands telling me that she's gone."

Annie wanted to be sympathetic. She wanted to walk up to him, wipe away the little tear that was threatening to fall. But all she felt was anger.

"Well, that sucks. And I'm sorry you went through that. But you know what? This isn't about you!"

Josh looked stung. "I'm not saying it is. I'm saying that at least you have answers. I'm trying to help you. I'm trying to show you the silver lining."

"Silver lining? You really think there's a silver lining to my mom's disappearing act? God, you can be such an idiot." Annie didn't mean it; the words flew out of her mouth before she could stop them. She was mad. And hurt. And Josh was *right there*. It was so easy to take it out on him. "Josh, I'm sorry. I didn't—"

Josh held up his hands. "You know what? No. I get it. You're hurt. You're angry. But I'm going to be honest. Maybe her leaving is for the best."

The words shocked her. It didn't matter that just a week ago, she'd thought pretty much the same thing. Annie *did* feel relieved she didn't have to hold on to the secret anymore. Despite all that had gone on, the house *had* been less dramatic since her mother left. But Josh had no right to say it.

She tried to think of something, *anything* to say. Instead, she turned the handle and walked through the door, slamming it shut behind her.

She ran upstairs and buried her head into her pillow. It was all too much. Josh, Laurie, Maddie, her mom. The list went on and on.

***

Her brother called the night before, and Annie filled him in. Apparently, no one bothered to call him. He was quiet on the line for a while then ended the call assuring her that everything would be okay. She lied, saying she believed him. Nothing, she knew in her gut, would ever be okay again.

***

She heard the front door open, and she wiped the tears from her eyes. She descended the stairs ready to convince her dad they should just hit the burger joint for dinner. It had been spaghetti and jarred sauce all week long, and she just couldn't take it anymore.

She stopped dead in her tracks on the bottom step when she caught a glimpse of her mother's platinum blonde hair flowing into the kitchen.

"Mom?" Annie croaked through a hoarse voice. "*Mom!?*"

Lisa opened cabinets and closed them again, frantically looking for something. She opened the cabinet above the microwave, retrieved a bottle of pills, and tossed them into her purse. She turned and headed to the stairs, toward Annie. Her eyes were blank.

"Mom?" Annie felt her throat closing up.

"Annie, I'm not having this discussion with you right now. I only have a few minutes."

"For what? Where are you going?" Annie followed her mother up the stairs and into her parents' bedroom, where Lisa was pulling a suitcase from the closet. She started throwing in undergarments. She pulled an armful of her precisely ironed suits off the rod in the closet and laid them on the unmade bed.

"Mom," Annie said again. "Why are you doing this?"

"We are not having this discussion, Annie. Richard is waiting outside. You can tell your father I've filed the separation papers with the court to make it all official. You can tell him I set the date as the last night I stayed here. My lawyer will be in touch with him shortly."

"No!" Annie felt rage boiling. "Tell him your damn self! Just once, face things yourself!"

Lisa stopped zipping her suitcase and looked at her daughter. "You have no idea what you are talking about, little girl. No idea at all."

"Apparently not," Annie said with tears pouring from her eyes. "So that's it, huh? You're just going to walk away from him? From all of us?"

Lisa said nothing as she pulled the garment bag shut and zipped it up over her suits. She swung it over her right shoulder by the hangers and lifted the suitcase.

She pushed past her daughter and descended the stairs. Annie heard the front door slam, and she crumbled to the floor in a fit of hysterics. That was it. Over, just like that.

When she calmed down, Annie continued to lie on the floor of her parents' bedroom. Her mind raced, but inside, she felt numb. She watched the fan spin as she lay with her back flat against the carpet that smelled like home. Her eyes blurred, and a memory flooded her vision.

***

She was ten. Her father and brother were out of town for the weekend on a Boy Scouts camping trip.

"Just us girls, huh?" Lisa said to a miniature Annie who was standing in the doorway of her parents' room. "What do you say we pop some popcorn and stay up past your bedtime and watch movies?" Lisa's platinum hair was piled on top of her head in a messy bun and her face was bare, beautiful.

"Mom, Laurie says that boys won't like me unless I wear makeup. But I don't know how to do that, you know, put makeup on?" Annie remembered standing there, truly concerned and nervous.

"Oh Anniebee, you don't need to worry about that for a good, long while. Trust me." A sweet, comforting smile lit up her mother's face, and Annie felt joy flush through her veins.

"But here," Lisa pulled the chair out from her vanity and flicked on the light that surrounded the mirror. "Have a seat." Annie smiled wide and sat in the chair and stared at herself along with her mother in the mirror. Lisa ran her fingers through her daughter's long, limp brown hair. "You, my Anniebee, are so beautiful."

***

Annie shook from her memory with the sound of the front door opening. She instantly felt sad, but for a moment she couldn't remember why. Then the last hour replayed in her mind. Her heart sank.

That day, that girls' weekend, was the last time her mother had looked at her like a daughter.

"Sweet!" Jason yelled up the stairs. "Burgers for dinner?"

Annie couldn't help but laugh at how alike she and her father were.

She picked herself up off the floor of the room that she would always remember as a room of lasts with her mother. Her face was flat as she descended the stairs, and tears stained her face.

"What is it?" her dad asked.

He took a deep breath. "Ahh," he said, nodding. "So, tell me. If I were to go on a trip right now, I'd find that a suitcase is missing, huh?" Annie nodded and walked past her father into the kitchen so she wouldn't see the inevitable tears. She'd been strong that year. Stronger than she'd ever thought she'd have to be. But seeing her dad cry would rip up her insides. She couldn't be *that* strong.

"And Dad?" Annie called from the kitchen, pulling the pot from the clean side of the sink and filling it with water for pasta. No way either of them could face a Burgette's' crowd that night. "I failed my math test."

The next morning, when Annie's alarm went off, she silenced it and rolled back over. She felt like she'd been hit by a truck.

Her dad tiptoed into her room a little while later and kissed her forehead before he left for work. She pretended to sleep. When she heard the front door shut, she opened her eyes and listened to her dad's car pull out of the driveway. *Alone.* She was totally and completely alone.

Her throat tightened when she thought about Laurie. It would have been so simple to just forgive her. Maybe it would eliminate all of this hurt. But the fear of getting hurt all over again stopped her.

She was hit with a sudden crippling realization. *Nothing* was forever. Not friendship. Not marriage. *Nothing.* How did anyone find someone they could rely on for their whole life? How could anyone expect someone to always be the same person?

Annie woke to the sound of voices outside her bedroom

window. She rolled over. The clock read 3:27. She'd slept all day. She wondered if Josh would stop by or if he'd given up.

She watched Laurie walk past her house without even glancing at it. Did she even notice Annie hadn't gone to school? She rolled back over and closed her eyes.

March 2, 2010

Listening to: Keri Noble *Piece of My Heart*

Is love even a real thing? I'm having a really hard time believing that it is. Honestly, it just seems like some kind of awful trick that life plays on us. Or maybe it's some grand illusion we all fool ourselves into believing because it seems so much easier than being alone.

This hurt that I'm feeling? It just doesn't even seem worth it. I'd much rather go through my entire life alone than to let people hurt me like this. If I didn't care it wouldn't feel like this. Not caring sounds so tempting these days. I can tell myself none of it matters, but everything hurts. And nothing makes sense.

All these TV shows make high school out to The Best Time Ever. It's totally false advertising. Nothing about any of this is good. Nothing.

DON'T BE SO DRAMATIC

"But he does totally miss you, trust me." Maddie sat with her legs folded underneath her at the foot of Annie's bed. Annie was feeling sorry for herself. She couldn't help it. She'd let life kick her down and she couldn't bring herself back up.

In the weeks since her mom left, she hadn't been able to get out of her funk. This was exactly what she had been trying to avoid by staying under the radar. Everything that happened with Laurie was just far too confusing and distracting. And the guilt she felt over how she'd treated Josh was overwhelming.

She couldn't quite convince herself that Josh actually cared, and she wasn't really sure why.

"Then why hasn't he called, huh?" Annie brushed her hair away from her face with her fingers. It was already March, and

Annie hadn't spoken to Josh since they'd argued on her front porch. She saw him in class, but she made it clear her wall was *up*. She watched him open and close his mouth as he would approach her, trying to find the words, but then he'd change direction. It was like he didn't know what to say to her. No one did, apparently.

Maddie adjusted herself awkwardly. "I don't know, girl. But I *do* know he misses you. He told me."

"I –" Annie sat up from underneath her covers and straightened the T-shirt she'd worn to school. The weather was finally warming up. It was the only thing making Annie feel even remotely happy. "I don't care."

"Uh, yeah you do," Maddie spit out flatly. "Why are you being this way?"

Maddie had a point. Why *was* she being this way? Happiness is a choice, a *mood.* Not a destination.

This wasn't the life she would have chosen for herself. But she could either sit in bed and waste it, or make the best of it. The latter seemed like a lot of work, though. "Because not caring takes less energy."

"Seriously?" Maddie said. "Isn't it, like, *way* harder to force yourself to be miserable?"

"Who's forcing?" Annie lashed out. "Maddie, you just don't have a clue, do you?" Maddie sat, stunned, at the edge of the bed. "Have you ever even lost anything? *Really* lost anything? All in one year I've lost my best friend, my mother, and probably my boyfriend, too. Not to mention whatever sense of direction I used to have."

"Oh, my God, please. Don't be *so* dramatic, Annie. So things have been, like hard. Whatever. That's life! Everything is hard. Suck it up." Maddie stood from the bed and collected her backpack from the floor, swinging it over her shoulder. "Let me know when you're done wallowing. There's a movie out I want to see."

Maddie turned and walked out, leaving Annie alone. It was a state she'd grown entirely too accustomed to. And maybe she had only herself to blame.

She lay back down and pulled the covers over her head, daydreaming about when things were simpler, when she and Laurie lived in their little bubble. Then, she always knew what to expect. She knew who she was, even if she was dancing in Laurie's shadow.

She was in a box, but it was a box she'd put herself in. The moment Laurie ripped the lid off and jumped out, Annie had been left flailing.

All that time, she'd been blaming Laurie. She blamed her for going out and living her life. Annie didn't want what Laurie wanted. So what? That didn't entitle her to keep Laurie from having what she wanted. Maybe *that* was why she and Laurie had drifted apart.

Laurie had changed, and Annie *hated* her for it.

But the drama with her family was too much to handle on her own. She needed her friend. Together they could tackle what seemed like The Worst Thing Ever.

That made her think about Josh and *his* mom. There was a story there, she knew. And yet, Josh didn't walk around letting it define him. If he carried the weight of it around with him, she hadn't been able to tell.

And then she realized, everyone had *something.* A story. Annie had been so caught up in the drama around her that she hadn't noticed how *her* story was changing *her.* And she'd been so busy blaming everyone else that she'd never taken responsibility for anything that happened.

She had to make it right.

She stood, waiting on Josh's front porch. She'd knocked, but it didn't sound like anyone was coming to the door. There weren't any cars in the driveway, but she couldn't bear the idea that he wasn't home. She needed to do this, and she needed to do it now.

She knocked again. When there wasn't an answer, she tried the door. Unlocked.

She pushed through the door and looked around.

"Hello?" she called out. "Josh?"

There was no response, but she could hear The Avett Brother's *St. Joseph's* spilling from his speakers. He was downstairs. Her heart raced as she passed his mom's bridal portrait and pushed open the basement door.

His bedroom door was open slightly. She knocked, but knew the music was too loud for him to hear. She pushed the door open gently.

Josh was face down on his bed, his shoulders shaking. He was sobbing, Annie realized. Without even knowing why he was upset, tears sprang to Annie's eyes. She ran over to his bed, sat gently beside him and placed her hand on his back. He jolted, startled.

"It's me, it's me. Josh, it's okay. It's just me." He placed his head back in the crook of his arm and continued to cry softly. She rubbed his back in circles and laid her head down on his shoulders.

They stayed there for what felt like forever, both crying. She had no idea why he was upset, but seeing him broken broke her, too. And not before long, she was sobbing. Everything she'd been keeping in released.

"I'm so sorry, Josh. I'm so, so sorry. I've been such an ass. I'm so, so sorry," she cried into his neck. "What *is* it? What's wrong? Oh, God, I'm just so sorry."

He shrugged her off and pushed himself up into a seated position next to her, cupped his face in his hands and took three deep, jagged breaths. When he uncovered his face, she smiled at him weakly.

"I've been such a jerk," she said, resting her hand on his thigh, hoping he wouldn't push it off. Instead, he rested his hand on top of hers.

"Yeah," he said, clearing his throat. "You really have been."

She nudged him with her shoulder. "I don't have an excuse. I'm just sorry."

"Sure, you do," he said, taking his hand off hers and wrapping his arm around her. He pulled her into a side hug and she rested her cheek on his chest. He kissed the top of her head. "I forgive you, in case you're wondering."

"You do?" She looked up at him, hopeful. He smiled through the tears that were still in his eyes.

"Of course I do." He squeezed her tighter and he rested his chin on top of her head.

"Josh," she asked, "what's going on?"

He released her and pulled one leg into himself as he turned to her. "I know where my mom is."

"*What*? That's—well, that's great, isn't it?"

Josh sucked his lips in and more tears welled in his eyes. "She's dead." He cleared his throat and wiped angrily at the tears that slid down his cheeks. "She died."

"Wait, what?" Annie couldn't make sense of what he was saying. That couldn't be right.

"What are you talking about? How do you know?" She was overwhelmed with questions.

"I finally confronted my dad. I told him I needed answers or I was going out on my own to look for her." He pulled his other leg up onto the bed and faced her.

"She had cancer."

"How did *he* know?"

"That's just it, Annie! He knew the *whole* time. She left *because* she was sick. He let her go. I mean, how do you do that? Let your wife die alone? How do you just not tell your kids what's going on?"

"He *knew*?"

"She didn't want Dave and me to see her sick, so she went to live with her best friend. Well, I guess she went to *die* with her."

"I'm sorry, I'm not sure I understand. She left because she was sick? Your dad knew she was dying?"

"He knew everything! He agreed that it would just be easier for her to disappear than it would be to explain how sick she was and for us to watch her get sicker and sicker. I mean, I think I get it, but what the *heck*? She was our *mom*. Yes, it would have been hard...it would have *sucked*! But this sucks more. Years of not knowing? Years of thinking she's a horrible person? Years of wondering what I might have done differently to make her stay? Wondering if it was my fault. I was a *kid,* Annie. And my mom *died*. And I didn't even know it. How the eff is that fair?"

"It's not," she said, leaning in to hug him. He grabbed her hard and sobbed into her shoulder. Her heart was absolutely breaking for him.

"I just can't believe she's really gone, you know?" He sniffled. "I just always thought, in the back of my mind, that I'd see her again." He was quiet a moment. "Part of me hated her for leaving. All this time I've been resenting her, and she's been *dead.*" He choked on the words and erupted into sobs.

She sat with him while he cried realizing everyone's version of real life had its own dose of screwed up. He pulled Annie down onto the bed and nuzzled into her neck. She lay there with him as he cuddled her. Soon his cries grew quiet.

"I'm sorry," she whispered into his hair. "I'm so sorry, for everything." He had cried himself to asleep. She closed her eyes and inhaled his scent. She cuddled into him.

When they woke up, they were both starved. Annie offered to order a pizza, but Josh needed to get out of the house. His dad was due back any minute, and he couldn't face him yet. She knew the feeling, so they walked to Burgette's.

The place was pretty empty, and she looked down at her watch, assuming they'd just barely beaten the dinner rush. They sat at a small table in the middle of the restaurant and ordered an appetizer of buffalo mozzarella sticks. The bell over the door chimed, making Annie glance up. Panic set in.

Brandon. Accompanied by Laurie, Maddie, and some guy Annie didn't recognize. Brandon spotted them immediately and approached their table.

"Dude," Brandon slapped Josh's back. "Way to go MIA, man!" Josh turned to Brandon, and shock registered on Brandon's face. "Whoa. You okay, man? Your face is … it's swollen. What'd she do? Slug ya?"

Josh didn't miss a beat. "Nah, just tired I guess."

"Well, you look like shit. You should sleep every once in a while." Brandon slid the chairs of the next table out and pushed it next to theirs. Annie's panic hadn't gone anywhere, but she thought back to the pep talk she'd given herself earlier. She had control over how she reacted. Plus, Olivia wasn't there, which definitely made things easier.

Laurie sat next to Annie with Maddie on her other side. The guy Annie didn't know sat across from Maddie, and Brandon sat next to Josh, across from Laurie.

"Well," Maddie said, leaning around Laurie. "You seem to have gotten your butt in gear since I saw you last. Everything good?" Maddie nodded towards Josh. Annie leaned behind Laurie, toward Maddie.

"Yeah," Annie whispered. "Sorry about earlier. Sorry about all of it, actually. Been kind of up my own butt lately. What you said really hit me. And I'm sorry."

"Well, good. It's, like, about *time* you get over your little pity party." Maddie giggled. "Anyway," she said, in her normal voice now. "This is Simon. You know, like, *the* Simon I was telling you about?" The guy Annie didn't recognize looked over and offered a shy wave.

"Ahh," Annie said. "*The* Simon. Well, it's nice to meet you. What got the two of you actually talking?"

Simon and Maddie shared an awkward glance, both of their faces flushing. "Let's just say Maddie *fell* for me instantly." Annie looked at him, confused. Maddie jumped in.

"Stupid Kate Tarlington and her *stupid* backpack. I tripped walking into class last week. Practically fell right into Simon's lap. It was mortifying. But at least it got him to say hello."

Simon and Maddie continued to tell their story. Something about exchanging numbers on the pretense of helping each other study for an exam. Then the next thing Maddie knew, Simon was asking her to be his girlfriend.

"I would have told you earlier today, but you were kind of

being a bitch," Maddie said. *Touché*, Annie thought. *Touché*.

Annie's panic disappeared. She was choosing how to handle the situation, and she chose not to make it bigger than it was. Laurie looked over to Annie with a weak smile. It was a start. Annie smiled back.

The food arrived, and Josh looked better. He and Brandon were talking about some video game, and Maddie was entertaining the rest of the table with a story about her mom's Bible study group. Apparently "Bible study" was code for "consuming lots of wine and dishing about the latest office drama." Laurie was giggling, but it was her real giggle, not the fake one Annie had grown so accustomed to hearing from a distance lately.

Someone near the door caught Annie's attention. *Olivia.* Annie froze.

"What the hell is going on here?" Olivia practically shouted from the doorway. "Having a little party without me, are we?"

Annie shifted her gaze to Brandon, who also looked frozen. Laurie frantically hopped up from the table and rushed over to Olivia.

"I tried calling you, Liv. We were just hungry."

"Yeah, well, I was getting a manicure. Can't exactly answer

the phone with wet nails." Olivia jerked her arm from Laurie's grasp and stomped towards Brandon. She made a big show of kissing him, and then glanced around the table. She waved her hands and exhaled in annoyance. "Uh, make room."

She was standing between Brandon and Simon's chair, and Laurie jumped to action. She forced Simon to slide his chair down, and she grabbed an extra chair from another table, sliding it between Simon and Brandon.

Things had been going *so* well. Annie had been a part of the group. And, for half a minute, she let herself believe maybe she could handle this.

But the problem wasn't the group. The problem was Olivia. She was such a miserable person. What did people see in her? Why did Laurie *cater* to her? She had forced Laurie to tell Annie's mom she was pregnant! How could Laurie still care about her? Why couldn't she see Olivia for who she really was?

"Oh," Olivia said as she snatched a menu from the waitress. "Annie, I'm actually glad I ran into you." Olivia flashed a fake smile, and her voice was dripping with sugary sweetness. "It turns out I had things *all* wrong." Olivia looked at Josh, then back to Annie. "Foolish of me, really. You know, to believe the rumors. Of course you couldn't be pregnant. You're still a *virgin.*" Olivia cackled.

Annie felt immune. "Is that supposed to be an insult? That I'm still a virgin? Really? And you're like, what? Open for business? Isn't there a word for girls like you?"

Olivia flashed red then tried to shake it off. "Turns out I had the wrong Mackey woman. You might want to give your mother a call. She might be the one with her feet up in the stirrups next." Olivia looked over to Laurie, and Annie did the same. Panic painted Laurie's face.

"Don't be ridiculous," Annie said. "How would *you* even know something like that?"

"Well, I just know what I know," Olivia said with a flip of her hair.

Annie stared blankly at Olivia. Where did she get off making everyone else miserable? And *why* did Annie feel so threatened by her all the time? If it wasn't one story, it was another. Annie didn't care what anyone thought anymore. What difference did it *really* make?

She stood up and dug in her pocket, then slapped a twenty on the table.

"Keep spreading rumors, Olivia. I really don't care if you talk shit about me. But the fact that you'd spread rumors about someone you supposedly care about? Wow. Just…wow."

Josh stood and put his hand in Annie's. "Y'all," Annie said to the rest of the table, "enjoy your dinner. It was nice to see ya." And with that, they walked out of the diner.

Once they were outside, Josh spun her into a hug. "What was *that*?" Josh asked.

She rested her cheek on his chest, feeling safe in his arms. "I don't have to take that, you know? No one does. She's a bully. That's it."

"You were *awesome* in there! Proud of *you*," he sang out in a silly tone, but it got Annie thinking. The girl she'd been at the beginning of the year would have sat and taken it. She would have quivered in her boots and worried what everyone was thinking. But the second she'd realized Olivia was *not* better than her was the second she'd freed herself.

"We don't have to go home yet if you're not ready," Annie said.

He was quiet for a moment. "Yeah," he exhaled. "I'm thinking frozen yogurt," he said with a grin.

"You know I'm down."

They filled their bowls with their toppings. Annie had all things chocolate: chocolate chips, chocolate sprinkles, and chocolate sauce. Josh filled his with every gummy candy known to man. She laughed at their contrast, but her heart swelled as she watched him. She loved his ability to live in the moment.

They sat down at a small table in the back of the shop where it was quiet. When the door opened moments later, Annie didn't even bother to look up.

She noticed people approaching their table out of the corner of her eye. She glanced up. Relief washed over her. Laurie, Maddie, and Simon.

Annie stood from the small table and the two girls grabbed her into a hug. "I'm so sorry," Laurie whispered into Annie's ear. "You were right."

Annie pulled herself out of the hug and cocked her head at Laurie.

"That rumor she's spreading? It's not just about you or your mom. It's about my *dad*, too. She's supposed to be my *friend*. Who would do that to a friend?"

Laurie's eyes filled with tears, but she blinked them back.

"So I'm done. Whatever. I'm just done."

Maddie draped her arm over Laurie and gave her a half hug. Annie smiled and grabbed Laurie's hands.

"I'm sorry I was right," she admitted, meaning it. She'd never wanted anyone to get hurt. That was what she'd been trying to prevent the whole time. "But hi," she said giddily, squeezing Laurie back into a hug.

Annie finally felt like her world was finally sorting itself out.

March 12, 2010

Listening to: Matt Kearney *Closer To Love*

Tonight was kind of awesome and kind of awful all at once. Things with Josh and his family are a little wonky. That's not my story to tell, though. But having all of that go on helps me understand the difference between Real Things and things that aren't important. What he's going through —what his family went through—that's Real Stuff. But it helps me keep perspective. Not everything is as big of a deal as it might feel.

Things finally came to a head tonight with Olivia and the other girls. She just can't go around making up stories that can ruin *people's lives. It's one thing for her to talk about me — but my family? That's unacceptable. And not just my family, Laurie's too. When she said what she did about my mom — I couldn't even believe she'd hurt Laurie like that. It makes me sick.*

And Maddie and Laurie are finally *fed up with Olivia, too. I feel like all year long they've been under her spell. I'm so glad they finally snapped out of it.*

Joey Hodges

WE NEVER LET THE BALL HIT THE SAND

"I don't know, Annie," Jason said, peering over his newspaper. "Who'd drive?"

"Dave, Josh's older brother." Annie poured the creamer into her coffee and sat anxiously across from her father. "It's only for the day."

"And what would y'all do?" Jason folded the paper and gave his full attention to his daughter. Annie noticed lines around his eyes that she didn't remember being there before.

She glanced past her dad to the stack of unopened envelopes on the counter. They were all from her mom's lawyer, a Mr. Frank Sylvagio.

"Well, we figured we'd all just pack a cooler and hang out on the beach for the day."

"Who is 'we'? And a cooler full of what?" Jason leaned back into his chair and laced his fingers behind his head.

"Da-ad," Annie sang with amusement. "The cooler's for soda and snacks. And the 'we' would be Josh, Dave, Amanda, and me. The same group from Homecoming."

Jason ran his fingers through his disheveled hair and stared past his daughter at the front door, a new habit Annie had noticed. Silence hung in the air for a moment, and Annie was vaguely reminded of the morning they'd spent together after her mother walked out. Finally, Jason broke the silence. "Allll-right," he sang, mimicking her. "You can go."

"Thanks, Dad!" Annie pushed the chair out from the table and began to stand.

"You'll be careful?" There was a fear in his eyes.

"Of course!"

The breeze was warm. Annie tilted her head back and closed her eyes. *Relaxed*. Completely and *totally* relaxed. She reveled in the feeling. It had been a while.

She scrunched her toes into the warm sand and daydreamed of staying in that moment forever. She could hear Josh and Dave talking about trucks; she wasn't interested. Amanda, who'd hugged Annie when she climbed into Dave's Explorer, was stretched out on a towel next to her. Amanda didn't talk much, and Annie liked that about her. She hadn't brought up Homecoming, which made Annie like her even more.

They arrived at Wrightsville Beach early, when the sun was barely peeking out from the clouds, and it was chilly. Annie was glad it had warmed up in the past hour.

She was surprised there weren't more people there. It was Willow Point High's spring break, and most of the public schools across the East were off as well. She hoped it would stay quiet. She wasn't in the mood for a crowd.

She opened her eyes and caught Josh staring. She ran her hand over her hair, smoothing the flyaways from her ponytail and blushed.

"C'mon! Girls against guys volleyball game!" Josh said, trying to drag Annie and Amanda off their towels

"Josh," Annie whined as she took her place on the opposite

side of the net. "Need I remind you I don't have an athletic bone in my body?"

"This should be a quick game," Amanda said. "I suck at anything that involves balls."

The guys laughed out loud, and Annie heard Dave mutter to Josh, "That's what she said."

The ball launched at Annie. She slid from side to side with her fingers laced, her thumbs parallel and her arms outstretched. She lined her hands up below the ball and punched. She heard a loud snap as pain shot up her arm.

"*Ouch!*" she screamed as she watched the ball sail over the net and land between the two guys, who looked concerned.

"What was *that?*" Josh asked, walking toward her. "You alright?"

Annie bent at the waist and cradled her left hand between her legs. "I don't know."

"You don't know what it was? Or you don't know if you're alright?" Josh approached her.

"Both." Annie placed her hand into Josh's. Despite the pain, her body still tingled at his touch.

"*What* did you do?" he asked, examining her hand.

"What do you mean? My finger is blue! And puffy!"

"I mean, how were you holding your hands?"

"Like this," Annie said, lacing her fingers and wincing at the pain.

"Oh geez, Annie." Josh let out a laugh. "You really don't pay attention in Gym, huh? The cardinal rule of volleyball: do not lace your fingers!" Josh nodded toward her hand. "I'm willing to bet your middle finger is broken."

Annie held it up to him with the rest of her fingers folded.

"So that's game?" Dave asked sarcastically.

"Guess so, but we won!" Amanda gloated.

"What? How do you figure?" Josh argued.

"We never let the ball hit the sand, unlike the two of you!"

"Yeah!" Annie chimed in. "We win! We win!" She danced around in a circle, pumping her fists with her left middle finger raised. Josh tackled her to the sand and smothered her with a kiss. "We win," she muttered into his mouth.

Josh asked Annie to stroll down the beach with him. He went to her right side so he could hold her hand.

As the day wore on, the beach got busier. Some of Dave's friends, who were staying at the beach for the week, showed up and

Amanda and Dave hung out with them. Annie didn't mind. The alone time with Josh was nice.

"You doing okay?" Annie asked Josh. They'd hardly discussed his mom since that night at Burgette's.

"Sort of, I guess." Josh strolled along quietly for a while just holding her hand. He rubbed his thumb over the top of it and sent shivers down her spine.

"There's something else," Josh said so quietly Annie could hardly hear him.

"Something else? What do you mean?"

"There's a letter. My dad gave it to me last night. He had to get it from the safety deposit box at the bank. It's from her."

"Oh, wow. Wh – what'd it say?"

"I haven't read it yet. I don't know if I want to." Josh stared straight ahead, squinting into the distance.

She wanted to tell him that he should read it. She wanted to tell him that maybe it would make him feel better. But she knew better. He had to make that decision on his own.

They walked to the pier, almost a mile from where they'd been sitting, in silence. People were everywhere, and yet, it felt like she and Josh were the only two people on the planet. And the world kept spinning.

Small tragedies, Annie remembered her dad saying. This thing with Josh's mom was a real tragedy, though, and she almost felt bad for mentally comparing it to her situation.

"What do you think you'll do?" Annie prodded as they made their way back to their spot. "I know it's gotta be hard, but isn't not knowing worse?"

"That's just it! I have no idea! When I didn't know…I hated her, Annie. I *hated* her for leaving. Maybe she had a really good reason. Or maybe she didn't. Maybe she was just a weak person who made a bad decision. The thing is, I have no idea. I have no idea what kind of woman my own mother was."

He was quiet for a bit. Annie could see Amanda and Dave in the distance, laughing with their friends. "She's in the cemetery in town."

"She's here?" Annie looked around. "In Willow Point, I mean?"

"Yeah. In fact, she apparently died at the hospital in town, too. Her college roommate lived just outside of Raleigh. My dad saw her up until her dying day. It's all so twisted."

Annie had no idea what to say. "Well, if you ever want to go, you know, I'd go with you."

"Thanks. Right now, I'd really like to just forget I know any of it, honestly."

"Understood. But whenever you're ready, I'm here."

Josh stopped walking and grabbed her into a tight hug. "Do you have any idea how thankful I am for you?" Josh said with his face buried in her hair. "I can't believe all this time you were right in front of me. And I missed out on knowing you. I love knowing you."

Annie melted into him.

Annie rested her head on Josh's shoulder. Dave pulled out of the parking spot. Their day at the beach had been nice, but Annie's finger throbbed and was now a dark purple.

They spent the rest of the afternoon lounging in the sun while Josh and Dave told jokes.

Annie adored how close Josh was with his brother, and she was glad they had each other. Dave seemed to be handling the news about their mom pretty well. Maybe he'd known more about the situation as it was happening. He was older. Maybe he had picked up on things Josh missed.

The water had been wintery cold, but the boys didn't turn

down the girls' dare to run in. Both Dave and Josh enveloped Amanda and Annie into wet, cold hugs once they emerged. The girls squealed and giggled. Annie allowed herself to live in the moment and enjoy the day, something she hadn't been able to do in quite a while.

She was almost asleep on Josh's shoulder on the drive home when he whispered. "I think I want to go to the cemetery tonight."

"You sure?" she asked, leaning her head into him.

"Yeah, I think I have to. It's eating away at me. We'll read the letter there."

"Okay," she whispered back. "Whatever you need."

It was midnight when Annie's phone vibrated. She'd been anxiously awaiting the text from Josh.

Josh: **I'm outside.**
Annie: **k. Gimme a sec.**

Annie slathered her skin in another layer of lotion. The sun had been veiled by a thin layer of clouds, so she never even felt her skin burning. But now it was red and hot. And itchy. *So* itchy. When she got home, she immediately hopped into the shower. The hot water stung, so she switched to freezing, which burned. No happy medium. She was miserable.

She threw her UNC sweatshirt over her spaghetti-strapped tank top. She'd been shivering since she'd gotten out of the shower hours ago. Stupid sunburn.

She peered out her window. Josh was pacing the width of her driveway with his head down. He was wearing khaki shorts and a navy T-shirt. Under the street lamp his skin looked perfectly golden brown. Her skin crawled, and she silently cursed him for tanning so easily.

She contemplated just walking out the door, but things were different in the house since her mom left. She scribbled a note for her dad and left it on the kitchen counter, just in case. She met Josh in the driveway. He was holding a folded envelope in his hand.

Josh shoved it into his pocket and took Annie's hand as they walked down the road. He held her hand extra hard. *Whoa.* Extra, extra hard. He was practically running down the street.

"Josh, God." Annie stopped short and snatched her hand from his grasp, holding it to her chest and rubbing it. "What the hell? Are you *trying* to break my other hand?"

He stopped briefly then started walking again, this time

slower.

"Wait!" Annie called out to him.

He kept moving forward.

"Josh! Stop! *Stop!*"

He stopped, but he didn't turn around. She caught up to him and tugged on his arm. "I'm not going any further until you talk to me."

He tried to shrug his arm from her grasp, but she was holding on tight. He stared at the pavement, which appeared painted gold under the street lamp. He yanked his arm from her and sat on the side of the road, hugging his knees to his chest. She sat next to him.

"I know this is impossible, Josh."

He didn't say anything.

"I really can't imagine how you're feeling, but I think you're doing the right thing."

Still, he said nothing. His bottom lip was quivering. He tightened his jaw.

"It's okay, Josh."

He glared at her, his eyes glassy. She looped her arm through his and leaned her head down on his arm, ignoring his glare. He could be as pissed as he wanted, but she wasn't going anywhere. She knew he wasn't actually mad at her.

They sat in silence for a long time. Her skin itched unbearably, but she didn't dare move to scratch it.

Finally, Josh turned into her. She collected him into a hug, and he cried into her. Sobbed, actually.

"I asked Dave to come but he said no. It's like he doesn't even care! Do you have any idea how much that pisses me off!?" He breathed out and sniffled, and she was pretty sure there was snot dripping down her neck. She squeezed him as tightly as she could, ignoring the tears that collected in her own eyes. His heart was exposed, and it was broken, and there was nothing she could do about it.

"Everyone deals with things differently." She squeezed him tighter.

When he collected himself, she could tell he was embarrassed. He stood, brushed off his shorts, and offered her his hand. "Listen," he said, clearing his throat. "I – I'm sorry about your hand."

"My hand is fine. Well, *that* one is." She held up her left hand and showed off the bandage her dad had rigged. She'd have to go to Urgent Care in the morning, her dad said.

Josh let out a pathetic laugh. More of an exhalation of air, but there was a tiny smile amidst the redness on his face.

"We don't have to do this," Annie said. "Not if you're not ready. No one will judge you for it. Maybe Dave will be willing to go with you once he's had some time to process?"

"Yeah, I don't think I want to do this. Staring at a headstone isn't going to make any difference to me, really."

"What about the letter?" At her question, he dug it out of his pocket and turned it over in his hands.

"I don't know if I can," he said, defeated. He flipped the unsealed flap open and then folded it back down. "Will it really change anything?"

"I don't know," Annie said honestly. "Probably not. I'm not sure there are any words that can take away the hurt you're feeling right now. But she's your mom. And she wrote *those* words," Annie nodded at the letter, "for you. For *this* moment. So I have to hope it can't make things any *worse*."

Josh handed the letter to Annie. "Would you?" He asked. "I'm not sure I can take seeing her handwriting. If I'm being honest, I don't know if I can take *any* of this right now."

"Are you sure?" He nodded. "Here? Right now?"

"Might as well. Rip off the Band-Aid," he instructed.

My sweet baby Josh,

Only, you are not a baby. You're not a baby at all. As I sit here and watch you, you're all boy. Nothing can stop you. You go after what you want, and you don't see any limitations. You are nine years old, and already I can see what kind of man you will be. You've always been true to yourself, and I hope that's still true when you read this. You are a good boy, Josh. You will be a good man.

Your heart is unlike anything I've ever seen. You might be all boy on the playground, but you are sensitive. You are compassionate. You can tap into the emotions of everyone around you, and that's what makes you such a good friend to the people who need you. I see you with Brandon. You're still just a boy yourself, and yet you give him the kind of support that most adults can't figure out how to give.

The way you open yourself up to people and the way you let people in – I hope to God you never, ever lose that. It is the number one quality I love so much about you. It's a rarity, Josh, that quality, and it's precious. It's something I am incapable of.

You're reading this, which must mean you are pretty angry with me right now, and I don't blame you. Be angry. Be raging mad. But only with me, do you understand? You do not have my permission to let this pain and anger ruin you. I know all of this must be so hard for you to understand. And I could tell you all of my reasons, but they will fall on deaf ears, Josh. Because no matter what I tell you, it won't be enough. Because you feel cheated. You feel deceived. And as much as I hate doing this to you, I cannot take watching myself die through your eyes.

The way you look at me? You see someone I am not. You see everyone as they could only ever hope to see themselves. You see strength where I am weak. You see bravery when I am terrified. You see me as a better person than I could ever be. And I love how you see me. And it is selfish of me to want you to still see that woman, even now. And if you see me wither away, that is all you will remember. I cannot be responsible for shattering your rose-colored glasses.

Because the way you see people, Josh? It'll change people. You make everyone around you better. And I'd rather you hate me than take that away from you.

You are my boy. You will always be my boy. And I am so sorry I had to leave you. But as your mother, I demand that you be bigger than this. I demand you find that strength you see in everyone else and rise above this. In the grand scheme of your life, Josh, this is a small tragedy, my boy.

You are stronger than this. You are stronger than me.

I love you,

Mom

Holy crap. Annie didn't make it two lines into the letter before she was crying herself. It took all of her strength not to look up at Josh when she heard his sniffles. She knew if she did, she wouldn't ever find the air to finish reading.

His mother was spot on. *Spot* on. She thought about their entire friendship, their entire relationship, and his mother couldn't have been more right. She smiled at the thought, despite the tears and snot dripping down her face. He was exactly the kind of guy his mom hoped he'd be.

Josh crashed into her as she wiped at her tears with the sleeve of her sweatshirt. He hugged her so tight she could hardly breathe. He completely broke down.

"Thank you," he kept repeating into her ear between sobs. "Thank you, thank you." He kissed the top of her head.

"I didn't do anything."

"You did *everything*, Annie," he said. "I couldn't do any of this without you." His face was soggy as he kissed her hairline, her cheeks, her nose. His lips crashed into hers, and what was left of her breath was taken away.

She pulled away from his face and looked up at him, resting her chin on his chest. "Are going to be okay?"

"I'm not sure, but she seems to think I will be."

The next day, Annie woke up with seriously swollen eyes, and her head felt foggy. The night before had been intense. *Way* intense. But she was glad she'd been a part of it.

After a trip to the doctor for her hand, Annie met Josh at Misty Lake. He was buzzing with energy. He was also carrying his guitar case.

"You promised," he said.

"What?"

"We're writing lyrics for your song."

"I made no such promise!" she protested.

"Please?" He made puppy dog eyes at her. "You know, I've gone through an awful lot in the last few weeks. This would really be an awesome distraction."

Great. He was *guilt-tripping* her. She rolled her eyes and laughed.

"Alright, whatever. Let's do this."

YOU'RE ALWAYS SO CRYPTIC

Lisa's new silver VW Jetta cruised down the highway. The trees blurred by as the little car headed west toward Boone. Even though it was a comfortable car, Annie resented it. Laurie's dad bought the car for Lisa the week after she'd moved out. Like it was a *reward* for leaving her family.

There was a question burning in Annie's throat, but she hadn't been able to bring herself to say hello to her mother, never mind ask what had been on her mind the entire trip.

When Annie got the bridal shower invite in the mail, it was addressed to her *and* her mother. Did Jamie know Lisa wasn't living at home anymore? Annie didn't want to hear her mom's voice, so she just texted the details and asked to be picked up at Burgette's. She didn't want to risk a run in between her parents.

Annie wasn't sure her dad could handle that. Not that it was *that* great a risk. Her dad wasn't home much lately. He was busy photographing couples in love, while his own marriage was dissolving. Before leaving, Annie poured out all the alcohol in the house, just as a precaution. The last thing she needed was an MIA mother *and* an alcoholic father.

A few days after the Burgette's situation, Sally asked Annie if she was okay. Annie had no idea what she was talking about.

"You know, the whole your-mom-Laurie's-dad-baby-drama. Everybody's talking about it."

Annie just stared at her. Apparently, Olivia wasn't backing down no matter how much any of them called her bluff. The word was quickly making its way through the small town, and Annie couldn't ignore it anymore. She had to know.

"Is it true?" Annie didn't even bother looking over at Lisa. Her blonde hair was perfectly curled, and her makeup was flawless. Her high heels were kicked off. She was driving barefoot in a beautiful, form-fitting yellow dress.

"Is what true?" Lisa replied, huffing. "You're always so cryptic, Annie. You really need to learn to communicate more clearly." Annie sighed. Of *course* her mother wouldn't waste an opportunity to take a stab at her.

She hated that she even felt like she had to ask, but Olivia had found a way to get into her head. She wished she knew and trusted her mother enough to not even *have* to ask.

"Are you—" Annie hesitated.

"Jesus, Annie. Spit it out already!"

"Alright, fine! Are you pregnant? Are you and Richard having a baby?"

Lisa was clearly caught off-guard. She glanced at Annie's face cautiously before replying. "Where do you even *get* these ideas, Annie? Of course I'm not pregnant."

Despite her mother's jab, Annie was relieved.

"But, I guess I *should* tell you that Richard and I have found a place. We're moving in together."

Annie sat silent. When she and Laurie were kids, they used to pretend they were sisters. They joked about how awesome it would be. And now it might actually be happening? Annie never realized all that would have to come crumbling down first for that wish to come true.

Lisa cleared her throat and kept her eyes forward. "That is not your news to share, do you understand me?" Annie understood perfectly, but her loyalty wasn't with her mother.

"Yeah," Annie spit. "Got it."

The rest of the drive to the mountains was painfully quiet. Annie never understood how her mother could drive anywhere without the radio on. Back in the day, when Annie asked, Lisa told her that music was nothing more than an annoying distraction. They couldn't be any more different.

When they got to Jamie's parents' house, there were cars spilling out into the street. Lisa had to park on the grass. The house was cabin-like and backed up to a cliff, which always terrified Annie. She couldn't understand how anyone navigated through this town on a snow day without sliding off the roads.

Annie grabbed the presents from the backseat of the car. Her mother was halfway up the driveway when Annie slammed the door shut. She considered running to catch up. But she didn't want to deal with her mother's fake smile as she enveloped her soon-to-be daughter-in-law into a hug.

Annie wondered what the wedding day would be like. She felt sort of bad for her brother and Jamie. They deserved a day that was all their own, and she just hoped beyond all hope that her mom would behave, leaving Richard at home. She also couldn't stomach the idea of what it would do to her dad to see her mom on Richard's arm.

Annie watched the door open from the end of the driveway. She waited as her mom entered. Annie leaned against the trunk of the car, her skin prickling in the cool breeze. She'd forgotten how cold Boone stayed through the spring. She wished she hadn't worn a sundress. She'd much rather be in jeans and a sweatshirt, but Laurie made it pretty clear that bridal showers were dressy affairs. *Dang it.*

When Annie got to the door, she tried the knob rather than knocking. No need for the over-the-top greeting. *Success.* Jamie saw her from across the room, and they exchanged smiles. Annie left their gifts on top of a growing mountain; she couldn't believe the number of packages that overwhelmed the foyer. Jamie grabbed her from behind, turning Annie into her hug.

"So happy you could be here!" Jamie gushed.

"Mmmhmm." Annie released her grasp. Jamie looked radiant and genuinely happy. Her dark hair was loosely curled, and her little white lace dress hugged her body perfectly. She was barefoot, which made Annie smile.

"Oh," Jamie squealed, startling Annie. "Before I forget. We've been meaning to ask you — we'd really like it if you would sing a song at our reception. Drew mentioned you were so talented, and it would just be *so* special for us!" Jamie's face was pink with excitement, and Annie's heart dropped into her stomach. The last thing she wanted to do was sing in front of all those people. But she didn't want to let Jamie or her brother down.

"Uh," Annie hesitated. "Uh, sure. I guess. If that's what you want." Jamie hugged Annie again.

"Oh, thank you! Thank you! It'll really make our day so special. Please, please help yourself to some food." Jamie gestured at the dining room table, which was crowded with fancy plates and tons of food. Annie smiled. The nerves that just surged through her entire body killed her appetite.

Jamie excused herself so she could mingle with her other guests. Annie scanned the room, snatched a fancy plastic cup of wine, and took a seat in a chair nuzzled in the far corner of the room. She'd never had any real desire to drink, but the idea of a blended family made the wine irresistible. She could use some numbing.

The warmth of the dry red calmed her, and she watched the other guests. They were all dressed in perfect outfits, spoke in perfect Southern dialects, and had perfect smiles across their perfectly lineless faces. Then, Annie saw her. What the hell was *she* doing at her soon-to-be sister-in-law's bridal shower, sipping juice and shoving Jamie's stuffed mushrooms into her mouth?

Olivia.

This had to be some kind of joke. Annie smoldered. She rose from her seat and glided, undetected, out to the back porch, overlooking the terrifying cliff. She needed some air and a chance to collect her thoughts.

Jamie came out with an armful of empty soda cans, which she tossed into an empty trash bag.

"Ugh," she huffed. "Nobody recycles!" She glanced at Annie. "Hey, you alright?"

Annie turned to Jamie with a wary smile.

"How do you know Olivia Hughes?" she asked. A confused expression danced across Jamie's face.

"Huh?"

"Olivia Hughes. She's in your parents' living room. She's drinking your punch and eating your food. What is she doing here?"

"She's my cousin," Jamie said, confused.

"Oh, my God." Annie felt like someone just punched her in the stomach.

Jamie nodded and half-smiled at Annie as she ducked back

inside. Annie leaned back into the deep lounge of the wooden chair that was perfectly placed to enjoy the view. Annie *wasn't* enjoying the view. She wanted to go home. She wanted to go home *immediately.*

She'd been outside for a while when she heard the glass door open and close behind her. Olivia plopped down in the chair next to her and cleared her throat. "Look, we can be friends, okay?"

"I'm sorry, what?"

Olivia rolled her eyes and scanned Annie like she was an idiot. "I guess we can be friends. Whatever. It's not a big deal."

Annie, stunned into confusion, just blinked. She narrowed her eyes. "Um, no?"

"*Excuse* me?" Olivia stiffened and cocked her head to the side.

"No. This," Annie gestured back toward the house, "doesn't change anything." She rolled her shoulders back and faced Olivia. "You can't just say something and expect it to happen. That's not how this works." Olivia stared at her.

"You're so used to intimidating people into giving you what you want. It won't work this time." Annie stood. She wobbled a bit from the wine that had gone straight to her head, the same wine that probably gave her the confidence to say what she did. She steadied herself and headed to the sliding glass door.

"You have everyone *so* fooled," Olivia spit out. "You paint yourself to be so innocent and quiet. Everyone thinks you're *so nice*. But you've got a little sass in you."

Annie twirled around. "Is that supposed to be an insult? Because from where I'm standing, it's never a bad thing to be a nice girl with a backbone." She spun on her heel and slid the door open.

"Wait," Olivia called out. Annie could hear the cacophony of the ladies inside, and that didn't seem any more inviting than Olivia's plea from outside. She hesitated, slid the door shut and faced Olivia.

"What?" Annie exhaled, throwing her head back in exasperation

"Would it matter if I said I'm sorry?" Olivia's eyes were filled with, what? Sadness? Regret? Hope? Annie couldn't tell.

"Well," Annie said, walking back to the chair she'd abandoned. "*Are* you sorry?"

Olivia got quiet and tossed her head from side to side as if considering Annie's question.

"If you want my opinion," Annie started, "I don't think you

are. I think you're just sorry that everything blew up in your face. And I'm sorry that it did, I am. But you brought all of this on yourself, so it's kind of hard for me to feel *that* sorry for you."

Olivia sat quiet, deflated. Annie worried that maybe she had been little too harsh and blamed the wine.

"I — I don't know what to do," Olivia admitted quietly. She was alone, without her loyal followers to make her feel invincible.

"You'll figure it out," Annie said, and she meant it. "You're a tough cookie." Annie exhaled a strained laugh, and so did Olivia.

"You think so?" That was the first time Annie had ever seen the human side of Olivia.

"Are you kidding? Uh, *yeah*. I mean, you poured *tequila* down my dress and still managed to get my best friend to think *I'd* done it. You're a resourceful little snot." The girls laughed an uncomfortable, awkward kind of laugh. Then silence settled between them.

They sat together for a long while with nothing but the sound of the screeching cicadas between them in the falling evening.

The sliding glass door opened, and Jamie's mother was all giggles.

"Oh, good! I'm glad you girls found each other! I told Jamie it would be good for the two of you to spend some time together since you're the same age."

Annie and Olivia shared a loaded glance.

"Anyhoo," Mrs. Christian giggled. "It's time for games! You girls get on in here!" She slid the door shut.

Annie stood and flattened out her dress. "You comin?" she asked Olivia, who was still sitting with her legs crossed looking out over the terrifying cliff.

"Go on, I'm just going to sit here for a few." Annie headed for the door and slid it open. She looked back over her shoulder.

"Listen, I know we're not friends or anything, but I *do* really think you'll be okay."

"I hope you're right," Annie heard Olivia reply as she slid the door shut and rejoined the party.

Joey Hodges

May 17, 2010

Listening to: Listening to: The Avett Brothers *Incomplete*

and Insecure

You won't even believe what happened this weekend. It would be my luck that Olivia is related Jamie. I can't really be sure, but I think I saw a human side to her. I don't like her or anything like that — but I don't know. She just seemed, deflated or something. I'd never seen her like that before. She was definitely a lot less intimidating without her coat of armor. She seemed ... lonely. I don't know if she's ever felt that way before: powerless. Part of me feels just a little bad. And I feel like maybe I should have just accepted her offer to be friends. But my gut says not to trust her. Not everyone approaches things the same way, I guess. It's just hard to think she'd rather be miserable than just be nice. And maybe that, right there, is the number one reason we couldn't ever be friends. I'd rather just get along with people.

I can't believe this year is practically over. I could sit here and go through all the stuff that happened, but honestly, I'm not sure it would be a good idea. I can say this. I am not the same kind of person I was at the beginning of the year. I'm still the same me I've always been—but I've grown. I used to think that being quiet wasn't a bad thing. And I guess really, it's not. But I think I used my quietness to mask the fact that I was weak. And I think it's okay that I was weak. I never really had to stand on my own two feet before. I always had Laurie in my corner. So maybe that's the silver lining to everything Laurie and I went through this year. It taught me how to be on my own. I'd never been challenged before. And I guess maybe that's a lucky thing that I made it 15 years with all kinds of support. But this year taught me things I never knew I needed to know. This year taught me how important it is just to be myself.

I learned the difference between changing and evolving. I also learned that adapting doesn't always mean that a person is changing themselves completely either.

A lot happened this year. To everyone. I spent a lot of time worrying about everyone else — and somewhere in the middle of all of that I just realized it's okay to worry about myself sometimes. It doesn't make me selfish or self-involved. It's healthy. It's important.

So if I could tell the girl I was on the first day of school one thing, it's that she's about to go on a wild ride. At times she'll feel

Joey Hodges

more alone and lost than ever before. But in the end, she'll be a better person and a better friend.

I'll be honest. I thought this project was going to be really easy. But I guess the point of was to see every situation from outside of myself. And that is never easy *— and I don't think it matters what age we are. What might feel like a catastrophe on the inside might just be a minor blip on the radar in the grand scheme of things.*

I hope that when I'm grown up and have a family of my own that I don't ever forget exactly how real *all of this feels. The things we go through are hard, sure. But I think for us (or at least for me) the hardest part is learning how to* handle *everything.*

RAINBOWS! BUTTERFLIES! RYAN GOSLING!

Annie flipped through the pages of her English project. The binder was overflowing with lyrics, receipts, and entries. She couldn't believe so much had happened in one year. Perspective was such a weird thing. When she thought back to the Bonfire, it felt like it was another lifetime. It kind of was.

The yearlong project was due in a week. Annie couldn't believe it was almost time to turn it in. She didn't feel like the same girl who'd written that very first entry about being a target. She'd pulled herself through so much that she wasn't sure she *could* be that girl anymore.

Everything she'd experienced through the year taught her just a little bit more about who she really was. And maybe that was the *real* point of high school: self-discovery. So that by the end of the four years you could stand a little more confident in your own skin.

Annie picked five of her most mild entries. They ranged from the sign on her locker that first week to her entry from last weekend after the shower. She felt safe with her choices ... as safe as she *could* feel sharing such intimate details. She'd unintentionally used the project as a journal. She kept forgetting that she would eventually have to share some of it.

"Our Gym final should be a breeze, but I'm really worried about my Geometry final."

Annie was hardly listening to Josh's rant through the phone. She hated when he talked about Geometry. She was basically failing Algebra I, and he sailed through a sophomore-level course.

"You'll do fine, I'm sure," Annie half grunted. It was Tuesday, and it was raining. That put Annie in a foul mood. She was stressed over the idea of having to sing at Drew's wedding. It was only a few weeks away, and the thought paralyzed her.

Everything that happened with Olivia over the weekend was

so strange. It was as if, for half a second, Annie could see her as a girl just like herself. She'd never seen Olivia anything other than poised and confident. It made her wonder how things would be at school now between them.

Also, she *really* needed to talk to Laurie. Despite what her mother said, she thought it was only fair to tell Laurie about their parents. Unless maybe her dad already told her. Annie had been so upset with Laurie for not telling her about the affair right away that she couldn't justify withholding her news any longer. She'd have to talk to Laurie in class. Annie and Josh were still eating their lunches alone in the library.

"How's all your studying going?" Josh asked, interrupting her thoughts.

"I don't know. I haven't started yet."

"You haven't started? Annie! You need to get on that!"

"Right, right." Annie didn't care. She was distracted.

"Listen." There was a lump in her throat. "Drew and Jamie asked me to sing at the wedding —"

Before she could finish her thought, Josh interrupted her. "That's awesome! You'll be great. What song?"

"Well, that's sort of the thing. I was thinking maybe if we

finish the song in time, that's the one I could sing."

"That's a great idea." He sounded hesitant.

"What?"

"Well, it's just—we've written it as two parts. A duet."

"Exactly." She was grinning into the phone.

"I'm asking if you'd like to be my date to the wedding. And sing with me."

There was silence on the end. Annie panicked, thinking maybe she'd spooked him.

"Sorry," he said after a minute. "Apparently it's really tough to talk when you're smiling really hard."

She giggled at his corniness. "Is that a yes?"

"It's a *hell* yes!"

The next day, Josh kissed Annie quickly when the bell rang, releasing them from lunch. She looked at him coyly. "You're not supposed to do that here."

"Oh, yeah? And what are you going to do about it?"

They'd been together for several months, and yet she still

loved flirting with him. They were so comfortable together.

"Yeah, okay. I liked it." She laughed and they went their separate ways.

She walked into Science. Laurie was already sitting in her seat behind Annie's, digging in her Vera Bradley tote for something. Annie breezed past her normal seat and plopped down next to Laurie, who flipped her hair up and turned.

"Hey buddy," Annie said giddily.

"Really?" Laurie's eyes were wide. "You're sitting with me today?" She bounced in her seat and clapped her hands.

Annie held up her hands. "Don't get too excited. I actually have to talk to you." Laurie's face fell and her excitement dissolved.

"Really?" Laurie said, deflated. "And here I thought we were doing so well."

"Oh, hush," Annie teased. "You and I are fine." Annie grabbed her notebook from her backpack and put it on the table in front of them.

"Okay, listen. My mom made it *very* clear I wasn't supposed to tell anyone. And I don't know, your dad may have already told you. I just don't want there to be secrets between us anymore."

Annie could feel the tension building between them. She

knew there was no easy way to say what needed to be said, and part of her questioned whether it was the right thing to do.

"My mom and your dad are moving in together."

Laurie pressed her lips into a flat line and slowly nodded her head as if processing the information. The classroom was rowdy around them, but Annie could really only hear Laurie's slow inhale and exhale.

"I'm sorry, you didn't know ..." Annie said. "I know this isn't exactly the best place to drop a bomb on you. But I didn't want another day to go by and not tell you. I didn't think that would be fair."

Laurie was still sitting quietly, slowly nodding her head. She took a deep breath and blew it out, turning to Annie in the process.

"Okay."

"Okay?" Annie cocked her head to the side, waiting for the rest of the response.

Laurie scanned the room around her, and then looked at the door, which prompted Annie to turn around. Mrs. Swanson was walking into the room. She called the class to attention.

Annie turned back to Laurie and whispered, "Are you okay?"

"Honestly?" Laurie whispered as she flipped open her

notebook. "I have no idea."

Class began and Annie regretted telling Laurie before class. She couldn't focus on a word Mrs. Swanson was saying, and she was pretty sure Laurie couldn't either. She looked over and saw tears collecting in Laurie's eyes.

Annie squeezed Laurie's knee underneath the table and Laurie reached down and grabbed Annie's hand, giving her the kind of sad smile that asked *well, now what?* with a little shrug and a deep breath.

Later that day, Annie was sitting in her living room watching the episode of *American Idol* she'd missed the night before. Josh had some chores to do at his house, but he was due over any minute so they could work on their song.

As she watched the contestants sing their hearts out on what had been live TV, she imagined her upcoming performance. Olivia wouldn't dare say awful things in front of all their family. Would she? She dismissed the thought, and the doorbell rang.

Wondering why Josh bothered with the bell, Annie opened the door. Standing on the front porch in the pouring rain was a soaking wet Laurie, sniffling.

She pulled Laurie inside and slammed the door. Her friend stood there, dripping wet and crying. She didn't have to ask because she already knew what was wrong. It was the same thing that had been on Annie's mind since the bridal shower.

Laurie's face contorted as Annie looked her in the eye, then the sobs took over and Laurie collapsed onto Annie's shoulder.

"Everything is so messed up," Laurie wailed between sobs. Annie ran her hand over Laurie's wet hair in an attempt to soothe her.

"I know, L. I know." Minutes passed as Laurie cried, and Annie rubbed her back. Laurie pulled herself away from Annie at an arms-length.

"What are we even supposed to do?" Her question was sincere and desperate. She threw herself back into her friend.

Annie contemplated Laurie's question. The thing was, Annie's mom had quit her family a long time ago. For Annie, this was a resolution. But for Laurie, it was just the beginning. While Laurie felt hurt and confused, Annie felt … relieved.

"I wish I knew," Annie admitted as she squeezed her friend tighter.

Laurie pulled away again, wiping at her eyes. She walked over to the staircase and sat down. She hugged her knees to her chest, burying her face.

"I feel like I want to hate everything right now. Him. Her. *You,* " Laurie said into her legs. Annie was stung by her words.

"*Me?* " Annie couldn't handle the idea of everything between them crumbling down again. Laurie looked up and offered a weak smile.

"I don't mean that I *do* hate you. I just want to." Annie let out a nervous chuckle.

"Honestly," Laurie said, extending her legs in front of her and folding her hands in her lap, "I just, I don't know. I don't *get* it. I thought my parents were happy enough, I guess."

Annie joined Laurie on the step and nudged her. "Yeah. I always thought that with grown-ups, things just got figured out, you know? This just goes to show that there's no stability in anything." Annie was quiet a long moment. "And that *terrifies* me."

Her emotions caught in her throat and before she could stop them, tears sprang to her eyes. She thought she was past all of that, the crying. Laurie draped her arm over her friend and leaned her head on Annie's shoulder.

Laurie took a deep breath. "Want a silver lining?" Annie wiped at her eyes as the tears fell and smiled despite herself.

"Sure."

"Well, we always wanted to be sisters."

Annie chuckled. "Yeah, I guess there's that." She smiled at her friend. "Oh, God. Do you really think they'll actually get married? I hadn't really thought that far."

"Who knows?" Laurie said. "But I wouldn't put it past them."

"Have you talked to your dad at all yet? Or your mom? Geez, how is your mom? Is she okay?"

"No clue," Laurie admitted. "It's not like I saw much of either of them before this. I mean, I knew ever since Valentine's Day that everything was effed up, but I honestly just thought they'd figure it out. I never thought it'd end up like this."

"I know," Annie agreed, leaning into her friend and getting comfortable. "I forget sometimes that they're actual people. I know that sounds stupid, but it's hard to imagine that any of them have lives outside of being our parents. And *oh my God!* Our parents were having an *affair.*" Annie emphasized the word in disgust, suddenly realizing what exactly it *meant.*

"Lauuuuuuurie," she groaned, "I can't even think about it. The whole thing just kind of grosses me out."

Laurie covered her ears and squealed. "Stop! Stop! I can't not think about it now!"

Giggling, Annie said, "Sorry! Rainbows! Butterflies! Ryan Gosling!"

Laurie shook her head violently to clear the thoughts from her mind. She laughed, threw her head back and groaned. "What the hell does this even mean for us?"

Annie swallowed her smile because it really *wasn't* funny. It was ... crappy. She shrugged. "I have no idea."

"I like my house. I like my little family bubble, even if they suck sometimes. I don't want any of that to change." The tears were back in Laurie's eyes, and she raised her shoulders. "I really just thought they'd work it out. Isn't that what parents are supposed to do? Fix everything?"

The tears slid down her cheeks, and she put her head in her hands. Annie rested her hand on Laurie's back and traced circles.

Annie took a deep breath, trying her best to ward off the tears that were threatening her own eyes again.

"I can't — I can't —" Laurie started to hyperventilate. Her

breathing was ragged, and she just kept repeating, "I can't — I can't
—"

The reality of the situation smacked Annie in the face as she
tried to calm her friend down.

She hadn't before considered that anything beyond her mom
moving out would change. Would she have to move? Where would
her dad go? What about her brother and the wedding? What would
holidays look like?

Suddenly, as the questions overwhelmed her, she couldn't
breathe. The thoughts choked her. She hugged Laurie, and they cried
together.

She wasn't sure how much time had passed, but when the
front door swung open it startled her. Her dad walked in and
immediately looked concerned. Annie frantically wiped at her face
while nudging Laurie, hoping she'd do the same and collect herself.
"Dad!"

He hesitated as he closed the door and shook the rain from
his hair. "What's going on?"

Annie and Laurie exchanged a panicked stare.

"Annie." Her dad approached. "What is it?"

She couldn't stand the idea of being the one to tell him, but she couldn't think of anything else to say. She'd never been any good at lying, especially under pressure.

"Uh — nothing. Nothing!" she said. She grabbed Laurie's arm and yanked her up, heading up the stairs. "Just — boy trouble," she called over her shoulder.

"Annette." She froze. "Turn around." She did. "Come here." She obliged.

He cradled her face in his hands and used his thumbs to wipe away her tears, then collected her into a hug. "What did he do?"

Annie's heart sank into her stomach.

"Mr. Mackey?" Laurie's voice was shaky and small. "I think maybe we need to talk."

SEE ME AFTER CLASS

The girls were seated at the kitchen table across from Annie's dad. Annie looked at Laurie and whispered, "I don't think this is a good idea." Laurie squeezed Annie's hand.

"Trust me," Laurie said with her normal confidence. Annie wondered how she did it. How she could go from broken to composed instantly.

"Ladies," Jason said hesitantly. "I'd appreciate it if you would fill me in on what's going on." He gave Annie a concerned look. "What happened?"

Making eye contact with her dad made Annie lose it all over again.

"No," she said, standing. "This isn't right." She yanked

Laurie up from the table. "Dad," she managed through tears. She took a deep breath. "I'm fine. And Laurie is fine. And Josh didn't do anything. But something did happen, or, *is* happening I guess. But, oh God. I'm going to be in so much trouble," she said to Laurie. "I wasn't supposed to tell *anyone*."

"Sweet." Jason's voice was soft and calm but full of concern. "One of you needs to tell me what happened because I'm about to have a heart attack here."

At that, Annie crumbled. "You need to call Mom," she sobbed. "Please? Just call Mom? I wasn't supposed to say *anything*. I wasn't supposed to *tell* anyone. She held her face in her hands. "Everything is *so* screwed up."

"Mom?" Jason questioned, and at that, his expression changed to one of recognition. "Okay. Sit down," he told Annie.

"You know." It wasn't a question. Suddenly, Annie felt great relief.

"Yeah," Laurie sniffled, folding her hands in her lap. "We know."

"I was going to talk to you about everything this evening," Jason addressed Annie. "Your mother and I had a conversation earlier today. However, she failed to mention that *you* already knew." Annoyance was in his voice. "Not that I'm surprised. Anyway." He reached across the table and took their hands.

"I know all of this is a lot for you girls to process, but listen to me, and I mean this; everything will be fine. I don't have a lot of answers for you either of you right now, and Laurie, you should probably have this conversation with your own parents, but I know all of this kind of..." he trailed off. "Complicates the lines between our families." He blinked back tears.

"Things are ... messy, and I know this seems impossible, but please let us adults figure it out, okay? I know it rattles your lives, but trust that we all will take care of you. This isn't your problem to handle."

The sound of the front door opening and closing interrupted him. Josh walked into the kitchen and took in the scene.

"Oh, I'm sorry," he apologized, holding up his hands. "I didn't mean to interrupt. I'll go –"

"No, no –" Jason released the girls' hands and called out to Josh, who was turning to leave. "Don't be silly. You're always welcome here."

Annie wiped at her eyes and looked at Laurie who was doing the same. They shared a smile.

Jason turned his attention back to the girls. "Listen, everything is under control, understand?"

"Yes," the girls said in unison.

"Okay, then." He cleared his throat, regaining his composure. "Josh." Jason offered the chair at the table he'd just vacated. "I'll be in the living room." He excused himself.

Laurie stood and wiped underneath her eyes at the mascara that had smeared down her face. "I'll go," she said quietly.

Annie reached for Laurie's hand to stop her.

"I'm fine, really." Laurie offered a weak smile. "Are you?"

Annie nodded quickly, and Laurie bent over to give her a hug.

"Thank you," Laurie whispered into her ear. "I mean it. I really needed you today, and you have no idea how thankful I am that I could just run over here. I love you."

"Anytime," Annie said, releasing her. "Love you too, L."

Laurie flashed her megawatt smile. "Man, I've missed you." She patted Annie's head. "Josh," she said in acknowledgment as she raised her eyebrows at him knowingly. She sauntered down the hall and called out, "Catch ya later, Mr. Mackey." With a bounce, she was gone.

Annie stared at the door for a moment, smiled, and rolled her eyes. Laurie's ability to just take a deep breath and move on baffled her. Annie's heart still felt heavy, but she was so thankful to have her friend back.

"Everything alright?" Josh asked, pulling her attention from the door.

She turned and laughed. "I have no idea."

Annie looked at the clock on her dresser. It was 9 p.m. She and Josh had been working on her song for the past three hours, and the distraction was nice. She filled Josh in on what happened when they got upstairs, and he offered to practice another day if she wanted to talk. But she really didn't have anything left to say. The situation was out of her hands, no matter how much it sucked.

"No, wait," Josh said as he jotted something down on the piece of paper laid out on the floor in front of him. He put the pencil in his mouth. He strummed the chords and hummed. He leaned forward, erased something, and wrote something else.

"I think this is it! One more time from the top." He flung the pencil across the room, marking Annie's wall. She laughed and picked up her guitar, strummed along and waited for her cue to sing.

They got all the way through it for the first time. She looked over at him, beaming.

"Thank *God*," she shouted. "Seriously? This is it?" She couldn't believe it. She had no idea Josh was such a perfectionist. Every time she thought maybe they had it, he panicked and changed a hundred more things. He slid his guitar strap off and laid the instrument next to him.

"Get your butt over here," he grinned. She put her guitar down and crawled into his lap, nuzzling her face into his neck. He kissed her hair.

"You let it happen... You did it! I'm so proud of you." He was practically whispering like he was afraid she might actually hear him. She backed away so she could look him in the eye.

"I'm kind of proud of me too." She giggled. "I couldn't have done any of this without you, though."

Josh opened his mouth to protest.

"No," she said, stopping him. "I mean it. If you hadn't nagged —" she smiled, "I mean *encouraged* me, this wouldn't have happened."

The final full week of school was weird. Quiet and weird. Everyone was so frazzled by exams that no one seemed to have time for anything but studying. Annie and Josh spent the week eating lunches out by their tree near the picnic tables. The weather was too nice to eat inside.

Annie was surprised when Maddie and Laurie both joined them. And she felt a *little* bad when she saw Olivia walk to The Elite table to find only Brandon there.

Luckily, exam week consisted of half days with two exams a day, so lunch wasn't an issue.

It was Tuesday, the last exam day, and there was a sense of relief and excitement among Annie's classmates as she walked through the hall to English.

She'd turned in her project, which was the final, on Friday. Mr. Beal would be returning it today, and her nerves were bouncing all over the place. Part of her soul felt exposed.

She worried she would be graded on how she'd handled all the chaos this year. Which hadn't always been very gracefully. As she entered the full classroom, the bell rang. Her throat was dry. Mr.

Beal made eye contact with her as she took her seat and gave her a nod. Her stomach unclenched.

The exam period was dedicated to discussing their favorite things to do over the summer. By the time Mr. Beal wrapped up the conversation and started handing back everyone's projects, Annie had relaxed, already in summer-mode.

Mr. Beal approached her desk and placed her binder down. He grabbed her shoulder and leaned in.

"See me after class for just a minute," he whispered, then moved on to the desk behind her. Her throat tightened, and she was too frightened to open the binder to check her grade. She couldn't begin to fathom what Mr. Beal wanted to talk to her about. Unless, *oh God,* he'd read more than just the five entries she'd selected.

There wasn't anything *too* serious, but she had gotten a little personal with some entries. She suddenly wished she hadn't been so candid with the assignment. She wanted to crawl under her desk and die.

The bell rang and the classroom cleared out quickly. Annie was left sitting in her seat in silence, her nerves going haywire. Mr. Beal collected some of the stray papers on his desk and straightened them before attaching a paperclip.

"Sorry to keep you, I'll be quick. I'm sure you're starving and ready for summer."

At that, Annie's stomach growled and broke the tension. She let out a little laugh, clutching her stomach.

"I guess so," she said shyly.

"I just wanted to congratulate you and actually, well, *thank* you." Annie sat bewildered. "Your project?"

At his indication, she remembered she hadn't even bothered to check the rubric. She'd been so certain he had asked her to stay behind because she'd *failed.* She opened the binder and saw a big, bright red A across the top. The detailed grading points blurred before her eyes in her excitement. She looked back up at Mr. Beal, who was deliciously adorable with his little grin.

"You were the *only* one to treat this project like I'd hoped. And the growth I could see in you through the entries you selected made me so proud of you. I hope you really got something out of the process," he said sincerely.

Annie's face flushed. "I did," she said as she stuffed the binder into her backpack. "It was …" She trailed off. "Sort of fun," she admitted.

"I hoped it would be. It seems like a lot of your classmates didn't think the same, though. So I just wanted to tell you that I appreciated your dedication to it." He stood, which prompted Annie to do the same. She swung her backpack over her shoulder and headed for the door.

"Thanks, Mr. Beal," she said, her heart racing.

"And Annie?" Mr. Beal stopped her from exiting. She turned. "It's been a real pleasure having you in my class this year. Best of luck next year. And ..." He trailed off. "Trust your gut. You've got a really good head on your shoulders."

"Thanks, Mr. Beal. I will." And with that, freshmen year was *over*.

SIMPLE BUT BEAUTIFUL

Jamie's mom helped her slide the dress over her head. Annie stood back and watched Jamie transform into a bride. Without warning, tears started spilling onto her cheeks.

Jamie's dark hair was loosely curled and pulled half-up. Her dress was nothing short of a princess gown. It was boat-necked with sleeves that hugged her shoulders. It cinched at the waist then poofed into a full skirt. It was simple but beautiful. *Very* Jamie.

Her mom zipped her up, and Jamie turned. Annie and Jamie's two sisters, Melissa and Audrey, beamed in approval. Jason snapped a million pictures.

***

When Lisa RSVP'd that she *was* bringing Richard to the wedding, Drew called Annie.

"We need to tell Dad," he said. "Right?"

"Yeah. I think so," Annie agreed. "He's not going to handle it well, Drew. This hasn't been ..." she had trailed off. "Well, it hasn't been pretty, to say the least." Jason had told Annie repeatedly that he was *just fine.* But Annie knew her father better than that. She could also hear him late at night, when he thought she was asleep, crying softly in the other room.

"I can't believe Mom," Drew said with disgust. "She can't leave it alone for just *one day?*"

"I know," Annie said. "It's really not fair. Listen, maybe it *would* be best for Dad to work. Don't you think?"

Drew took a minute to respond. "I don't know. You don't think that could get ... *awkward?*"

"Oh, I'm sure it could. But I honestly think it might be best for him to have some sort of distraction. Is it too late to cancel your photographer?"

"Oh, for sure," he said. "We put a deposit down ages ago." He paused. "Okay, I'll talk to Jamie. What if we did both? What if we kept our photographer *and* had Dad? They could shoot different things? Get different angles?

"I'm sure Mom is going to want pictures of her pinning my

boutonniere and whatnot. Maybe Dad could photograph you girls getting ready, and our guy could be in with the guys and me. That would save *some* of the awkwardness, right?"

"That's a good plan," Annie said. "And I think Dad would like that. A lot."

***

Earlier that day, Laurie insisted on doing Annie's hair and makeup before they all went to the bridal suite. "It's an important day," Laurie said. "You can't have your makeup dissolving halfway through." She used things like primers and setting powders and waterproof liquid eyeliner. When Annie looked in the mirror that morning, she felt silly. Her hair and makeup were perfectly done, but she was still in yoga pants and a tank.

As Annie stepped into her gown, she was careful not to get makeup on it. Laurie zipped her up. Annie stared at her reflection in the full-length mirror. Laurie stood behind her, beaming.

"Seriously? You look amazing," Laurie gushed. "I'm so glad I get to be here."

"All right, ladies," Annie's dad said, looking at his watch. "It's show time."

The ceremony was beautiful but quick. Annie couldn't believe that after all that planning, it was over so fast.

While on the altar, Annie noticed Olivia sitting with her family. Olivia gave her a weak smile and shrugged her shoulders, as uncomfortable with the situation as Annie was.

Annie also made the mistake of making eye contact with Josh. He was looking at her with such love that it made her cry half her mascara off. She couldn't get a handle on her emotions!

She was in the bathroom reapplying when Laurie swung the door open. It hit the wall startling Annie so much she poked herself with the wand.

"Crap, L!" Annie reached for a paper towel and started wiping at the mascara all over her nose.

"We have a problem." Laurie was panting against the door. Panicked, Annie finished erasing the mascara then followed Laurie out into the cocktail hour. Her heart was racing.

"Okay, what's going on?" Annie asked.

Laurie pointed across the room to the bar. Richard was holding a glass of red wine and a bottle of Coors Light. Standing in front of him was Jason, his face red.

"Crap!" Annie exclaimed, already sprinting across the room.

"Okay, Okay," she said, yanking on her dad's arm as he talked in Richard's direction. Annie could now see that the redness in his face wasn't from anger but from tears. He jerked his arm from Annie's and reached out toward Richard. Annie feared he was going to slug him.

Instead, Jason flicked the glass of wine and it spilled all over the front of Richard's suit. Annie couldn't hold in her laugh.

"Okay, hot shot," she said to her dad, pulling him out into the hallway of the venue. "Let's let you cool off." He wiped at his eyes. "Was that really necessary?" she asked.

He leaned against the wall and then slid down until his knees were up by his chest.

"It really was, Sweet."

Annie laughed.

Jason leaned his head back against the wall. "The thing is, Sweet. This feels like the worse kind of betrayal. I considered Richard a friend."

Yeah, Annie knew a little about that.

Her dad's broken heart would mend in time. And Annie knew he was much better off without her mom. In the years leading to their split, her dad had been left *so* neglected. He did all he could for Lisa only to be left with nothing.

She hoped that someday her favorite guy would let himself find someone who could make him as happy as he deserved.

Jamie's sister, Melissa, came looking for Annie. It was time for introductions and then ...

Annie told her dad to *behave* then followed Melissa. Her stomach knotted up.

She was as prepared as she could possibly be, but that didn't mean she *felt* ready. And the fact that Olivia was there didn't help matters.

As she was introduced, holding onto the arm of a groomsman, she spotted Josh next to the DJ's set up. She joined him, and they waited for Mr. and Mrs. Andrew Mackey to enter.

"You've got this," Josh whispered, handing her guitar to her.

She took a deep breath, "I sure hope so."

The DJ announced her brother and new sister-in-law. Drew escorted Jamie, with her gown flowing behind her, to the center of the dance floor. He caught Annie's eye and winked. That was their cue.

The room grew dizzyingly quiet. Annie's tongue felt numb. Her blood was pumping so loudly in her ears she could hardly hear either of their guitars as she and Josh started to play. She took three

deep breaths.

> *I was in the darkness*
> *I couldn't see the light.*
> *Everything was shadows*
> *And nothing felt right.*
>
> *I was all on my own*
> *In a world of instability*
> *There was no use even trying*
> *To make any sense of me.*
>
> *Sorted through the feelings*
> *And found the layers to peel*
> *To finally find out*
> *If love could be for real.*
>
> *But together we climbed*
> *Out of the darkness I was in*
> *And you forced me to find*
> *All my strength from within*
>
> *And now there is no question*
> *If love can exist*
> *We found out the truth*
> *The night we first kissed.*

Her voice mingled with Josh's, and their guitars echoed

through the reception hall as they played the last chords. Her heart

wasn't tight anymore; her vision wasn't blurred. Her tongue wasn't

numb, and her hearing was crystal clear.

When the song was over, she looked out over the crowd.

Everyone was on their feet, applauding. In the mix, she spotted

Olivia doing the same.

There was nothing to be afraid of anymore.

EPILOGUE

August 2010

"*Girls!*" Lisa yelled from the bottom of the stairs. "*Josh is here!*" Laurie mockingly fluttered her eyelashes at Annie. Annie threw a brush at her.

"Shut up!"

"I didn't *say* anything," Laurie antagonized. Laurie was in a cute sundress, but she'd left off her full arsenal of makeup, settling for just a swipe of mascara and some lip-gloss. Her now chin-length locks were pulled into a small pony at the nape of her neck. She looked natural and beautiful. And *happy*.

"Wait, you have those Target gladiator sandals here, right? Or are they at your mom's?" Lisa and Richard moved in together the week after Drew's wedding. They chose a house on the opposite side of Misty Lake Park. Annie and Laurie each had their own rooms and, thanks to joint custody, they spent two weeks of every month living as sisters.

Annie wasn't thrilled with the arrangement at first. She hadn't even *considered* the idea of joint custody. Originally, the idea of living anywhere besides *her home*, even if only for a couple weeks a month, pissed her off. She *hated* the idea of leaving her dad alone in that house. And she *especially* hated the idea of spending *any* time with The Homewreckers.

But it was sort of working out. Annie and Laurie spent the summer rebuilding their friendship, and it was *almost* back to how it used to be.

Annie also got some real time with her mom. Now that the affair was out in the open, Lisa spent a lot more time at home – with the girls *and* Richard all together. Apparently, sneaking around was a full-time job.

Surprisingly, the divorce had been unifying for Annie's family. For the first time in a long time, Annie had *two* parents present and involved, even though they were on their own.

***

Around midnight on one of the first nights Annie stayed at the new house, she found her mom at the kitchen table, sitting in the dark with a glass of wine. Lisa admitted that sometimes she just liked the quiet of the dead of night. It helped her re-center for the next day.

Annie sat across from her with a glass of water and summoned her nerve. "Are you and Richard going to get married?"

"Not any time soon," her mom assured her. "That's where this is all heading eventually, but everyone needs a little time to adjust before we make anything permanent."

***

"Top shelf of my closet." Laurie laughed.

"What?" Annie was half out the door to get the shoes from Laurie's closet but stopped.

"Nothing. I just don't think I've ever been ready *before* you."

Annie rolled her eyes. She'd cut her hair, too. She and Laurie went together after three days of rain and boredom. She loved her new bob, but it required actual work, like with a hair dryer and straightener. She pretended to hate it, but part of her liked looking *done* every day. It added a level of confidence and made her feel more grown up.

She searched through Laurie's closet and finally found the sandals under a pile of discarded clothes on the floor. She rolled her eyes, *top shelf my butt.*

She stood in the doorway to her bedroom. "Okay, all set." She was wearing one of Laurie's sundresses, per Laurie's demand. Some things *never* changed. But Annie had to admit it *was* pretty cute.

Laurie tilted her head to the side and put an earring in as she met Annie at the door.

They found Lisa and Josh talking in the foyer as they came downstairs. It had taken a few weeks, but Josh finally seemed comfortable at the new house. Annie knew, though, that he would always prefer to be where her dad was. Plus, it was a monster walk. He said to give him some time. He'd figure out a shortcut. Or buy them both bikes. He *had* to be joking, Annie thought. No one rode bikes anymore!

     ***

Her dad seemed much happier and kept busy with all the things he loved.

A few weeks into the summer, Annie came home from midnight bowling and found him and Mrs. Wentworth sitting on the front porch drinking. She raised her eyebrows at them, said hello, and went on up to her room. The next morning, Jason was sure to

. inform her that the two were just friends.

"She and I have something in common," he said. "We're both mending broken hearts. And sometimes that's a little easier to do with a friend. *And* Jack Daniels."

Annie just shrugged her shoulders. Things were already as weird as they could be, *so what* if he ended up with Laurie's mom.

***

"Sorry," Annie huffed as she landed at the bottom of the steps. "Couldn't find my shoes in Laurie's tornado!"

"*Your* shoes?" Laurie interrupted.

"Oh, whatever. Fine. *Your* shoes. But your closet's a disaster!"

"About that," Richard said, joining them in the foyer. "I take it you're planning to clean up that pigsty tomorrow?

"Yes, Daddy," Laurie said sheepishly.

The summer had been fun, but Annie was nervous for sophomore year.

She and Laurie were back on track. And they'd spent a good amount of time with Maddie, but there hadn't been a peep from Olivia.

Not entirely surprising, since the girls made it pretty clear at the end of last year that they were done with her. Maddie even quit cheerleading. It never really was her thing, she'd admitted. Olivia bullied her into doing it originally.

Josh told Lisa that he'd have them home by curfew, which, luckily for Annie, had now been extended by an hour.

They were out the door and halfway down the front walk when Richard swung the door and bounded after them. He handed Josh some cash.

"Treat the group to Burgette's after the Bonfire," Richard said, and then disappeared back into the house.

The group. Annie smiled. She'd found her place and she *actually* belonged.

Laurie looked at Josh. "How much?"

Josh unfolded the bill. "$100," he said, his eyes wide. "So I guess he means the *whole* group," Josh laughed.

The *whole* group: Annie and Laurie, Josh and Brandon, Maddie and Simon. *Her people.* Brandon and Olivia broke up just after exams. She told him if she was going to be a Varsity cheerleader, she needed a more mature boyfriend.

He was crushed at first, but the more time everyone spent together, the closer Laurie and Brandon got. They weren't going out or anything, not yet. But Annie guessed it was just a matter of time.

As they approached Misty Lake Park, Annie heard someone running up behind them.

"Hey," Maddie huffed, bending at the waist to catch her breath. "Have y'all seen Simon?"

"Not yet," Annie answered. "I'm sure he'll be here soon." Maddie gave Annie a look.

"Are you kidding?" Maddie laughed. "You know he's already here. We're talking about Simon here. He can't *ever* be late for anything."

"Yeah," Laurie laughed, nudging Maddie as they all walked into the party. "And how's that working out for you?" she teased. Maddie was habitually late, so it made for a fun dynamic.

They found Simon by the keg, chatting with one of his friends from the yearbook staff. He looked at his watch. "It's about time y'all showed! He wrapped his arm around Maddie and handed her his drink.

Brandon walked up, interrupting Simon.

"Dude!" he yelled at Josh, slapping his back. "Where were you earlier, bro? I tried getting up with you."

Over the summer, Josh spent a lot of time with his dad

learning as much as he could about his mom. Oddly enough, tonight was the anniversary of her death. Josh spent the entire day with his dad and brother. They went to her gravesite for the first time. He'd asked Annie to join, but she knew that some things were just for family.

"Yeah, sorry. Family stuff." He performed an elaborate man-handshake with Brandon and didn't explain further. Annie was still the only one who knew the details.

Annie spotted Olivia across the park, gathered with some cheerleaders around the bed of a rising senior's truck. She was dressed to the nines and wearing even more makeup than usual if that was possible.

Her loud cackle and the way she wobbled on her five-inch heels were evidence she was already a few drinks in. Annie's heart tightened. *How long will it take for that to stop?* It hadn't taken Olivia long to move on to a new crowd. But whatever kept Olivia away from Annie worked for her.

Josh returned with two Solo cups and handed one to Annie. She hadn't even noticed that he'd slipped away. She took a sip and smiled. *Water.*

He draped his arm around her shoulders and pulled her close.

How she felt tonight was a dizzying contrast to how she'd felt that night a year ago.

She wouldn't say she'd changed, necessarily, but she'd definitely adjusted. She'd fostered new friendships and repaired old.

The group stayed for a while, long enough to see Dave's farewell speech to the graduated seniors and welcome the rising seniors. He and Amanda were heading off to NC State.

Annie wondered if Dave being out of the house would change much for Josh. The boys spent so much time just the two of them while their dad traveled. Maybe now she'd get some golden alone time with him. They were still taking things slow in *that* department, but ...

After Dave's speech, the noise level rose by 100%, and Annie didn't have the veil of a buzz to soften it.

"Y'all up for Burgette's?" she yelled over the crowd to her friends, who had taken over a picnic table.

The group migrated toward the street. They were all a little extra loud and silly. Annie fell behind, watching them. Josh slowed to match her pace.

"You okay?" He put his arm around her.

"Yeah," she said. "I really am." Laurie turned and flashed her megawatt smile, calling for Annie to catch up. And she did.

Joey Hodges

ACKNOWLEDGEMENTS

All of my thanks…

To Jennifer Wright, my sister, editor, cover designer and lighting specialist! Your encouragement, expertise, and the *many* hours of hard work mean the world to me. I'm pretty sure my love for words is your fault, too.

To Sarah Buchanan, one of my editors, for your unending patience with my many, *many* questions, for talking me down from every ledge, and for all of your hard work to help out your old high school friend.

To Jonathan, my husband and best friend, for paying the bills while I chased my dream! For pretending to care about teenage girl drama when I'd enlist your help to hammer out story details. For putting up with me, and most importantly for *always* believing in me. I kind of like you.

To my mom and dad, for not laughing in my face when I told you I wanted to spend your money on a degree in Creative Writing, for dealing with *my* stupid girl drama, for all your constant support, and for always knowing I'd get here someday even when I was a fish out of water.

To *ALL* of my family, *JUST US,* for always having my back!

To Eileen Bucklen, my sister, for taking my author photos and sparking my love for reading. To Jacob and Lanning, my nephews, for your assistance even in the pouring rain.

To Zoe Weaver, my neighborhood turned school BFF, for volunteering to be my accountability partner, for getting this ball rolling all those years ago, and never, ever letting me give up.

To all the friends who offered unending support, weighed in on a title, and just make life more fun in general! Abby Carbaugh, Kelly Sweet, Andrea & Matt Smith, Amber Rhodes, Courtney Ligon, Cori Nilsen (and Atomic Salon in Raleigh), Matt Belvin, Meg Lindley, Gaby Shelow, The Christian Family, Our GA Crew, Emily & Patrick Hodges, Corley Cole, and many, *many* others.

Joey Hodges

To all my blog friends for your constant enthusiasm, support, and for always pushing me whenever I was ready to give up.

About the Author

Joey Hodges was born into a large family in California in June 1986. Just after she was born, her parents loaded up their five kids and moved them to Raleigh, North Carolina where Joey grew up.

She marched in her high school marching band and fell in love with a football player, who would later become her husband. Joey graduated from Appalachian State University with a degree in English with a concentration in Creative Writing.

She now resides in a Charlotte, NC with her husband, Jonathan Hodges, their dog, Bailey, and *her* cat, Campbell.

Yeah, maybe is Joey's debut novel.

She blogs at www.joeyhodgeswrites.com

Follow Joey on Twitter & Instagram at @Joelizabeth

If you liked the book, feel free to tell your friends and leave a review on Amazon and Goodreads.

Joey Hodges

Made in United States
North Haven, CT
22 April 2023

35743861R00221